Arlington Hts., Illinois · 1990

Night Visions 8

Afterword by
Robert R. McCammon

· all original stories by ·

John Farris

Stephen Gallagher

Joe R. Lansdale

illustrated by
Paul Sonju

Trade Hardcover Edition   ISBN 0-913165-57-3

NIGHT VISIONS 8 Copyright © 1990 by Dark Harvest, Inc.

Illustrations Copyright © 1990 by Paul Sonju

These stories are works of fiction. Names, characters, places, and incidents are either the product of the author's imaginations or are used fictitiously. Any resemblence to actual events or locales, or persons, living or dead, is entirely coincidental.

"Little Jimmy" Copyright © 1990 by John Farris.
"Hairshirt" Copyright © 1990 by John Farris.
"The Girl Next Door" Copyright © 1990 by John Farris.
"Good Morning, Daddy" Copyright © 1990 by John Farris.
"Folk-Naif' 1942" Copyright © 1990 by John Farris.
"More Than Mischief" Copyright © 1990 by John Farris.
"Revenge" Copyright © 1990 by John Farris.

"The Back of His Hand" Copyright © 1990 by Stephen Gallagher.
"Comparative Anatomy" Copyright © 1990 by Stephen Gallagher.
"Dead Man's Handle" Copyright © 1990 by Stephen Gallagher.
"Hunter, Killer" Copyright © 1990 by Stephen Gallagher.

"Incident On And Off A Mountain Road" Copyright © 1990 by Joe R. Lansdale.
"Steppin' Out, Summer, '68" Copyright © 1990 by Joe R. Lansdale.
"The Phone Woman" Copyright © 1990 by Joe R. Lansdale.
"Drive-In Date" Copyright © 1990 by Joe R. Lansdale.

"The Judge" Copyright © 1990 by Robert R. McCammon.

All Rights Reserved

Manufactured in the United States

FIRST EDITION

Dark Harvest / P.O. Box 941 / Arlington Heights, IL / 60006

TABLE OF CONTENTS

JOHN FARRIS

Little Jimmy 11

Hairshirt 13

The Girl Next Door 43

Good Morning, Daddy 47
Illustration 60

Folk-Naif: 1942 77

More Than Mischief 79
Illustration 82

Revenge 91

STEPHEN GALLAGHER

The Back of His Hand 95

Comparative Anatomy 107
Illustration 118

Dead Man's Handle 129
Illustration 132

Hunter, Killer 151

JOE R. LANSDALE

Incident On And Off A Mountain Road 177
Illustration 190

Steppin' Out, Summer, '68 199
Illustration 212

The Phone Woman 219

Drive-In Date 233

ROBERT R. McCAMMON

The Judge 249

The Publishers would like to express their gratitude to the following people. Thank you: Ann Cameron Mikol, Stan and Phyllis Mikol, Wayne Sommers, Dr. Stan Gurnick PhD, Gary Fronk, Linda Solar, The People of All American Print Center, Raymond, Teresa, and Mark Stadalsky, Tom Pas, Tony Hodes, Greg Manchess, Stan Wiater, Rick Hautala, James Kisner, Thomas Tessier, F. Paul Wilson, and Kathy Jo Camacho.

And, of course, special thanks to the most important people to this book. Without them NIGHT VISIONS 8 would not exist; John Farris, Stephen Gallagher, Joe R. Lansdale, Robert R. McCammon, and Paul Sonju.

John Farris

Prelude: Little Jimmy

Little Jimmy
walking   the west field
with dad and the birddog
ground opened
like a wizards pocket
and Jimmy slipped   in
out of the optic yellow

Never made a sound and
like   that
there was no pocket neither
Only five fingers stood out
withered pegs
stripped by grackles
to the numbbones

Wish
I had one
in my museum of chance

Hairshirt

He's Mel McGiveney, Jr., and he's feeling pretty good about himself this spring night, two weeks before graduation from high school. There's the ten thousand dollar Rotary International scholarship, for one thing. College of his choice. (His choice was Georgia Tech; they accepted him in April). There's the new Nissan Sentra he's driving, gift from mom and dad. And, last but not least, he just got laid, in the snug back seat of the Sentra; after several months of will-she-or-won't-she Vandy gave in and gave out and now, a little after the fact, she's being a good sport about the whole thing although Mel suspects she didn't enjoy herself all that much. Partly his fault. Well, no, mostly his fault, but next time . . .

Their trysting place for most of their senior year has been the driveway of an unfinished, quarter of a million dollar home in a bankrupt subdivision in East Cobb County, Georgia, where they live and go to school. It's a hilly area, and this particular house is high above the paved street in a neighborhood where only six of fifty planned homes are completed and occupied. The concrete driveway rises at a steep angle and they've enjoyed complete privacy up there, inside the doorless three-car garage with curls of shaved wood in the corners, a bird's nest in the light fixture.

Mel, getting his second wind in a hurry, as highly sensitized 18-year-olds are apt to do, suggests to Vandy that he can probably do a much better job of satisfying her on a second attempt, but

Vandy has already wriggled back into her pink-striped cotton underpants (Jockeys for Her). She strokes Mel on the cheek and smiles and says, No, it's late, etc., and bites her underlip delicately, as if she's felt a twinge. And he says, Did it hurt much? and Vandy goes Well, I guess it's something that takes a little getting used to, but it was fine, really.

Fine, really, is almost a promise that they're going to do it again, and Mel is satisfied with that. Next time maybe they can do it in a bed, Vandy's house, probably, and Mel is confident he'll perform a lot better in bed. It was the condom. He'd practiced putting them on at home, but coping with the damned thing in the back seat with a compliant and heavy-breathing Vandy almost on top of him had provided a little too much stimulation.

They both get out of the car; Mel, with a certain bravado (Mel McGiveney, Jr., was here, armed and dangerous), tosses the sploshy rubber on the garage floor and they hurriedly share a joint—Mel doesn't want the tell-tale smoke permeating his new Sentra. They hold each other around the waist and Vandy pretends to be weak in the knees and gets the giggles. Then they each have a stick of Doublemint gum. In the car again Vandy says, Do it fast, and Mel goes down the precipitous curving drive as if they are on a roller coaster. And Vandy goes

"Whooooooooops!"

all the way down. Then spits the lump of gum into her palm and looks at him with adoring dreamy eyes as if that was it, she finally had her orgasm.

It's a semi-rural area they're driving through, once they leave the unfinished sub-division. Narrow two-lane blacktop bumpy as a bad complexion that winds through countryside, past horse farms, with more look-alike swim-and-tennis communities every half mile or so. Ashbrook. Dover Highlands. Eton Woods. Narrow bridges over small streams. At one particularly sharp curve in the road there is a home-made memorial, whitewashed stones piled high by the side, to five teenagers killed in a crash there. Mel is going fifty. He cannot imagine a world without Mel McGiveney, Jr., in it. His tires squeal a little, thrillingly, on the curve. In the seat next to him Vandy Trohmann has her eyes closed. Her head lolls on the seat back as the Sentra niftily negotiates the tight curve, hugs the road without a tremor. Vandy licks her full lower lip. She is riding low in the seat, knees wide apart, hem of her skirt well past mid-thigh. Mel is wild at the sight of her. Randy for Vandy. It's as if they had never screwed, as if their brief intercourse was something that had only occurred—again—in his fevered imagination.

They are heading up another dark hill. A church cemetery on one side, old tombstones on the nod, the church long since relocated. There is no one behind them. No cars are coming from the other direction. The high-beam headlights of the Sentra pick up a dog by the side of the road.

Kind of a mud-colored dog, like a Labrador. Nearly a hundred yards away. In the blink of an eye they cover half of that distance. Mel has only a glimpse of the animal, of eyes looking back and lit up by the ambient light, sparkly yellow eyes with small red pupils. Then Mel is glancing at the inside of Vandy's love-warmed thigh and wanting to reach out and put his free hand up under her skirt where the springy little cushion of cinnamon hair is pressed down, defined by the close-fitting pink cotton, but instead he twists the wheel slightly to the right and wipes out the mud-colored dog.

Vandy opens her eyes at the moment of impact and sees the dog flying past the car and there is a sudden swish of blood across the window, she flinches: goes, Shit! and looks around quick as Mel puts the outside wheels back on the pavement, touching the brake, Vandy rising up with hands clutching the back of the seat trying to see, goes:

"Stop, Mel! Stop!"

"What for?"

"You hit a dog!"

"Yeah." They are near the crest of the hill. He is a little breathless. Tingling.

"Stop!"

"I don't want to. I mean, what's the point?"

"What's the *point*?" Vandy, kneeling in the seat, face turned to him. Her generous mouth, usually smiling, is out of shape, a clown's mouth. Her normally serene blue eyes in shadow, it's all he can see of her, the anguished clown's mouth. "Go back, I said! Go back!"

"Vandy, it's—it's gotta be dead, I killed it."

"*Why?*"

"What do you mean, why?" He has slowed without realizing it. Oncoming vehicle, one headlight dim as an occluded moon. Pickup truck. Rattles by. Vandy's hand is on the wheel. Grabbing it, trying to make him pull over.

"Vandy, don't do that!"

"Are you going to stop, or what?"

"Yeah, I'm stopping. What are you so upset about?"

He's off the road. Narrow shoulder. Vandy flings the door open.

"Hey!"

"Come on if you're coming," she says furiously, with a high-headed shake of her abundant brown hair, and goes running back over the top of the hill. *Running*, he can't believe this. Farmhouse set in the pine woods, porch light on, another dog barks. Mel backs up, slowly, left wheels on the blacktop. Seeing her in the mirror. The flash of her bare long legs in the backup lights. She ran cross-country for three years. Pulling steadily away from him. He backs into a rutted red clay driveway, turns, follows her on the wrong side of the road. Blood on the window, he winces. Didn't think about that. The fucking dog *splattered*. Usually when he clipped them just right they were flung away with a high-pitched scream. Or died on impact beneath the wheels, not a sound except for the crunching thump. Mel's jaws work painfully hard, teeth grinding his wad of gum.

Vandy is down in the gully twenty feet from where he ran over the dog. Mel parks with the lights flashing, takes a small flashlight from the glove compartment and goes down there with Vandy. Shuddering, she shies away from him. He casts around with the light and there's the dog, lying on its side. Eyes open, teeth bared. But it's dead. Never knew what hit it. Vandy draws a long breath.

"You saw it, didn't you?"

"Vandy, come on, let's—"

"Just tell me the truth!"

"Look at it. Half-starved. An old stray."

She turns slowly to him. Running fingers through her hair. Stares at Mel. He tries to take her by the arm. She yanks it away and almost loses her balance on the slope of the gully. There is a fecal odor rising from the dead dog.

"You did it on purpose."

Faced with her inexplicable hostility, he doesn't want to admit it. But his shoulders twitch. And his face can't lie.

Vandy goes, "Fuckhead." There are tears on one cheek. Vandy only cries on one side of her face, the right side. But the eye is streaming. Her mouth is locked in a brutal grimace of contempt.

HAIRSHIRT

What is this? Mel thinks, outraged. *Fuckhead?* As soon as the epithet was out of her mouth he came within a heartbeat of slapping the hell out of her. Fifteen or twenty minutes ago she was nearly upside-down on the back seat of his car, bare-assed and gasping against his neck. His Vandy. They've had little disagreements since they started going together; Vandy can be contrary and Vandy can pout, but she has always catered to him. His whim is her command. Mel's jaw muscles bunch where he has clamped down on the chewing gum. He looks at the dead dog again, whose fault it is, and realizes that if he can just get Vandy away from here and make some kind of apology she'll come around; if she loves him, and he knows she does, she'll come around. But it is not his nature to be conciliatory. Mel McGiveney, Jr. never backs off, which is why he was such a damn good linebacker until he blew out a knee his sophomore year.

"I run over 'em," he says coldly. "Cats, too. What difference does it make? If nobody want's 'em. They're better off being road pizza. Come on, let's get out of here."

"Fuck—"

Before she can finish he throws down the flashlight and has Vandy by the arm above her elbow. Jerks her hard toward him. His right fist is cocked. Her face with the streaming tears looks almost expressionless by moonlight, her lips are loose, he feels the bones of her arm, he senses a certain willingness on her part to be in pain, he is learning a lot of new things about Vandy tonight.

"You won't hit me," she says.

"No, but I'll whip your tail, Vandy, if you ever cuss me again."

She looks steadily at him, breasts rising and falling. A car comes up the grade, slows. Some spillover from the headlights illuminates her face. She doesn't blink. She looks almost hypnotized to Mel. He relaxes his grip on Vandy, looks back at the road. A woman's face. Middle-aged, hair a streaky gray mop.

"Are you chirrrun all right? Did you have an accident?"

"Sort of," Mel says. "I ran over a dog."

"Oh, dear."

"He's dead," Mel says, shaking his head. "Can't do a thing for him."

"Oh, that's a shame!"

"Yes, ma'am. He just run in front of my car. No way I could've missed him."

"If you're sure you don't need any help."

"No, ma'am, thanks for stopping. We're going on now ourselves."

The other car drives off. Mel looks back at Vandy as the light fades from her face, leaving it heavily shadowed except for the tearglaze. She is still breathing hard. He resists an impulse to shake her.

Goes, "Well, that's the way it is. You want to get back in the car?" Harsh, a little rude. What she deserves.

Vandy doesn't stir. She stands there swallowing and licking her lips and holding herself with one hand between her breasts where she keeps a little gold cross tucked out of sight and finally Mel says in a subdued, more kindly tone of voice, Well, Jesus, Vandy, just come on, you're not going to have a fit over this, are you? And that seems to do the trick, gets her moving anyway, up the slope to the shoulder of the road. He opens the door for her and she settles into the seat, still with that vacant gone-off look in her eye, like she's on a head trip.

Mel looks with distaste at the drying dog blood on the window, but he doesn't have a way to get it off. There's a Texaco mart on Wade Green Road just off I-575 where he can clean the window and buy them a couple of Pepsi's. He could use the caffeine fix, because he's still smarting and sore thanks to Vandy's attitude.

* * *

They've gone about a mile when Vandy opens up, talking, in a low whispery voice, more to herself than to him.

"We have to do something about this."

"Vandy, I don't want to talk any more about it. It's over and done with, far as I'm concerned."

"But you'll do it again. And again. I didn't realize that was part of your nature. I just didn't realize. Then you raised your hand to me. You did that, Mel." She speaks, as a dull child reads aloud, in a tense monotone.

"Well, you lit into me for no good reason, so how was I supposed to take it?"

"I guess the blame's mine. I know it must be. But the fact is, I can't be in love with you any more if you don't change."

Mel goes, "Jesus," whistling between his front teeth for emphasis.

"It's just like it's happening again. All over again, the same way."

She isn't looking at him. Her expression is pathetic, entranced. Mel chews gum savagely and drives too fast. Although neither he nor Vandy—as far as he knows—touched the dead dog, the odor, of mayhem and blood, is vivid in his nostrils, as if it is seeping through the glass of the window next to Vandy.

"What does that mean?"

"Cousin Rayford ran over animals in the road too."

"Who's Cousin Rayford?"

"Mama's second cousin. He came to stay with us to help out after Daddy was killed in that construction accident. Then he and mama had a thing going so he stayed on longer. I always liked him. About the time I turned twelve I got a crush on him and let him know it."

"What?" Mel says, alarmed and fascinated.

"Well, one night when mama was laid up I went to the drive-in movies with Rayford, in his pickup truck. During the movies he wanted to, like, handle me and I let him. He was remorseful about that. He cried and said he was a sinner. Then he handled me again, and himself at the same time, and put his tongue in my mouth when he kissed me. On the way home there was this big old tomcat on the far side, and Rayford drove clear across the road to run over it. He said tomcats were bad news. He was acting real ugly. He sat down when we were home and got drunk big-time. I cried in my room and prayed for him. Then about the time the sun came up I had a vision, and knew what I must do."

Vandy turns her head slowly as Mel pulls into the Texaco mart on Wade Green Road. He feels her eyes on him, feels the hairs erect on the nape of his neck. Something like a shock runs down both forearms as he stops.

"I still want to be in love with you, Mel," she says sorrowfully.

"I—I want you to love me too, pigeon."

"Well, then. There's something you have to do for me."

"Uh-huh. Sure. Could you do with a Pepsi?"

"Okay, I'll have a Pepsi. Mel—it's somebody I want you to meet."

Mel shrugs and opens the door.

Vandy reaches out and lays a hand imperatively on his arm. He glances at his senior ring, that she has taped so it will fit her own third finger on her left hand.

"I mean tonight. It has to be tonight."

"Getting kind of late."

"He'll be there. He's always there." Her fingers tighten, bonding them. "You will, Mel? Promise? Then I can go on loving you, and not feel guilty, like I'm a part of what's bad in your nature."

"How long will it take? Who is it you want me—"

"It won't take long. And he's not far away. Just up the road a few miles, in Cherokee. And I'll feel so much better, after you've talked to him."

"Sure. Anything you want. I'll just run in and fetch the Pepsi's, babe."

After he squeegees the dog blood off the window and the side of his car, Mel, his spirits somewhat lifted by the jolt he gets from his can of Pepsi, decides to go on humoring Vandy. In the car, northbound on interstate 575, they share a bag of artificial onion rings and a bag of fried pork rinds. Vandy tells him to get off on 92 highway in Cherokee County and take 92 to Bells Ferry. This far north Bells Ferry is strictly redneck country, another narrow, curving, hilly stretch of blacktop. Vandy, leaning forward in the seat as if she isn't quite sure after all where she's taking them, says, Well, it's been a while since I was up here. And Mel says, spirits lagging, his passion an anchor, We're close to Allatoona already, pigeon, and she goes, Yeah, that's where it is, almost to Allatoona—Allatoona being a popular local recreational lake with sandy swim beaches. The pork rinds have made him thirsty again. Mel sighs.

"Okay, now," Vandy says. "Where the blinking light is on up the hill? I recognize that old store. Well, it'll be on your left just a little bit past the feed store and that tarpaper beer joint where all those pickups are."

"Who is it we're going to see?"

"Brother Ezar."

"Oh, didn't know you had a brother," Mel teases.

"He's a spiritual advisor."

Mel doesn't like the sound of that. "How do you happen to know—"

"I told you that already. When I was twelve years old I had a vision, and that vision led me straight to Brother Ezar. —There it is!" In her excitement Vandy bounces on the seat. "Told you! Everything'll be all right now."

Mel sees, off the main road in a thick stand of tall Georgia pines, a house trailer up on blocks, with an orange-striped awning over the door midway in the side of the trailer, and above the awning a pale blue neon sign about the size of the Budweiser logo in the window of the roadhouse they just passed. The tired, flickering sign says *roadside chapel*. The words are bracketed by neon crosses.

"Vandy—would you listen to me for just a minute—"

"All I want you to do is talk to Brother Ezar! For five minutes. That's *all* I'm asking. Tell him what you did. Brother Ezar won't condemn you for it. He'll be real helpful, I swear."

"It's getting to be after midnight."

"Brother Ezar won't mind. He doesn't own a clock. He doesn't have a calendar. He doesn't care what time it is. He's just always there, for those who need him." Vandy's hands are clenched in her lap; she licks her lips. Her eyes are the simmering unearthly blue of the blinking, beckoning neon.

They get out in silence. There is a small porch of uncemented concrete blocks in front of the trailer door. Through the screen Mel sees a candle burning. And the glowing tube of a very old black-and-white TV. Canned laughter from the TV. A rumbling chuckle in response to the laugh machine. The show is *Mr. Ed*. Vandy takes Mel's hand firmly in hers. They go up to the screen door. *A horse is a horse of course of course*—Mel finds himself humming the recalled theme song.

"Brother Ezar?" Vandy says, and raps on the aluminum frame with her free hand. A mosquito whines around the back of Mel's neck. He smells warmed-over snack food. Pizza, or canned spaghetti, or both. A cat gazes out at them from a cushion on a well-clawed corduroy sofa.

"Come in, come in."

Vandy gives Mel a reassuring smile and opens the screen door, goes in first. The cat reacts to Mel's entrance by backing to the other end of the sofa and hunkering down there.

Brother Ezar rises from his lounge chair in front of the television console, on top of which he has placed religious statues. Christ crucified, and beside Him in His agony, Buddha, looking fat and piously contented. There is one other Divinity Mel can't identify. This one has sinister slant eyes and tits and an extra pair of arms. Brother Ezar is tall and gaunt, nearly as bald as the unknown divinity, with salt-and-pepper stubble that is almost, but not quite, beardlike. His eyes are a soft, benign brown, magnified by lenses to such a size it seems nothing could be hidden in them, even if he had the soul of a devious man. But there is an angry red sty on one lid, also cruelly magnified, so that it glows like a fleshy cobuchon in the semidarkness of the house trailer.

"Welcome, welcome," he says, leather sandals creaking as he comes toward them, wearing a russet cassock as voluminous and crumpled on his frame as bearskin is after the bear's long hibernation. Brother Ezar has a brash but not obnoxious odor about him. His shinbones gleam palely as the too-short hem of the cassock swirls around his legs.

"I don't know if you remember me," Vandy says diffidently. "It's been about three years since I was here last."

Brother Ezar stops and studies her momentarily, grinning, rubbing the back of a tattooed hand across his chin. Both hands are tattooed but without artistry, crude Greek letters on the left, a vividly bleeding sacred heart on the right. He wears several chains around his neck, some beaded, some gold, with small mesh and leather bags dangling from the chains.

"I remember your pretty face," Brother Ezar says, "but not your name."

"Vandella Trohmann."

"Oh, yes."

"And this is my boy friend Mel McGiveney."

Mel nods and smiles weakly. The gaunt bird of prayer smiles back.

"I was wondering if I could speak to you privately for a few minutes, Brother Ezar?"

"Are you troubled, Vandella?"

"Sorely troubled, Brother Ezar."

"You will excuse us, Mel? Please make yourself at home." Brother Ezar is staring at him, then suddenly he looks beyond Mel at the cat on the corduroy sofa, frowning, and Mel turns his head quickly. The cat, a black-and-white tabby, fifteen pounds if it's an ounce, is crouched in a cloud of erupted cushion stuffing with front paws tucked under, eyes half closed. But Mel has felt something on the back of his neck like a tiny crawling spider and his stomach begins to cramp, maybe from the fried pork rinds; he thinks, *No, I don't want to be in here—with that.*

But it isn't as if he has a choice; Brother Ezar has pulled aside a swagged velvet drape over a doorway and in another room of the house trailer Mel has a glimpse of an altar, religious paintings, a few metal folding chairs, more lighted candles. The flames flicker as the air is disturbed by the swishing movement of the heavy drapery. Vandy steps through the doorway ahead of Brother Ezar, her hands folded together below her breastbone, and Brother Ezar follows, pausing to pull the wine-colored drape across the doorway again. Leaving Mel alone with the cat.

He's sorry he let Vandy talk him into this. He hears their voices, low, murmuring, but can't make out what is being said behind the drape. He hears the cat too, a rasping purr. The cat is standing, digging its front claws into what is left of the sofa cushion, staring at him. Mel opens the screen door quickly and goes outside. After a few moments of gazing vacantly in the direction of the road, hearing pickup doors slam and raucous voices from the roadhouse parking lot, he strolls around to the back of the house trailer.

There he finds an old-fashioned pump on a concrete slab. He's still thirsty. He works the rusty handle up and down a few times, and suddenly there's a gush of cold water in the moonlight. He tastes it. Artesian well water, clear and unexpectedly satisfying, with only a faint aftertaste of iron. He drinks his fill.

"Mel?"

Vandy is calling him. Mel answers, then walks around to the front of the trailer where the blue neon is fizzing and popping. She holds the screen door open for him, smiling, as if she feels wonderful all of a sudden. Seeing her smile like that, he supposes their visit to the tacky roadside chapel was worthwhile.

Before he can ask her if she's ready to leave, Vandy says, "Will you go to Brother Ezar now?"

He starts to protest, but the love-light in her blue eyes, her reverential smile, gives him pause. A couple of minutes more, he thinks, then they'll be on their way, and maybe there'll be a reward for him if he can find a good place to pull off before they reach

Vandy's house. Hell, even in the driveway; nobody can see them from the street and her mother seldom waits up. Mel nods.

"Sure. I guess you told him all about it."

"Yes. Brother Ezar understands. There's nothing to be afraid of."

Vandy comes down into the clay yard and takes both his hands in hers, presses them against her breasts in a moment of private ecstasy. Mel swallows. He is aroused.

"I'm going to wait in the car." Her look of ecstasy is replaced by something bleaker. "I'll be waiting, Mel," she repeats, slowly. "I know you can do it. My love goes with you."

Do what? He is both perplexed and amused by her show of solemnity, and then when he thinks about it, irritated by her routine of Brother Ezar this, Brother Ezar that, as if he is something other than a crackpot hermit in a tawdry trailer. Mel is about to kiss Vandy to demonstrate who really counts in her life, but she turns her face aside. Not spurning him exactly, but as if he is no longer there, and she can see him only in memory. She lets go of his hands and walks straight to the car.

The heat in Mel's groin fades and he swallows a small soft lump in the throat, thinking how much he loves Vandy too, and how he wishes tonight sort of never happened, at least after the moment of the stray dog in his headlights and his savage, overwhelming urge to run over it.

He goes up to the screen door trying not to be sulky about keeping his end of the bargain. Just as he steps into the trailer the cat screeches, freezing his blood. Mel flinches and scowls. The cat's ears are flat to its head and it looks ready to spring at him from the far end of the dilapidated sofa when the drapery twitches and Brother Ezar looks out, clucks in disapproval at his pet, then beckons smilingly to Mel.

In the other room the odors are of warm melted wax and incense. The incense bothers Mel's nose, and he chokes back a need to sneeze. Brother Ezar offers Mel a metal chair with a shabby cushion on it and sits facing him, one bony knee showing through a threadbare spot on his rust-red cassock.

HAIRSHIRT

Brother Ezar looks at Mel for a long time, patiently; Mel looks at the floor and then at the walls where there are a couple of interesting pictures. In one of them a comely nude woman holds a newborn babe to her breast in a leafy sun-drenched forest setting surrounded by animals—lions, wolves, lambs. All with identical round, staring eyes. In another picture the forest is darker, storm-wracked, ominous. A hunter on a rearing black horse fires arrows in a volley at a creature of some sort—part man, part beast, while a pack of snarling dogs surround the cliff on which the creature has become trapped. The picture is ugly, violent, fascinating. In contrast to the dark greens, earth tones and blotches of crimson in this painting, the huntsman's face is as blue as a summer sky.

"None of us," Brother Ezar says, aware of Mel's scrutiny of the allegorical hunt scene, "can hope to regain our primeval innocence. But it is possible to scourge ourselves of base instincts, if we are willing to endure the necessary trial. Mel?"

"Oh—uh, sorry. What—"

"A trial, Mel. Absolution by ordeal. Are you interested? It's for Vandy's sake, as well as your own."

"Ordeal?" He doesn't like the sound of it. He's ready to get up and walk out.

Brother Ezar smiles broadly, sympathetically. But when Mel looks at Ezar all he really sees is the shiny bulbous sty that has taken over much of the left eyelid. Like a freak in a carnival sideshow, it has Mel's full attention. He can't look away from that grotesque sty.

"Perhaps 'ordeal' makes it sound worse than it actually is. Individual reactions vary, depending on one's stamina and spiritual strength. You're young and appear to be quite strong. I think you may do very well."

"What is it I—"

"Let me show you."

Mel tenses warily as Brother Ezar rises from his chair, ready to knock him on his butt if Ezar gets funny. But Ezar, still smiling, goes to a painted wooden chest with a vaulted top in a corner behind the altar of his chapel; kneeling, he opens it. He rummages inside for a few moments, murmuring to himself.

"It *has* been a year or more—but I know there's another one. Now where did I—oh, yes. Here it is."

Mel has turned in his chair to watch him. Brother Ezar stands and closes the lid of the chest. He has something in one hand, rolled up in a sheaf of parchment-like paper. He unties the leather string from around the paper and smooths it out on the altar, saying something in a language that Mel thinks might be Latin. Ezar's eyes are closed, but the sty by candlelight looks gross, ready to erupt.

With this brief mysterious liturgy out of the way, Brother Ezar steps down from the altar and holds out to Mel what appears to be the dried, stretched hide of a red fox. Or a couple of foxes, their cured skins sewn crudely together to make a vest. Wooden toggles and leather loops confirm to Mel that it's something meant to be worn. He looks skeptically at Brother Ezar.

"It's a penitential garment," Ezar explains. "Commonly known as a hairshirt. I've blessed it. Now all you need to do is wear it, for twenty-four hours. Then you will be scourged. And twice-blessed. Because—as you already know—Vandy's love is conditional on your acceptance of your penance."

"I have to wear that?"

"Next to your skin. You may wear anything you like over the hairshirt. A sweater, perhaps, or a school jacket. No one has to know."

"For how long?"

"Once you've put the hairshirt on, you may not remove it for twenty-four hours. Or the act of penance is violated and nullified. Do you accept?"

Mel turns away, sneezing violently. Either the incense has finally got to him, or it's the hairshirt, which has no obvious odor. Looks harmless enough. Vandy, he thinks, is fucking *nuts*. But he has never felt more tenderly toward her, so in love, so—protective. And, okay, he did upset her tonight. Think of it, Mel advises himself, as having lost a bet, or something.

He sniffs a couple of times, but the sneezing is under control. He's impatient to get out of there. He'll wear the hairshirt; if it's what Vandy wants he'll even fuck her while he's wearing it. But when he gets home, straight into the garbage it goes.

Okay, Mel gasps, I'll put the thing on. But Brother Ezar corrects him gently: Do you accept? Mel goes, I accept, sure, I accept, come on; and he doesn't waste any time stripping to the waist so he can slip into the vest, hair side next to his skin.

It doesn't feel as itchy as he anticipated. The hairshirt is not soft, exactly, but sufficiently pliable so as not to affect his movements. It'll be okay. He buttons his long-sleeved blue Polo over the hairshirt and tugs on his sweater. He feels lumpy. But it's only for a little while. Twenty-four hours? Bullshit to that. He checks the time routinely on his LED watch. It is nineteen minutes after twelve.

He turns to Brother Ezar, but Ezar is kneeling at the altar with his back to Mel, and Mel doesn't feel like hanging around until he finishes his prayer, or whatever it is he's mumbling. It's warm in the tiny chapel and his nose is running from the pall of incense. The hairshirt is already causing him to sweat. He pushes the heavy drape aside and walks through the trailer to the door, looking uneasily for the cat. Doesn't see the cat. Opens the screen door and as he does so the damn cat streaks out of nowhere behind him and goes squawling between his legs, shoots off the porch to the left. Mel stumbles outside, swearing, heart pounding beneath the hairy vest, which almost feels alive against his damp skin: an unpleasant tickling sensation. He scrubs with both hands, fingers digging in, looks up angrily, looks for Vandy. Not there.

Not there? His car is gone too. No Vandy, no Nissan Sentra. No trace of tire ruts where he parked. For that matter, the road has vanished, there's unbroken pine forest in front of him.

Came out the wrong door.

Goes, "Vandy!"

Sounding shrill to his own ears as he turns back to the bulk of the house trailer he has just stumbled out of.

That's gone too, with nothing left of it except for the faint blue vein of neon spelling out *roadside chapel* in the air. But the letters quickly become shapeless to his astonished eyes, unreadable, they grow fainter still and twist slowly into nothingness like cigarette smoke adrift on the wind.

Mel turns a full circle, and another, for the moment anesthetized by shock against the nagging discomfort of the hairshirt. The spring night is still on the warm side, with a three-quarters moon shining high above the piney woods. The tops of the trees sway in a lively breeze. He hears himself panting, his breath catching in his throat, again and again. A cat squawls, far off in the darkness. Nearer to him there are insect sounds: cicadas. And a lot of frogs. He hears a full-throated response to the first lusty squawling. Cats, they seem to be all around him in the darkness. But they don't sound to Mel like ordinary housecats on the prowl. There are still bobcats in these north Georgia woods, or so he has heard from friends who go hunting. Mel McGiveney, Jr., is no outdoorsman.

There is no smoke or haze left in the air, his vision is clear, but disorientation has him in a state of shock. So they must have done something to him, somehow, doped him. When? He doesn't know, he didn't eat or drink anything except water from a well. It tasted okay. Nothing in well water to knock him out—and he hasn't suffered a loss of continuity. Just a minute ago he walked through the trailer after putting on the hairshirt—then he started outside—and that was when the cat ran between—he was distracted, off balance, but he didn't fall—or did he? A little gap in time at that point, two seconds at the most, he can't focus sharply—then—the car gone, Vandy—what are they trying to *do* to him?

Mel closes his eyes tightly, which makes him even more jumpy when the cats sound off again. Mating season. When he stops breathing noisily through his mouth, gulping air, he panics at the notion that he will never be able to draw another breath, he is going to suffocate. He bends over as far as he can, but the hairshirt, bulking rather inflexibly at his midsection, makes it difficult for him to get his hands down as far as his knees. He breathes through his mouth again. Finally he sinks down on one knee, head bowed. That's better. If the blood would just stop pounding in his head. If he wasn't sweating so much. But with freshets of perspiration drenching him he still feels cold. Just take it easy a minute or two, then—Vandy, God damn her, a little sex and it's as if she turned into a different person! She's never acted like this before. What possessed her to run off with his car, leave him stranded in the woods? It had better be a joke. She had better be just down the road waiting

(*What road?*).

Mel lifts his head. When he gets hold of Vandy—but as he reviews his grievances, he can't even be angry. He just wants her. Vandy's absence is torment to Mel, he's never felt so lonely.

Now he can breathe without gasping, his head is okay; he opens his eyes and is aware of the time on his LED wrist watch: 12:21. It must have stopped, Mel thinks, after another unwelcome jolt to the heart. Just two minutes ago (he clearly remembers checking the time) he was fixing to leave Brother Ezar's—the time changes. 12:22.

HAIRSHIRT

So they reset his watch too, that's part of it, Vandy's really serious about giving him a hard time because he ran over a useless dog. He's smarter than she is, though, he'll just wait here and sooner or later she'll repent and come back for him . . .

Instead of feeling more confident, superior to the situation, Mel thinks, *It didn't happen that way.* And he's colder than ever, suddenly, from the cold of terror: *I don't know what happened, I can't explain it.* Mel stands up a little too quickly and staggers, rights himself, goes plunging off across the somewhat marshy clearing and is sobbing before he covers more than a few yards. His Air Jordans are leaking water. There's a big windfall at the edge of the clearing. He pulls himself up on the partially rotted hickory trunk and perches there, trembling. Rebuking himself. Can't just go off in a panic; he needs to find a road, walk that road, find a house, ask for the use of the telephone. Call Buddy or Parks or one of the other guys to please come pick him up, no questions asked. And if anything happens to his new car while Vandy's driving it, the Lord help her ass because for sure he'll take his belt to it.

He sees something plump and dark near the other end of the windfall and after a stunned frozen couple of seconds recognizes the masked face of a raccoon. More than one of them. A family. They aren't particularly interested in him; each of the coons lifts up in turn, sniffs the fear-laced spoor Mel is broadcasting, and moves on.

Time for Mel to move on too. He stands on the windfall and looks around, hoping to see something—a light, a utility pole, a billboard. All he sees is forest, mixed pines and hardwoods, a lot of dark understory, the trees rising steeply off to his right to the crest of a ridge. Fine. From the ridge he should be able to see at least a mile in any direction. With the moon in a clear sky providing enough light for good contrast, he'll locate one of the wide slashes that mark the right-of-way of the monster TVA pylons, which crisscross this part of the Georgia countryside. Following the right-of-way, it'll be easy going south, toward the lights of Metropolitan Atlanta, which also ought to be clearly visible against the sky on a cloudless night.

It bothers him, leaving the sanctuary of the pocket-size marsh to try to reach high ground. When the woods close on him, where it's bound to be darker than it is in the open—Goddamn cats yowling again—he could get lost. But he knows the stars, and spends a couple of minutes staring at the sky, recalling some of what he learned in his astronomy elective last year. Mars, because of its red color, is readily identifiable. Then the North Star, Polaris, which he locates adjacent to the Big Dipper. Polaris, Casseopeia—north is that way, the moon is in the eastern sky—he hears a horse.

No mistaking that sound, a nasal snorting. His sister has owned hunter-jumpers since she was six. Mel withdraws from the stars and looks around gladly—a horse, a rider, he'll be out of the woods in no time.

"Hey! Who's that? Where are you?"

Can't see a thing, and no one answers him; Mel's initial excitement dwindles rapidly and he shivers again. But maybe there's a farm nearby, which he can't see from this perspective. A horse or two spending the mild night outdoors.

"Hey!" Mel says again, hopefully, listening, hearing a crackling sound like a large animal, or a man, walking in the woods; and again, the slobbery exhalation. He can't tell where it's coming from.

Mel gets down from the windfall. The frog population has quieted. So have the whipporwills in the pine woods. The flow of the wind quickens through the trees, a rushing, ghostly sound as if a floodgate has opened. As he moves he's reminded of the hairshirt, that prickly, nettlesome scrubbing against his skin. What is he still wearing that stupid thing for? Mel pulls his crewneck sweater over his head and hangs it on a broken branch, unbuttons his Ralph Lauren dress shirt, a gift from Vandy. Hears the horse again—and this time—he's sure of it—a creak of saddle or stirrup leather. They can't be that far away, they must be aware of him too.

"Look, I want some help! Wait just a minute? I need to know how to get out of here, that's all!"

He drapes his shirt across the windfall and grasps the hard leather toggles of the hairshirt. Twists and pulls, but can't seem to get the hairshirt unbuttoned. It feels stuck to him. He can't budge it. It just won't come off. And the more he struggles, the tighter it seems to get, inhibiting his ability to breathe.

(*Do you accept?* said Brother Ezar.)

"Shit! Ohhhh, *shit*," Mel whines. A knife. He'll cut the hairshirt off if he has to! There's a small penknife on his keyring. He's trying to find his keys in the pockets of his khaki slacks when he remembers. *Vandy.* He left the keys in the ignition, and she took his car.

Sound of a horse champing at the bit, and now in his heightened state of anxiety Mel gets wind of it. Spins around as if expecting the animal to be breathing down his neck.

He can hear it and smell it, but still he can't see it.

(Do you accept?)

Accept? Accept what, for Christ's sake? And then Mel remembers, something about an ordeal, a penance, vowing to wear the hairshirt for twenty-four hours; but he would have said anything just to get out of—

He tries again, frantically, to rid himself of the hairshirt, pulling hard at the toggles, ripping a fingernail to the quick, but the hairshirt is still stubbornly there, *his,* a part of him until—

The horse is coming steadily toward Mel. From the sounds the hooves are making, splashing with each step, it is in full gallop along the fringe of the marsh. The wind has come down the ridge and through the trees and the tangled understory shrubbery and is now in his face, turning the beads of sweat at his hairline to droplets of ice. He stares into the darkness where a fog seems to be rising: streaming upward from the pools of black stagnant water and the hollows of gaunt stumps, accompanied by tiny flickers of pale blue fire.

Suddenly he can see it, materializing full-bodied from the foggy tempest: the huge stallion and its rider, who is less distinct although he has a glowing face, blue itself and wreathed in ghostly blue Saint Elmo's fire. In contrast to the huge appalling horse's head, all black and with fiery distended eyes as large as Mel's fists, the rider's face has a deathlike tranquility, with hooded heavy-lidded eyes and hollowed cheeks. His mouth is expressionless, unspeakable as a scar. Yet Mel knows, instantly, that the horseman is not dead. He wears a black hat with a wide soft brim and a flat crown; there is a hunter's horn on his chest, an old-fashioned bow across his back.

They are less than thirty yards from him. Mel's instinct is to duck low behind the windfall. Moments later the stallion leaps, showering Mel with slimy mud, the trailing hooves just missing his head. The stallion lands hard enough to shake the ground and gallops on as Mel cringes and shudders.

When he looks up again the horse and rider have disappeared

into the woods. There are wisps of fog in the understory that appear to mark their passing.

Mel gets up slowly. The wind is still strong, sweeping through the trees, stirring up the fetid vapors of the marsh. Despite the purity of the moon, golden-eyed in space, he can't see more than a few feet behind him. Ahead, deep in the thrashing woods, is the dark form of the standing horse, and, turned toward Mel, the blue lantern of the horseman's severe, ascetic face.

Which isn't the worst of it, as far as Mel is concerned, because something else is coming, panting, slogging across the marshy ground, making nearly-human sounds of despair and grief.

Mel looks quickly side to side; he can't see a thing.

From deep in the woods where the blue man abides, he hears the prolonged, eerie lowing of the hunter's horn. The sound is doleful, and ominous; Mel feels an impulse toward sorrow and tears. Then the urge to run is wild in his blood, he is choked with dread.

He scrambles up across the windfall, glances back at the woods to see—and is jerked down from his perch by a vile pair of hands. He lands hard on his back, and a knee is thrust into his belly near his groin, pinning him down. He sees, a foot from his own, a hairy brutal face. Manlike, but he can't be sure. There is a hand on his throat, not quite choking off his breath.

"Don't move!"

"Uhhh—"

"Who are you?" The voice is hoarse; his breath is abominable.

"Uhhh—"

The hand at Mel's throat loosens. "Shhhh! Don't make no sound. Did he see you?"

"Who?"

"The blue man, idjit! Who do you think I be talkin' about?"

"I—don't—know."

"There goes the damned horn! Callin' his dogs, he must've seed you. Oh, God! When's it going to end? When will it ever end?"

The evil-smelling man slumps to one side, leaning against the windfall, and Mel sits up slowly, staring at him, disbelieving his senses, that a human being could be so filthy and degraded.

"Blue man? Dogs? What—"

"You're new, ain't you? You just got here. Just a kid, huh? Well, you stupid son of a bitch, if that's a hairshirt she done talked you into putting on, then you're about to regret the day you ever met up with little Vandy."

"You—you know Vandy?" The mournful, chilling sound of the hunting horn seems to bring to life, like a violated ants' nest, the hairy hide that Mel no longer merely wears, but is a loathsome part of him.

"I knowed her—but maybe not as well as you." The grossly pelted man laughs softly and meanly, then lapses into a coughing fit. Mel discovers, staring at him in the moony dark, that he is naked. And there is a broken shaft of what might be an arrow protruding from his side.

"Wha—what's your—"

"Name's Rayford," the savage answers, when his coughing subsides. "Don't reckon she ever had occasion to mention me."

"Tonight—she did. She told me that you—"

Rayford seizes him with unexpected speed and strength, given the condition he's in. "It's true! Something compelled me, a demon of lust, and I couldn't keep my hands off the child! She was all rosebuds, and clean-smellin' hair. I dirtied her. The filthy things I whispered in her ear! I should've cut out my own tongue that same night. But they give me a hairshirt 'stead of a carving knife. Oh, that'd be enough, they told me. All smiles. Just wear it for a little, Rayford, and scour away your sin. What a fool I was! Tell me—what else did Vandy have to say? Did she say—'I forgive him. I forgive old Rayford?'"

". . . No."

Rayford's hands loosen; he covers his face in a paroxysm as the horn lows anew. And now, answering, Mel hears the croupy belling of hounds.

"Oh, God! If Vandy didn't send you to release me, then I ain't never going to be released! It'll go on forever. You don't know—you're new here—but in six months you'll be just like me! The wounds that won't heal but won't kill me neither. The bugs and the infernal itching, so I can't get five minutes' rest without jumping up in torment! What is it you done? Never mind. No need to be a-tellin'. All I need know is, you got yourself a hairshirt."

"It won't . . . come off," Mel says, and suddenly he begins to blubber, out of control. "I can't get the fucking thing off! Help me."

"Help you? Only Vandy can do that, you little bastard. Gonna *pay*, now, ain't you? What'd she say? What'd she tell you? 'Til I *forgive* you?' That what she said? Well, she ain't never going to forgive you, neither, if I know my sweet Vandy."

"Help me!" Mel pleads, grasping at a bare arm that he can't get a grip on: it is unpleasantly larded with sweat, grease, the corruption from unhealed wounds. He feels the stump of another arrow embedded in Rayford's forearm and jerks his hand away.

"They don't never get tired," Rayford gasps. "They track you til you drop. Then they rip and tear at you awhile, and maybe the blue man lets fly a few of his arrows. God, don't they sting, though! Then they all just . . . fade away, like ghosts. But not for long. A day or two. Until they miss their sport. That's when you'll hear his damned horn again. Iff'n you don't choose to run, hell, they'll *make* you run! Running's not the worst part of it anyhow. The worst part is knowing you can't never run far enough, climb high enough, to get away from them for long."

Something dribbles and squirms from a corner of one of Rayford's eyes; bright as a tear, but it's a maggot.

"Where's . . . Vandy? I . . . I've got to talk . . . to Vandy!"

Rayford pushes Mel away. "Get to runnin'! Lead 'em away from me! You're young. You're fresh. I'll see you again—some day, maybe, when you're so much like me even a dog's nose can't sort us out!"

"No! Twenty-four hours—they said—I only had to wear it for *twenty-four hours!*"

"That's when you'll see her again, idjit! By then maybe if you're bloody enough—if you crawl on your belly in your hairshirt—if you plead with her for mercy, Vandy'll forgive you. But don't make the mistake I did."

"What mis—"

"I wouldn't crawl! I had repentance in my heart, but there wasn't nothing but spite and bitterness on my tongue when I come face to face again with that silky devil's bitch. Now look at me—have you a good whiff, younger, and know what it is you're in for!"

The dogs are closer, the long-winded horn calling them to the chase.

"Get away from me!" Rayford howls. "Now there's two of us, so you do your part! It's only fair! Spare me some of the misery I've suffered!"

Mel is shoved over backwards. On his hands and knees he shudders violently. *The dogs!* How many dogs? But it is the presence of the blue man, with his hunter's bow and quiver of arrows, that most terrifies him.

Getting to his feet, bumping against the windfall, Mel runs away, splashing through the marsh, only half aware, by the misty light of the moon, where he is going. For all he can tell, the dogs, formidable in their concerted belling, are everywhere in the woods. And, in his panic, he must also contend with the dreadful knowledge that there may be no way out for him, that he has been cast into a primeval hell at the whim of—

He trips and falls, rises drenched and moaning, looks back, sees the body of the great stallion framed in open space between walls of the forest; sees the melancholy radiant face of the blue man. His horn is silent. The horse stands eight feet high and wheels slowly in a pawing dance. Suddenly there are dogs all around them, a milling, surging pack, dark and indistinguishable except for the glowing brimstone of their eyes.

Mel stumbles into the woods, tearing himself from the grasp of branch and vine and web. Somewhere ahead of him a frightened buck crashes from concealment, he sees the quaking tail-tuft, the velvet glint of spring rack in moonlight. He is on a path of sorts. He runs, runs. Behind him the savage yapping of the dogs, Rayford's luckless scream. They have his scent, not Mel's. He rips through thorny underbrush. His face is lashed and blood flows. His lungs are heavy in his chest, brimming like lava. Rayford screams again. By sheer willpower Mel keeps going, thinking of arrows in his flesh, the horror of dogbite. He once knew a boy in scouts who thought all dogs liked him. But the trusting boy got too close to one who didn't. A hundred forty stitches, blind in one eye. Mel climbs higher, drops into a shallow stream, follows it against the flow. Can *they* follow him, in water? He doesn't think so.

When he can no longer hear the dogs or their anguished victim he stops to rest. Have they had enough of Rayford, and vanished, like he said they would do? Mel doesn't know if he believes Rayford. Near him water rushes through a crevice between boulders. He thrusts his burning bloodied face into the stream. So poundingly cold it's like an anesthetic. Soon his face is numb, but the rest of him shakes violently. He crawls out of the stream onto a bank thick with ferns and lies down. Teeth chattering, he huddles in pain and misery. But before long he feels a spreading warmth, front and back, could it be the quick-drying hairshirt? The tremors cease gradually. Lying on his back, knees up, he shivers at the upstart stare, the Luciferian grimness of an owl. Then Mel gazes at the sky, nearly as pale as dusty glass beyond the dark umbrellas of trees. He falls asleep.

Bird cheer; daybreak. Mel awakens with a start that painfully snaps his knee joints. His face feels stiff from healing cuts. He scarcely has the energy to kneel and pee. By his watch it is a little past six. The sky is pink and cloudless.

He makes another attempt to get the hairshirt off. It won't budge. As if it is glued on. But he doesn't find it all that uncomfortable. Real discomfort lies now in the pit of his empty, growling stomach.

Mel is alert to every forest sound without having to think about potential peril. Could it be that the blue man and his pack of dogs only hunt at night? By day he might be safe, if he's careful. How long has it been since he heard an airplane, a car, another human voice? Not counting Rayford's. That much of his recent ordeal is almost like a dream. But he can still smell, too powerfully, Rayford's stinking pelt. Feel the stubs of arrows in the man's oozing flesh.

They didn't get me, Mel thinks, and is cheered by his resourcefulness. *They didn't get me! It's only another day*—But less than a day, he reckons, more than six hours have passed. Eighteen more hours, and he will have fulfilled his penance. Vandy will release him—but where, and how, will he find her?

He might not have to look for her, though. She'll find him. There is some logic in this, considering the circumstances. He is easily able to convince himself that it will happen just that way. Vandy will find him, and oh God, there is no anger in his heart, he will be so happy just to see her face again, and tell her how much he loves her.

Meanwhile he could use something to eat. His wallet is in his back pocket, nineteen dollars in cash; thoroughly dampened, but it's still legal tender. If there's a place to spend it.

It hasn't really occurred to him before. The woods, the stream, the birds flickering noisily from branch to branch, the sun rising as it always does, everything except the blue man and his hounds is so natural, commonplace, it just hasn't occurred to him that over the next couple of hills there won't be a road, a town, a MacDonald's or a Wendy's or an accommodating motorist to give him a lift.

Two hours and four hills later, he's exhausted and even hungrier and nothing's changed at all except the sun is higher. The woods stretch on, endlessly, without a break. One stream is like another. No sign of habitation: not a weathercock, a well, a fence, a hovel. Old but virgin countryside through which he wanders, leaving behind his telltale, fleshy taint. Heart thumping, breathing through his mouth, he slumps down to rest. The hairshirt itches, but it's become so familiar he digs in with his fingers without giving it a thought.

The crooning of the hunter's horn snaps him from a momentary doze; at first he isn't sure he actually heard it. The sound of belling hounds convinces him otherwise.

His first impulse is to run, but he is already footsore; the undergrowth all around him allows for steady penetration, but not flight.

Hide.

Mel looks around frantically. Nothing but trees, some of which look as if they can be climbed. Would the dogs be fooled if he takes to a tree? He doesn't want to learn the hard way.

Maybe, he thinks, *it's Rayford they're after again.* But almost immediately he knows better; Mel knows it's his time and he struggles up from the ground with a low cry of distress.

The hounds of the blue man are on his track for nearly an hour before he glimpses them, as scary by daylight as they were in the dark.

He has reached, with the last of his strength and wind, the relative safety of a boulder the size of a small island in the rapids of a mountain river. Clinging helplessly by his fingertips to the high rock, Mel glances over his shoulder at the redbacked, crop-eared dogs as they appear in two's and three's by the water's edge, jostling one another, their hoarse cries louder than the roar of the river. The dogs are huge. They seem to be quarreling among themselves as the blue man appears on horseback, bow in hand; then two of the dogs take the plunge into the wild river and, as Mel has done, struggle from one precarious outcrop to another, heading toward him. The sun is electric on the surface of the river. More dogs follow the first two. A couple of them lose their footing and are swept downstream by the strong current.

Mel pulls himself higher, inching backwards up the boulder. His eyes are on the dogs as they maneuver closer to his sanctuary. When he shifts his attention to the blue man, Mel sees him standing in the stirrups, holding his bow at a 45-degree angle to the ground, tautly aiming. The arrow arches up and for a couple of seconds Mel loses sight of it, as it flys against the background of rugged sky-high pines on the side of the gorge. He is barely aware of the flickering downfall. When he sees the arrow again, it is standing out, with a slight riffling of sharply trimmed blue feathers, from the meat of his left leg four inches above the knee.

He screams at the sight of it, the lethal actuality, and not from the pain, because, numbed from his passage through chilling water, he is slow to feel pain. Another steelhead arrow goes skipping off the rock with a little spurt of sparks a few inches from his head. And a drenched hound has arrived, humpbacked, with sprung and hungering jaws.

Mel kicks at the hound, ineffectively; his ankle is seized. It's as if a large trap has snapped shut, he feels teeth nearly meeting through the ankle bones but again, curiously, pain is absent. There is a great white snowfield of shock around his heart, he views the clinging hound with blurred detachment and tries to get to his feet, shaking the trapped foot and the ninety-pound dog.

An arrow rips through his chest with great driving force and Mel is torn, dog and all, from the boulder, plunges insensibly into the spume and current, loses the dog in a deep trench between downstream rocks, erupts in a geyser of frigid water, knows nothing more . . .

Until well past moonrise.

He awakens to the tone of soft lapping water, the isolated cries of nocturnal birds, the hoo-haw bark of a barred owl.

Mel's resting place is a sandbar along one shore of the flattened, tranquil river. He is lying on his back with the broken shaft of an arrow protruding from his chest, another from his left thigh. Moonlight is diffused through a thick mist. He sits up slowly, fingering the

HAIRSHIRT

remains of the arrow. He should be dead, but he realizes with an emotion worse than terror of death that in his state of ungrace he cannot die.

Shuddering, he drinks from the shrouded river, listening keenly for the sound of the hunter's horn, the crooning of dogs.

If I—

If I can only—

But he doesn't know what to do next.

Belatedly, it occurs to him.

Twenty-four hours.

Mel looks at his watch. It is still working. The time is ten thirty-five.

Almost made it, he thinks. But where is he? And how can he hope to find Vandy?

His lip quivers and he begins to cry. Vandy'll find *him,* won't she?

But he can't be sure of that.

Maybe the best thing to do is walk.

The hairshirt, nailed to his chest by an arrow, is one incentive. When he is still, even for a minute, it torments him like a skin disease. On the move, he doesn't notice it so much.

One ankle is badly lacerated; Mel can feel sharp bits of bone grinding against flesh and muscle. But, although the pain should be excruciating at his slightest attempt to put weight on the ankle, he finds he can hobble along like a derelict: like old Rayford, child-molester. That seems to be part of the penance: always to be moving when conscious, never to be still. No wound so dreadful he can't serve as prey for the blue man's perpetual hunt.

Mel makes his way through shallow water to the rocky bank and follows the river in the fog.

Eleven-ten. Eleven-twenty.

Through the fog comes the lowing of the blue man's horn.

No! It isn't fair! Mel checks his watch frantically. He has only thirty-eight minutes to go.

"Vandy—!"

The sides of the river become steeper, more difficult to negotiate. The fog in this ravine is as dense as curdled cream. He cannot see obstacles until he runs into them. He stumbles and creeps on all fours. He is deathly tired, breathing hoarsely and in pain. But the hounds themselves are tireless, ecstatic in the nose-deep flow of his spoor.

Mel pauses, staring at his wrist watch.

Thirty-eight minutes left.

But that was—it's been at least—

His watch has stopped. Time is frozen.

"No fair!" Mel screams.

Up and stumbling, blindly, he runs into a concrete culvert. The belling of hounds nearby is like a chorus from hell.

But he hears something else in the fog: a droning, the unmistakable swish of tires on sweating asphalt.

It's a truck; a big one, maybe an eighteen-wheeler. Looking up, he sees headlights, running lights, phantoms in the fog, peaking, fading.

He's back; Godalmighty, he's back—!

Even so the blue man and his dogs are still in pursuit, unerring in the dismal fog, their voices echoing from the high concave walls of the culvert.

Mel scrambles higher. Something else whisks past him on the unseen road, a car or a small truck.

"Stop! Help me!"

The ground levels suddenly beneath his feet. He is, at last, by the edge of the road. He hears the frenzied panting of hounds on the slope behind him, the blue hunter's brute halloo. Opposite him something glows through the fog. Pale blue crosses.

Roadside chapel.

Sluggishly, then with a bouyant heart that seems to float him along, he runs. Before he can cross to the other side the swiftest of the pursuing dogs takes him down from behind.

"Vannnnnddddddy!"

Shock, again; the teeth of the hound are buried in the calf of his right leg, tearing the muscle. Mel drags both of them toward the shabby house trailer. He sees the doorway, then her pale intent face behind the screen. *Vandy.* She has heard him.

"Please! Please!"

Another hound has him. Snarling hounds are tumbling over one another in their eagerness to get their taste of blood, their fill of his flesh. Mel's scalp is torn, his neck bitten. Useless to struggle any more. Weeping, he tries to keep Vandy in focus. The fog . . . she appears to be drifting silently away. But there is a smile on her face. She raises her right hand slowly, a gesture of benediction, or farewell. Mel screams and screams.

Until it's all he hears. Until his screams fade to hoarse pitiful bleatings.

He is alone, his fingers digging into the surface of the road. The dogs have vanished, along with Vandy.

But for how long?

He gets slowly to his feet. Weak-kneed, filled with tremors, but okay. He no longer smells the rankness of hounds, or his own blood. His hands grope at his breastbone. The broken-off shaft of the arrow is not there.

The hairshirt seems loose. He snatches at the hard leather toggles. Frees one of them.

It's coming off!

Blood roars in his head. Vandy. Her upraised hand, a blessing, not goodbye. *Forgiveness.*

Pulling awkwardly at the hairshirt. The sun coming up through the fog behind him, he almost has it off, a loud droning, he feels a prickle of warning on the back of his neck, can't . . . quite . . .

As Mel turns awkwardly into the glare of the oncoming eighteen-wheeler he hears the dreadful hooting of the air horn, the locking of brakes; his mind is paralyzed by cacaphony, by the glitter of chrome before impact and a vision of Vandy's mild contemplative eyes in the sudden void.

The rig's driver manages to stop in a straight line midway on the bridge. After waking his partner in the sleeping compartment they both go back along the road with their flashlights and emergency markers and flares, the driver swearing and sweating coldly, but of course—his partner reassures him after hearing what happened—no way is it his fault.

They find Mel McGiveney, Jr. lying in his tangle of hairshirt on the shoulder fifty feet back of the rig, his eyes open. His body is a loose bloodied bag of shattered bones. He can't be alive, but he is; and the driver almost faints. Be still, don't try to get up, buddy, we called they're coming you'll be—but as he speaks he is aware that Mel is gazing with a look of fatal fascination at the rear of the trailer with its How Do You Like My Driving? sticker, and the company's sizable logo. Mel raises a trembling finger and points, then falls face down in a dark gout of his own insides. Both men turn away from the sight and the driver shines his strong light on the rig, on the tall painted figure with the leather jerkin and hunter's horn and sturdy bow. On the face with hooded eyes.

    The face, and the legend:
Blue Man Van Lines.

Interlude:

the Girl Next Door

The girl next door was frequently mad.
She wandered naked, blond on top but brown
between her legs, among
the family cows, until her father
and mother came to throw a shift over
her head and lead her
home on a leash. Much of the time
she eluded them: she was the whitest bird
of sunset, a blacksnake speeding
through spring grass
like an eel of the sea, a blue eyed
mole
     moonlighting
in beastly fields outside my bedroom
window. When they left her alone
she lived in a shattered tree furnished
with old nests, rocking
her tarbaby with the calico bonnet
and singing
     "My Jay, my Jay."
Placid bees
     hummed in the rough locks
of her hair.

Did I tell you her name? It was
Ivory Diane.

The bad boys of the neighborhood hunted
her with slingshots and cruel
barkings. But she was not the easiest
of prey: heady wolf-howls
and her midnight spoor had them going
in circles plenty of evenings
until one of them tripped and fell
on his Scout knife, bled a soft
river to daylight where no one
could hear him whimpering.

After that the hunter was the sheriff,
white-haired, scary as old Jesus.
Ivory Diane hid from him in a burrow
beneath the holyoak
til hunger drove her out and into the trap
he had fixed and waiting.

Must have been well into the witching
hour when I heard the tarbaby tapping
at my window. I took down the lamp
and followed him, jerky
through the dark, until I saw
her.
A shock-cord of silvery wire
gave her the jumps, lighting up
her pale, exhausted face
                        and mangled neck.
O Ivory Diane, the soul
of her speeding through
that quickened wire! I touched it
with my lamp:

                    "My Jay, my Jay,
I'm going with you."

So it was meant to be. An egg-tooth
of lightning pecked apart
her fragile skull and tarbabe melted
in her arms, inky
as a signature.
More amazed than frightened,
I carried the lamp back to my room
and there she lived
for over a year within that chimney,
fading so slowly
                    and at peace,
the whitest bird of sunset.

Good Morning, Daddy

I was finishing my laps around the lake about seven o'clock when Doyle Kindor's youngest boy Ricky Gene shot me in the head with Doyle's old Colt Woodsman.

Ricky Gene was only ten, and probably shouldn't have had the gun at all without Doyle or one of the older boys along with him for safety's sake. As I found out later, Ricky Gene sneaked the Woodsman out of the house to do some target shooting with a couple of his fifth-grade friends. The how and why of it weren't important to me, of course; the fact is a .22 caliber bullet went astray and struck me six centimeters from the temple, just above the left eye, penetrating the skull at a slight downward angle, splitting apart on impact with the bone (I have well-calcified bones). Pieces of the bullet then plowed through the left hemisphere of the cerebral cortex, lodging variously in the motor cortex and Broca's area. One small fragment traveled as far as the cerebellum.

I didn't lose consciousness. I went down in a heap with a bloodied face, partially paralyzed and unable to speak. Spud Morris, doggedly trying to drop thirty pounds, was trudging along the lakeside path about forty yards behind me. I know he'd heard the little firecracker pops of the Woodsman too, and as soon as he crossed the shelf of limestone that juts out over the weedy cove where the bream are most likely to be biting early in the morning he saw me and realized what had happened.

I could see and hear Spud okay. At first I didn't know, or maybe want to believe, that I was shot. I thought I'd run into something in the twilight, like a dead branch protruding from a tree. But Spud, a Vietnam vet, left no doubt. "You've been shot, you've been shot," he said. "Damn careless kids!" Sweat dripped from the tip of his nose. He told me not to move, dabbed at the blood on my face with one of the terrycloth sweatbands he always had with him, and yelled for help. His voice carried across the lake to the homes on Thornhill Road. The neighborhood that Caroline and Sharissa and I had moved to not quite two years ago, after a decade of hard work, planning, and a lot of scrimping to make it all possible. We were in our dream house, and now this had to happen.

The paramedics from the fire department got to me in under ten minutes. The emergency medical unit was something new in Sky Valley. Caroline, my wife, was largely responsible. She'd spent three years lobbying the City Council, getting the necessary community support: four thousand signatures on a petition. We had a fine hospital, too, for a city our size.

My head was swelling fast and my left eye was nearly shut. On advice from the trauma center at the hospital, the medics put me on oxygen, sodium pentothol to decrease the brain's metabolism and lidocaine to reduce intracranial pressure. My brain was rapidly filling up with blood. I still didn't feel much pain, and I couldn't feel anything at all on my right side. I was blinking and woozy, the lashes of my left eye sticky from blood and leaking brain tissue, but as they carried me, sitting up, around to the other side of the lake, I saw a couple of cops talking to Ricky Gene and his friends. Those kids had the sickest, scaredest faces I'd ever seen. Unlikely as it seems, I wasn't worried about myself—shock, I suppose—but I felt sorry for Ricky Gene. He was a good boy. It was always "Yes, sir" and "No, ma'am" with Ricky Gene.

I guess the sodium pentothol took affect quickly, because I was drifting off by then. Spud Morris kept shouting at me as they hurried to the ambulance with the gurney I was strapped to. Something about finding Caroline and Sharissa right away. It was a primary month and Caroline was off in another congressional district working on Claude Gilley's campaign for the United States Senate; she hadn't expected to be home before ten o'clock. Sharissa, I thought, might still be at the country club playing tennis after her shift as a lifeguard. I assumed she'd probably arrive at the hospital first. But I didn't want my baby to see me with a hole in my head.

The traumatized brain always swells from bleeding. Most

severe head injury cases arrive at the hospital with no neurological functions, and if they don't get fast expert treatment, the swelling brain herniates, forcing the brain stem through the bottom of the skull and compressing it to the point where it can no longer function. Then the lungs and the heart stop. Pure oxygen to slow down the heart, regulate the violent pumping of blood to a brain that already holds too much, is the first requirement. Then emergency surgery to relieve internal pressure, suction off the necrotic tissue, all the bone and bullet fragments that can cause trouble later if the patient survives the initial trauma. After that the neuro team replaces the bone they removed to get at the brain, and hopes for the best.

I came to in the IC unit. At first I couldn't make any sense of being wired up to a respirator, some monitors and drip-feeds. I also had drains in my head. The last thing I remembered was dropping the Honda off at Ed Reedy's for an overdue brake job.

My lips felt caked and dry. My throat was painfully dry too. My left eye was still swollen shut. I couldn't lift either of my hands. I was barely able to move my head.

The first face I saw was Dr. Jesse Fernando's. We used to play racketball doubles at the Y until his back went out on him. Since then he'd put on weight, added a chin, some gray hairs.

"Do you know me, Greg?" he said. "I realize you can't talk. Just blink once for yes."

Why can't I talk? I said, or thought I said. I know that my lips moved. My tongue felt old and dry and wasn't very mobile.

"Just blink."

I blinked my right eye for him. There were a couple of nurses at bedside, checking this, checking that, jotting things down.

"Caroline and Sharissa are outside," Jesse said. "I'll let them see you for a few minutes. But I wanted to talk to you first."

One of the nurses put a sponge to my lips. I was able to suck. But she didn't let me have much of the tepid water. Just enough to moisten my lips and tongue.

Jesse explained then that I'd been accidentally shot in the head, that the little bullet had fragmented and done a lot of damage, but that I was going to survive.

He didn't go into paralysis or permanent speech impairment or any other expectable consequences at that point; he grasped my left hand reassuringly and smiled and said, "Here's your family."

I got some idea of how long they'd been waiting from the puffiness and discoloration around Caroline's eyes. She'd probably been without sleep for twenty-four hours. Sharissa was trying to be brave, but her lips were pale, the skin ragged from being chewed. They both kissed me and I smiled and I don't think either of them had much to say, except that they loved me and I shouldn't worry. I couldn't worry about anything; I was in twilight by then.

The next face I saw was one of the nurses, a slim mocha-colored girl.

"Good morning," I said. "Or is it morning?"

She just stared at me. She looked shocked. She went away quickly. When she came back there was a doctor with her.

"Mr. Walker, I'm Dr. Kiddfield. I understand you spoke to Ruby."

"Sure I did," I said. My voice sounded all right to my ears. "Why not?"

"Well—" Kiddfield consulted my recent trauma history on his clipboard, grimacing a few times as he read. "According to this, you suffered extensive damage to Broca's area."

"What does that mean?"

"Broca's area controls the necessary muscle movements in order for you to pronounce words. There's more to speech than that, but in a nutshell—"

"Maybe I'm not hurt as bad as everyone thought. I feel pretty good, actually." I reached up with my right hand to rub the stubble on my cheek. "Could use a shave."

Kiddfield watched me, then pored over the information on his chart again. He looked as thoroughly confused as any human being I'd ever seen.

"I'll be back," he said. "I just want to have a good look at your EEGs."

That afternoon, after another CAT scan, I was moved to a

GOOD MORNING, DADDY

private room. Except for a persistent headache, I felt good. My head was still bandaged but the swelling had gone down. I could move my right hand at will, and feeling was coming back in the leg. I spent an hour with Caroline and Sharissa, until three doctors showed up for an audience. Two of them had helicoptered in from Atlanta. They had the look of heavyweights in their field, and Jesse Fernando tended to be somewhat deferential.

Jesse said to me, "Good buddy, we can't figure out if you're just lucky or good."

"I don't know what you mean. When do you reckon I'll be getting out, Jess?"

Jess glanced at the eminent neurosurgeons. The eldest, a man with crewcut white hair and the ruddy complexion of a construction foreman—I believe his name was Kogen—then gave me a concise summary of the usual expectations when a bullet of any size passes most of the way through the human brain. The unfortunate victim has years of physiotherapy ahead of him, and is never a hundred percent functional thereafter. In my case nearly all the symptoms of neurological impairment had vanished after four days; my memory, despite the loss of approximately two tablespoons of frontal lobe, was as good as it had ever been. Most men, I was told, would still have been in a coma so soon after surgery.

"But there are always exceptions," I said.

Kogen shrugged slightly, smiling. "I was a field surgeon in Vietnam for three years. I'm confident I've seen almost everything, including one soldier who came back from the dead as they were about to prepare him for burial. But the adaptive and recovery powers of your brain is unique in my experience."

"What about the bullet fragments?" I said. "Could they cause me trouble later on?"

"That's hard to say. Dr. Fernando recovered the bulk of them. It wasn't worth the risk of trying to get all of the fragments out. You're, what, forty-five years old?" I nodded. "You have the constitution of a man twenty years younger. That may be a factor in your—umm, unprecedented recovery time."

"I've always tried to take care of myself. Most of my life I've worked two jobs. I always like to say, I'm too busy to get sick." I chuckled and they smiled, but I still didn't care for the way they were looking at me. As if I was some sort of insult to their education and experience. "This is the first time I've been in a hospital since I was born. Hope it's my last."

The reverend Bob Justival from First Iconium Baptist Church had a little different slant on my narrow escape.

"It's a miracle, Greg!" Bob said, or rather, exulted; he has that bully, holy look of the fatted friars of old. His fervent style can wear you down, after a while. Most parishioners of First Iconium refer to his wife Beth Ann as "shy," but to me she looks sort of stunned most of the time. "Jesus heard our prayers, good buddy."

"God has surely touched me," I agreed.

"A special favor," Bob beseeched me. "Would you testify at our next revival meeting?"

There was no doubt about it, I was the local celebrity of the week. Or month. Front page of the Sky Valley *Tribune*. I just hoped it would stay local. I had a lot of visitors, including the repentent perpetrator Ricky Gene Kindor, and his family. I had my picture taken for the *Trib* with my arm around Ricky. We smiled at each other. No hard feelings. Just be careful where you point that thing next time, Ricky Gene.

I didn't know until much later that the Associated Press had picked up the story, and the photo, and it had been reprinted in papers around the country, as well as in Canada. So far away. But these are modern times, a world of instant communications. We are a global village.

Headaches were never a big problem, and after about a week they stopped. After a couple of spells of fever there were no complications. On the Monday following the accidental shooting I was released from the hospital. Jess recommended another week of recuperation at home, and I was in no hurry to go back to work until my hair grew in; not knowing in advance of surgery how many entries into the skull he'd have to make, Jesse's team had shaved my entire head. But my hair has always grown quickly. To keep it the length I like it, I need to have it trimmed twice a month.

Fortunately I had a boy named Bisco working for me at Walker's Authorized RCA Servicenter, a junior college dropout who was a genius at locating the trouble in TV's and stereos that have been blitzed by sudden power surges—most people have no idea of the damage that can be caused if they leave their sets plugged in during an electrical storm, even if the set is turned off.

If Caroline hadn't been working eighteen hours a day to get Claude Gilley re-elected, we might have taken some time off and driven down to Calloway Gardens or even Hilton Head for a vacation we both badly needed. Sharissa was lifeguarding days at the country club and working four nights a week at Burger King, but even so I saw more of her than I did my wife. Sharissa made it a point to spend time with me, having sensed what I was doing my best to hide: a post-trauma depression, a deep uneasiness at having come so abruptly to the stark realization that it was all going to end for Greg Walker, sooner than I had anticipated. Although it was certainly not my nature, then or now, to brood about death.

Caroline alternately slaved over her typewriter in her tiny office off our bedroom trying to come up with speeches that would put Claude back in the good graces of his disenchanted constituents, and running off to whatever club breakfast or civic forum he was scheduled for. Sharissa and I spent several weekend hours scraping and repainting the front porch. Looking back, I realize that they were some of the happiest hours of my life.

I'd been married to Caroline for eighteen years; Sharissa, our only child, would be seventeen in October, a senior in high school, where she was Miss Everything. She deserved all of her honors. She was a lovely girl who had inherited my slim build, Caroline's hazy gray eyes and Georgia peach complexion. She never wore makeup and didn't need any. Her closest friends, boys and girls, were from our church. They were all active, personable youngsters with high ideals and rigorous moral standards, no trace of the soiled insolence that characterizes so many young people these days. In an age where numerous nut cases are on the loose and smut is a national blight, we never had a moment's worry as to where Sharissa was, who she was with or what she was doing.

No matter what time of day I needed to be up—and for years I'd awakened at four-thirty a.m. to deliver the Atlanta *Constitution* locally for extra income—Sharissa was always in the kitchen ahead of me, the coffee would be perking, and she'd greet me with a cheerful, "Good Morning, Daddy." She always had her own reasons for being up and around that early, but I suspected her primary motivation was just to spend those few extra minutes with me. We were no longer under severe financial pressure—Caroline's spells of nervous debilitation were few and far between these days—and breakfast was now at a more reasonable hour, but Sharissa had never abandoned the small ritual that was so precious to me.

Caroline's nerves and melancholia—well, it had been a strain on the family union no matter how hard Sharissa and I tried to pretend otherwise. Who could blame Caroline? She was simply one of those high-strung individuals with more nervous energy than is good for them. More than one member of Caroline's large family, going back a hundred years, had been subject to what they referred to as "sinking spells." In the old days the Crowder family manics dosed themselves with patent medicines liberally infused with cocaine, and were, perhaps, the better for it. Caroline's treatments had been more complex and of limited value. In addition to our unyielding trust in God, what seemed to benefit Caroline most was the passage of time, and, of all things, an early menopause, which occurred when she was forty-six. Sharissa had been spared this glum and potentially dangerous inheritance, although like any teenager she could be moody. Since we'd moved to Thornhill Road Caroline had suffered only one crisis, after a tongue-lashing from the senator, whose home-district office she managed while he was away in Washington. Caroline put up with Claude, not only because the pay was good, but because she believed he still had value to our state—a point I was always careful not to argue with her, although I and numerous of his colleagues in Washington considered Claude to be a four-flushing son of a bitch.

We finished the tedious job of hand-painting the latticework beneath the porch by moonrise, cleaned and put away the brushes. I was standing on our flagstone patio looking out over the placid silver lake and a twinkle of birds at the water's edge. Burgers were sizzling on the charcoal grill. Sharissa came down the steps from the kitchen with the hamburger buns, potato chips and catsup. She put the stuff on the picnic table and came over, slipped an arm around my waist, laid her head on my shoulder. As always I was ravished by the power of her art, which is called youth. I clasped her hand and sighed contentedly.

"What were you thinking just now?" she asked me; she used to ask that all the time, when she was much younger, but was out of the habit now. It was one of those special privileges and freedoms of childhood that seems to be lost once they enter the prison of puberty.

"I was thinking that life is good."

"Amen," Sharissa said, and tightened her grip on me, laughing, a joyous laugh that expressed more eloquently than any words or prayers the miracle that had kept us together.

Two days later the madwoman came to town.

It was unfortunate that this was also the day Caroline was able to steal enough time from Claude Gilley's campaign so the two of us could have an early dinner at the Ovenbird.

I first saw the woman earlier in the day outside my store, which is just off the courthouse square in downtown Sky Valley. I noticed the car she was driving before I paid any attention to her. It was a vintage Pontiac that had seen plenty of miles and a lot of bad road. Mud caked in the fender wells, cracks in most of the windows, a redneck's squalid car. I was on the floor trying to convince Carmack Knox to splurge and buy the big-screen projection model he'd been hankering after for months. Lord knows he could afford it. The woman drove her Pontiac past my store at least four times, slow enough to annoy the drivers behind her. She looked almost too elderly to be driving at all. She was obviously looking for something, or someone, but she probably couldn't see inside the store: on sunny days I don't keep all of the overhead lights on, to pinch a dollar or two.

Carmack procrastinated. I made a service call out on Balm of Gilead Road, returned to town at one-thirty. The dirty red-and-white Pontiac eight, one of those with the Big Chief ornament on the hood (which does go back a few decades), was parked in one of the diagonals that surround Lonzell Freely Square, named for a local boy posthumously awarded the Medal of Honor in the Vietnam conflict. I didn't see the woman who owned the Pontiac on my way to the bank. She might have been eating her lunch with other retirees on one of the benches around the town gazebo. Or shopping at Goldblum's. Goldblum was slashing prices again at his old-fashioned clothing emporium, hoping to lure customers away from the new mall. He's been on the square for sixty years and is always crying the blues. Fact is he owns half of the choicest commercial property in downtown Sky Valley.

Mindy Lockard, one of the loan officers at Sky Valley National, came over to chat while I was in line to make a deposit.

"Did she find you?"

I was wearing a Braves baseball cap and I still had a big caramel-colored elastic patch covering much of my forehead. The cap was new and making my fuzzy scalp itch, so I took it off briefly.

"Who, Mindy?"

"The woman who was looking for you. She came in to cash a traveler's check. Royal Bank of Canada. She had your picture that she cut out of a newspaper. Your famous picture. Hey, your hair's really coming back fast. Without that part on the left you look young enough to be one of those kids who hang around the mall wearing suspenders and paratrooper boots."

"Wish I felt that young, Mindy."

"Don't we all. I'm not kidding, though. You look terrific." And Mindy looked wistful. She was forty, and played tennis nearly every day to keep her figure. Her weight was down, but she had serious sun-wrinkles to go with her coppery tan. Mindy also had a crush on me and I wasn't exactly disinterested in her, but an affair was out of the question.

"By the way," I said, "thanks for the flowers."

"*De nada*. God, you really scared us, Greg. You're one for the books, I guess."

"I've heard of men who have survived worse. Did she tell you what her name was?"

"Oh, the woman who—no, Sandy cashed the TC for her. Sandy could tell you. But it looks as if she's on her break right now."

"Well, whoever she is, I guess she knows where to find me. What does she look like?"

"Old. White hair. Seventy or better."

On my way back to the store I cut across the square. The Pontiac was still in the same slot. The red flag was up on the meter. She'd be getting a ticket as soon as Alma the meter maid cruised by on her scooter. I looked at the license plate in passing. It was as dirty as the rest of the lower half of the Pontiac, but I could tell that the car was registered in British Columbia.

I had the uneasy feeling I was being watched—but a lot of people had been staring at me since the gunshot accident. As if I was a freak of nature. I didn't like it, but what could I do? Go about my business and assume it would all be forgotten soon.

GOOD MORNING, DADDY

* * *

They had a good crowd in the dining room of the Ovenbird by the time I got there, at a quarter to seven. Caroline was late, but we both had expected her to be. Our favorite table is the one in the center of the high windows overlooking the walled garden, in a nook away from the traffic patterns. I sat where the quarter-inch of stubble on my head wouldn't be conspicuous and had a Campari and soda, the only spirits I ever take.

Caroline showed up ten minutes later, escorted by Fog Hatley, one of the Ovenbird's owners.

"How 'bout them Dawgs?" Fog boomed. His standard greeting. He's such a big fan of UGA football he even goes to intrasquad scrimmages—the college football season wouldn't start for another three weeks.

"Heck of a recruiting year," I said, as if I hadn't said it a dozen times already. "Two high school All-Americans. How's Casey handling that switch to tight end?"

"He's a gooder; and he's gonna be a-better. What can I get you, darlin'?"

"Coke and four aspirin," Caroline said with a husky sigh.

"Gonna pull old Claude through this time around?"

"It'll be a squeaker," Caroline said, confidentially. And added, "You didn't hear it from me."

"Gotcha," Fog said, and went away. We heard him say, "How about them *Dawgs?*" from across the room. Caroline and I smiled at each other. She'd lost a few pounds in the past couple of weeks, which was to her advantage, but her cheeks looked sunken as a result and the lines around her mouth had deepened.

"You're coming straight home with me tonight," I said. "I'm taking the telephone off the hook and locking up your typewriter."

She smiled again, gratefully. "I just keep telling myself, Tuesday, Caroline, it'll be over Tuesday. Win the primary, we're home. November'll be a breeze."

"Love you," I said.

Caroline reached for my hand on the table.

"I know I've been impossible these last couple of months. But if it wasn't for politics, well—"

"We don't have to talk about it. Sorry I gave you such a bad scare."

"Scare?" She squeezed my hand. "That's the understatement of the century. But we're not going to talk about it. We're good people. We deserve to be blessed."

"Not another word," I agreed.

"Pardon me," the madwoman said. "This man is my husband, and I need to talk to him."

Caroline and I looked up simultaneously. She was standing a little behind me, a large woman with permed white hair. Her eyebrows were newly plucked and penciled; in fact she looked as if she'd just had the works at Luralee's downtown. But she had on too much rouge and a purple eyeshadow that was not becoming. Her upper lip was pleated like a boudoir lampshade. The sunlight splashed our way by the fountain in the Ovenbird's garden revealed liver spots through her vivid peach makeup base.

She was looking at Caroline. We were still holding hands across the small table. The woman smiled, showing gold-lined teeth that didn't appear to have been worth saving in the first place.

"Let go of him," she said, still smiling, but corrosively. "He don't belong to you. I staked a prior claim; honey, and believe me it'll hold up in any court of law."

Caroline blinked; she's a quick-witted woman and almost never at a loss for words. Her hand, covering mine, twitched a little, the diamonds in her wedding band reflecting a dancing light over the small enameled rose in the bud vase.

"Excuse *me*," I said. "This is our table and my wife and I are having a private conversation. Whoever you are—"

The woman looked at me. She had a strong beaked nose and cheekbones bold as a squaw's. I could see that, much younger, she would have been a rough-hewn beauty. But longing was weighty in her, and toxic as a tumor. I was rapidly becoming more concerned than indignant.

"Stuff it, Frederick," she said. "It's been a long time, but the giveaway is, see, you haven't changed a bit. Always been the problem with you, hasn't it?"

She laughed. Her voice hadn't carried, but the laughter—coarse, uninhibited—attracted attention. It was almost impossible to detect that she was putting on an act. But blue veins showed on each white knuckle of the hands that gripped her purse. And something—a long-held sorrow, remorse—ghosted the dense black pupils of her eyes.

"Greg—"

The woman turned her head sharply when Caroline spoke. "Not Greg. Not *Walker*. That's all hooey, sweetheart. His name is Frederick Sullivan. I'm Mrs. Roxanne Sullivan. We were married April 3rd, 1952, in New Lost River, British Columbia. Married eighteen years. Until—until—" It was then her voice cracked, almost undetectably. She sniffed. "Do you want to tell me what happened, Frederick? I sure God deserve . . . an explanation, don't you think?"

I swallowed and looked at Caroline, furrowing my brow significantly. She got the message and stood up at once. "Excuse me," she said, and left the table. The woman turned to watch her as I unobtrusively moved my chair so that I was not sitting trapped sideways between her and the windows.

"Didn't do so bad for yourself, huh, Frederick? Of course she's beginning to show her age some. I guess I did too. Was that it? Was that all there was to it—" and now she looked sharply at me with one of those disconcertingly quick turns of her head, "—you bastard?"

"I don't know you. I don't know what you're talking about. I'd advise you—Mrs. Sullivan—"

"Got a proper Southern accent, 'n everything," she sneered. "But I'm not fooled. As for your advice, hooey. You can stuff that too. You're coming back with me. To New Lost River. Nothing's left. The house, the lounge. Gone. But we can start over. I've got some good years left, Frederick. I knew as soon as I saw your picture in the Vancouver paper I was willing to forgive you. All you need to do is tell me—"

Caroline was coming back with Fog Hatley behind her. Fog is six-five and stopped weighing himself when he hit three hundred pounds. I relaxed at the sight of him. I didn't know if there was any danger in her or not, but Fog would have the woman out of his restaurant in a matter of seconds.

Possibly she sensed, from my eye movements, what was going on. She moved quickly for her size, slipping into Caroline's vacated chair. At the same time she drew a small nickeled automatic from her purse. Her eyes flickered to Caroline and Fog. When they were ten feet from the table I waved them off.

"Tell that tub of guts to stay put," the woman said. "Or I'll put one through your eye, and we'll see how quick you get up and walk away from that! Remember how good a shot I was, Frederick? Maybe you don't think I've still got what it takes."

"This is really—not very smart of you."

"I'm smart, all right. I'm *very* smart. It was me who made such a big success of the lounge, remember? All you ever did was tend bar and fool around with the strippers. Couple of those young slim-hipped cowpokes too, as I recall. Never mind. It's all bygones with me. Got myself all fixed up for you this afternoon." She preened, her smile striking gold again. "I still love you, Frederick, or I wouldn't be here."

Her gaze swarmed on me, like a cluster of bees around a honeyed fingertip. Quite obviously, in my own eyes she saw nothing but disgust.

She stopped smiling. There was a quirk of malevolence to her mouth. She made an odd clucking sound. "What happened to Bonnie? You know where she is? She never came to see me even one time, after they put me away."

"I don't know anybody named Bonnie," I said, looking at the muzzle of the pistol and ready to explode from frustration.

"Don't know your own daughter?" She clucked again, out of the side of her mouth. "Fat chance. Well, you're crafty, Fred, I'll give you that. But I've got the goods, lover. Tell those two to get over here toot sweet, and let's get this show on the road."

"What show?"

"Don't try my patience! No more bum steers. What's her name?"

"My wife?"

"I'm your wife! She's—she—doesn't count." The woman faltered then; there were flecks of saliva at the corner of her overly-colorful mouth, the side that tended to fly out of control when she made the clucking noise. She had the slick devoted expression of someone who is listening, suspensefully, for her heart to start pumping after a hiatus. But her grip on the automatic was still solid.

The tables on either side of us were empty; so far the madwoman hadn't attracted much attention. The fist with the little automatic in it was on the table in front of her, the muzzle angled up at my face. A waiter approached and Fog Hatley sent him off with a curt motion of his head. We looked at each other. Fog backed off a step but Mrs. Roxanne Sullivan caught the movement out of

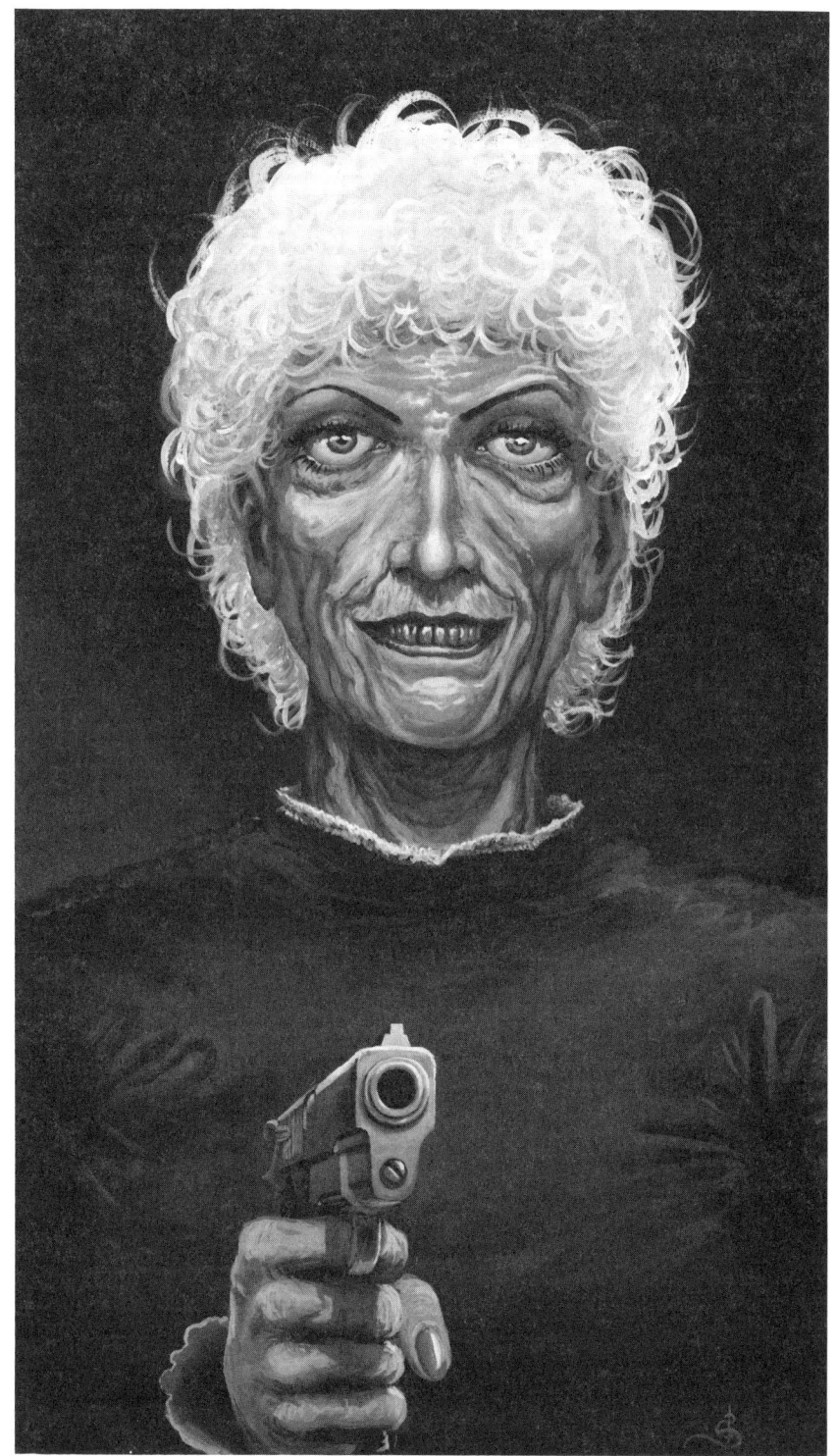

the corner of her eye and said, "Stay standing where you are right now, fat stuff. You—Mrs. Bogus—come on over here."

Caroline advanced slowly to the table. I could tell, by the tightness of her eyes, how frightened she was. I knew I'd better do something, and quickly. I could shove the table toward the Sullivan woman, knocking her off balance, maybe out of the chair. But if there was a possibility that the shiny automatic would go off . . .

"If you've convinced yourself that I somehow mean something to you," I said to the madwoman, "why threaten to kill me?"

She looked vague for a few seconds. She licked her lips. "That's a bum steer," she said finally. I didn't know what she meant. But I wasn't particularly skilled at talking to, trying to reason with, the mentally disoriented. To Caroline she repeated, "Open my purse. Take out the envelope. Like I said, it's all there. Marriage license. Pictures of me and Frederick together. Have a look, then tell me if you still think your claim's any good."

"Please—I wish you wouldn't do this—please, he's been hurt already, put your gun away."

"Fat chance. Mrs. Bogus, I said open the envelope! And get set to piss in your pants." A tremor of excitement agitated her garishly-painted features. I was, for the most part, keeping an eye on the pistol.

Caroline did as she was told. There was a large packet of photos secured with a thick rubber band. A newspaper clipping fell to the table and I carefully reached for it. The familiar photo of Ricky Gene and myself in the hospital room, reprinted in a Vancouver newspaper. I was wearing my post-operative turban. The quality of the photograph wasn't exceptional. How Mrs. Roxanne Sullivan could have decided I was her long-missing husband was beyond my ability to comprehend. I have strong features—a Roman nose, high cheekbones, heavy eyebrows, rather penetrating eyes the color of weak tea. So do a great many men.

Caroline passed me a black-and-white photograph. This showed a far younger, busty Roxanne standing in front of an ordinary-looking corner beer joint with glass block on either side of the padded doors, her arm around the sought-after Frederick. He resembled me, superficially. I didn't care for the way he grinned at the camera. The cocky, lady-killer type. I could read a history of a knock-about life in his face. There was a row of B-girls behind them, bartenders, kitchen help. The lounge was called The Pigalle. A hand-lettered *Grand Opening* banner hung from a tacky marquee. There were snow-covered mountains in the near background.

I laid the photo and the newspaper clipping down wearily. Caroline was shaking her head, trying not to cry.

"When did the Pigalle open for business?" I said.

"1954. As you very well know."

"How old was—Frederick, then?" I asked the madwoman, seeking a chink in the hard fortress of her self-deception, a means to yank the entire edifice down.

"You were thirty-four, lover."

"Then I—I mean Frederick—would now be nearly seventy years old. Didn't you ever stop to think about—"

"Sure I thought about it! Being as how you never aged a day in the eighteen years we were married, I didn't see any special reason why you would have aged since then."

I reached for a glass of water. The muzzle of the pistol snapped up alertly. The madwoman clucked, and clucked again; some spit flew from the corner of her twitching mouth. Her eyes looked different to me. They seemed to be peering backwards, past old ecstasies into the darkness of her pathetic soul. I looked at Caroline, who was totally befuddled. A tear had squeezed onto one cheek. Fog Hatley loomed behind her, close enough to grab and hurl her aside if Mrs. Roxanne Sullivan aimed the pistol her way.

The madwoman's eyes flicked back to the here and now.

"Time for the *piece de résistance*," she said. She pronounced it correctly. "Nobody believes their own eyes, hey? Okay, Frederick. Remember how you earned your living at the sawmill before you cozied up to me and got your hands on my nest egg? You almost cut your arm off once. Left a wicked scar midway of your left forearm, didn't it?" I heard Caroline react, a sharp intake of breath. And I heard, from the madwoman, "peel back your sleeve. Here comes proof positive you're who I say."

I unbuttoned the left cuff slowly, and rolled it back. She clucked again, triumphantly. "That's how you always did it, just before you tended bar! Peeled back those cuffs in such a dandified manner. Still keep your hands nice, don't you, Frederick, the nails all buffed and—"

I suddenly pulled the sleeve back as far as my elbow. Of course there was no scar.

She stared at my unblemished forearm, then reached quickly

with her free hand and clutched at me. I could have disarmed her then with little potential danger, but as she touched me I looked deeply into her eyes and saw her mind fall apart, almost like a slow-motion study of a calving glacier. A momentary churning, then nothing left back of her eyes but a great white void. Her fingers on my forearm had no strength. I easily took the little automatic from her other hand. She was leaning forward against the table. Her mouth had sagged open, and she was drooling. She didn't make a sound.

The Ovenbird's patrons had scarcely been disturbed by the drama taking place in our alcove. Fog Hatley had a screen set up around the table, and the police came in the back door, took Mrs. Roxanne Sullivan away in the chair she sat in. She was completely catatonic.

Caroline and I had lost our appetites. The detective in charge of the investigation, a man named Boyer, talked to us in Fog's office. He looked at the photos the madwoman had brought with her from British Columbia, and studied me thoroughly without appearing to look too hard. He was a speed-reader of character, absorbing volumes of nuance and personal history in a single glance. We asked him what would happen to the Sullivan woman. Judging from the state she was in when they carried her out, detective Boyer's opinion was that she'd wind up in the state mental hospital. Of course the authorities would try to track down relatives or friends in British Columbia who might be willing to be responsible for her. At any rate, he said, we shouldn't be concerned about Mrs. Roxanne Sullivan showing up in Sky Valley again.

On the way home I broke a bad silence by saying, "Another close call."

Caroline had her hands over her face. "Stop," she said. She hissed when she breathed. That made me uneasy. It was a habit she had, when emotionally things were going badly for her. "It's just been too much, don't you see? I don't even want to think about it."

As soon as we were in bed I began to make love to her. We've always had a good sex life, except for those down times when it was useless to approach Caroline. We started all right, she was very responsive, and then she just turned off, her eloquent fingers poised lifelessly at the base of my spine, as if she had forgotten, not how, but why. She didn't ask me to stop, knowing I was closer to my climax than she had been, but, burdened with the sudden blankness of her flesh, I couldn't keep on, so it was one of those rare fizzles for us. We lay side by side on the bed with the moonlight on our bodies, holding hands.

"You haven't changed, either," she said.

"What, honey?"

"We've been married eighteen years, too."

"I thought we weren't going to—"

"Look at me. Everything sags, or puckers, I have to have a rinse twice a month or I'd look like my own mother, because of the gray—"

"Don't," I said.

"But *you're* still the same. Your body is—"

"I run thirty miles a week, minimum."

She was quiet for a long time, but because of the rhythm of her breathing I knew she hadn't fallen asleep.

"Ever been to British Columbia?" Caroline said.

"I was up there just last week, scouting for a nice little topless lounge to buy."

She rolled to her right, then rolled back and hit me with a pillow, her usual response to my occasional absurdities. I tickled her. Finally she begged me to quit.

"Sharissa'll hear us."

"I don't think it'll do her any harm to know we have fun in bed. After all these years."

Caroline snuggled against my chest, and reached lower.

"I could—if you want—you know—what you like."

"And I'll do what you like." Although, after eighteen years of marriage, she was still too bashful—prudish, I suppose—to admit she liked it. The mutual act we performed to our complete satisfaction, is still a felony in the state of Georgia, and men—but no women that I know of—have done long stretches in prison for their pleasures. The Baptist Church was against it too, I'm sure. I tithe, and attend our church faithfully. But no sensible man would allow his religion to regulate his sex life.

"How did you ever learn to make love like that?" Caroline murmured, when we were finished. She had said it many times before, not really expecting an answer. Just grateful, I liked to believe.

And my stock reply was, "Curiosity and unlimited opportunities with the woman I love."

Because we were so warm and close and loving at that moment, what happened not long after was especially disturbing to me.

I awoke about three in the morning. Since the shooting I hadn't jogged, and the missed exercise caused me to be restless at night. Caroline wasn't in bed with me. The bathroom was dark, but there was a light on in the hall outside our bedroom. I smelled smoke.

I found Caroline in the living room sitting cross-legged on the sofa in her short nightgown, hunched over a large photo album in her lap. There was a pack of Marlboros on the coffee table. She was smoking a cigarette, holding it with a sort of pinched craven intimacy, and there were butts in the coffee mug she was using for an ashtray. A hunger for tobacco had always been a prelude to one of her manic phases. She turned the stiff gray oblong pages of our wedding album with a robotic, mildly distressed monotony, her eyes glazed. She smiled sadly between puffs on her cigarette.

"'Til death do us part,'" I heard her say.

"Caroline?"

She looked up, not surprised. "Oh, hi." Her gaze wandered; she cocked her head, as if my image had appeared, mysteriously, near the crown molding. Or some other image of great interest to her.

"Where did you get the cigarettes?" I asked from the doorway.

"Oh, Jim Shively gave them to me to hold. He said absolutely not to give him one, he was turning into a human chimney."

"So now you're turning into a human chimney."

"I'm just having this one, then I'll quit." She returned her attention, slowly, to the wedding album. There were other photo albums on the coffee table. She had taken them all down from the shelf in the hall closet. Making visual contact with the flash-frozen past. First car, first home, first and only precious child. I wondered if there was any Prozac in the house.

"How many did we have at our wedding? A hundred sixty-eight

guests? Look at this. Here's Maceo Hubbard and Roy Starks. I went to school with both of them. Maceo's dead."

"I know. Heart."

Her breath hissed hotly as she smoked. "I saw Roy the other day. He looks bad. Most of his hair's gone. He's fifty pounds overweight. I think he said something about varicose veins."

"Sweetheart, please come to bed."

"In a minute," she said sharply. "And here you are."

"No," I said. "This is me; and that's a picture in a wedding album. And I'm not just the same as I used to be. I'm older and better."

Caroline methodically turned another page.

"One hundred sixty-eight guests. Each of them a friend or relative of mine. Where were your relatives?"

"I didn't know then, and I don't know now. What are you trying to do, Caroline?"

One of the pages came out of the album as she turned it. She held up the page with an apologetic smile, and mumbled, "Coming apart."

I walked over to the sofa and took the page and the album it had come from out of her hands. She didn't resist me. I put the wedding album on the coffee table with the others. I sat down beside her. She handed me the cigarette, holding it upright like a tiny torch, and I took that too, put it out in the coffee mug. We sat side by side, touching at the hip.

"The long and short of it is," Caroline said, "I don't know who you are. You're somebody from Baltimore, Maryland, who did his service at Fort Rucker, got out of the Army, and settled in Sky Valley."

"Because I loved it here. The first time I saw this town, I knew I was going to stay."

"And I fell for you like a ton of bricks. Didn't care where you came from, even though mama and daddy had their objections. I married you because you were a kind, decent, loving man, and you've taken wonderful care of me. Sharissa and I adore you, Greg. But *who are you?*"

"Just a guy who's had a little luck in his life, after a bad beginning."

"Did you ever make any attempt to find out who your father was, what happened to your mother after she abandoned you?"

GOOD MORNING, DADDY

"No."

"Why?"

"Obviously they never cared about me. Why should I care about them? I have all the family I've ever wanted, or needed."

She glanced at me uncertainly, mollified if not content. I took her hand in mine. Caroline touched the bandage that covered my forehead. It would be coming off in another day or two; then I hoped there would be no further reminder of that unfortunate accident.

"A little luck," she said. "Yes. That's all there is to it sometimes . . . isn't there?"

"Good morning, daddy," Sharissa said. She was poaching eggs and toasting crumpets. I kissed her on the cheek.

"Good morning, babe."

"Mom's gone already?"

"The senator's barnstorming north Georgia today. Five stops."

"That old fool," Sharissa said, which was uncharacteristic of her. "Mom's wasting her talents. I wish she would go back to work for the *Tribune*."

"So do I. But she loves politics."

Sharissa looked over her shoulder at me. Her gray eyes were startling in her smooth tanned face and I thought with a wrench of the heart that no one should be that lovely; it lasted for such a short time.

"I heard the two of you talking last night. Mom sounded . . ." She waited for me to finish, to confirm her suspicions.

I decided to tell her about our aborted evening out, the close call with Mrs. Roxanne Sullivan.

"Weird," Sharissa said, setting out our breakfast. Tight-lipped, she blinked at me, as if she were trying to communicate in code. "Were you scared?"

"Sure I was. Having a gun pointed at you so soon after being shot is not an experience I'd recommend."

Sharissa hugged me. "Don't let mom . . . you know. Crash dive again. I don't think I could stand it." I thought I could feel her heart beating as I held her. Or maybe it was two hearts together.

* * *

The bandage came off and the stitches came out of my forehead. Jesse Fernando had done a neat job of sewing the big flap of scalp back. He told me that in a year or two the scar would barely be noticeable, a thin, white, sealed doorway into the brain.

On primary day Claude Gilley held off the challenge of the earnest young lawyer from Dalton who had sought to get the democratic nomination. After the primary night party, flushed with victory and apparently her old self again, Caroline went up to Washington for several days to meet with Claude's staff at the Capitol.

Detective Boyer of the Sky Valley police department dropped around to see me at the store. I wasn't particularly pleased to see him. I had pretty much put the whole distasteful business at the Ovenbird out of my mind.

"We got some information back on the Sullivan woman," he said. "Thought you might like to know."

"Not really."

He smiled. Boyer had a cheerful air, a fleshy face, a gap in his grin. His eyes had the steely calm of a pond with alligators coasting just beneath the surface. He changed the subject with a flick of his hand over a lapel of his loud sports jacket.

"I was on vacation when that kid shot you. Near miss, huh?"

"It still makes me shudder to think about it."

"You look a hundred percent now. I reckon you're just about one in a million. Several million. My daddy was a boxer in his heyday. But he took his share of jabs to the head. Died years later of an embolism nobody was aware of."

"That's something to think about," I said coldly.

"I wasn't aiming to upset you, Mr. Walker." Boyer looked far from contrite. He changed the subject again, swiping at the other lapel of his coat. "Mrs. Sullivan was diagnosed catatonic schizophrenic. Same illness that put her in an asylum in Canada for years. She was, we hear, a borderline alcoholic all her life, but when her husband, what was his name?—Frederick, walked out on her, she really hit the stuff hard. We couldn't locate much in the way of family up there. She and Frederick had a daugher, Bonnie—"

"So she said."

"Who was adopted when she was a baby. Frederick's idea. Story goes he insisted on the adoption; Mrs. Sullivan couldn't bear children. He wanted a girl, too; had to be a little girl. Anyway, Bonnie split with Frederick after he cleaned out the joint bank account. This was a few days before her sixteenth birthday. Frederick, he was okay with the RCMP; local law didn't have much on him neither. Some misdemeanors. He was just another good-looking low-life, according to all reports. But I wonder. Something about Frederick Sullivan purely intrigues the hell out of me."

I found myself looking, not into dark placid pond eyes, but eager alligator eyes. I shrugged and said, "So Mrs. Sullivan is likely to remain in Georgia?"

"Locked up. As I said, she's catatonic. She could snap out of it tomorrow, they tell me; most likely she'll remain that way for the rest of her life. Which probably won't last much longer. Her liver's failing. All that booze, I reckon."

"I think it's sad. On the other hand, I think she might have killed somebody."

"I wouldn't doubt it. Mistaken identity." He shook his head. "Ironic, in your case. You just happen to closely resemble a man she was in love with almost forty years ago. Odds are he's six feet under by now."

I didn't say anything. Boyer dusted his lapels again, slowly. "Well, that's all I had. Just thought you'd be interested."

"No, I'm really not."

"Well, maybe I'll be seeing you. Morning, Mr. Walker." He started for the door, then snapped his fingers, regaining my attention. "Oh, I meant to ask you. Sharissa Walker—one of the lifeguards at the country club? Is that your daughter?"

"Yes, she is."

"Beautiful girl. Any more at home like her?"

"No. We couldn't have more children."

"Good tennis player, too. My wife and I don't travel in those circles, but she does get invited to play out there at the club from time to time."

He waved a hand at me and went out, whistling between his teeth. I watched him jaywalking in the heat haze to where he'd left his car near the square. I watched until he drove away, thinking over everything he'd asked me. Random questions and musings. He was a policeman, after all. He just had one of those inquisitive minds. I wondered why I disliked him so much. Why his interest in my daughter had cast such a pall over me.

On Friday I drove the seventy miles to Hartsfield airport to meet Caroline's flight from Washington. A storm front was moving in from the Gulf coast, and a severe weather watch had been issued. The concourse was crowded and the airline switched gates at the last minute; by the time I reached the new arrival gate the passengers were getting off. Caroline must have flown first class. I saw her waiting for me in the smoking area by the check-in counter. She was lighting a cigarette. Her hands were unsteady. She turned her cheek when I tried to kiss her. She looked starkly tired.

"Everything all right?" I asked. "How was Washington?"

"Humid." I couldn't interpret the look she was giving me. "I don't know how anyone could live there during the summer. But some of us went for a cruise on the Potomac a couple of nights ago. That was fun. You don't mind if I smoke? Just one. I won't smoke in the car."

It was raining when we left the terminal. Caroline said she wanted to drive. She's a better driver than I am, particularly in bad weather, so I let her take the wheel. We headed west on Camp Creek Parkway to I-285. Caroline couldn't, or didn't want to make conversation. It was raining harder. There was lightning all around us. If she was exhausted, it didn't show in her driving.

"What is it, Greg?" she said abruptly. "Is it something so bad you can't let anyone know? Are you a fugitive? Did you kill somebody? Am I really Mrs. Greg Walker, or did you have another name once?"

"What have you been up to, Caroline?" I asked after a few moments.

"I'm a journalist by trade. So I did what any good journalist would do when—when she thinks the man she loves has lied to her all these years."

A glaring light filled the inside of the car. Thunder cracked. I stared through the windshield.

"Go on," I said.

"I checked with the Pentagon first. There've been several

Gregory Walkers in the various services, but no one of your age and description at the time you said you served. There was never a Lieutenant Greg Walker of the 24th Field Artillery posted to Fort Rucker, Alabama. Anyone can buy an officer's uniform, have papers forged; and phony drivers' licenses are so easy to obtain, aren't they—Greg."

"I suppose so."

"I still wasn't—satisfied, so I spent a day in Baltimore. Looking through birth records, checking with the welfare agencies. The date and place of your birth on our marriage certificate checks out okay —but the infant Gregory Walker, whose name you took, died at the age of six weeks. Needless to say, you weren't shunted from one foster home to another in your youth. I doubt if you've ever been to Baltimore."

"I've been there," I said.

"For how long?"

"A week. Long enough to familiarize myself with the city, and pick up an identity."

"Mother of God!"

"Please don't, Caroline."

Her breath hissed. "I suppose I should be grateful for one thing. Your fingerprints aren't on file with the FBI. You're not on the National Crime Information Center's computers."

"I've never been a criminal. Some occasional indiscretions, misdemeanors. You did a very thorough job. As for gratitude, you should be grateful for many things. I've been faithful to you, Caroline. We've had a good marriage. What else do you really need, or want to know?"

"*Everything.*"

"You're going too fast," I cautioned her.

Caroline eased off on the accelerator. I shook my head. "It's just human nature, isn't it? The hardest lesson life offers is learning to leave well enough alone."

"Tell me! I want to know who you are."

"Frederick Sullivan," I said.

"Oh, no! Jesus! I don't believe *that!* The bullet in your head! I think it must have—you've gone completely—You're talking like a—a psychopathic—"

I went on, calmly, "Psychopathic liar? You know better. You've lived with me for eighteen years. I'm a perfectly normal, ordinary human being. Except for one crucial difference. Once every nineteen years I'm required—compelled, if you want to put it that way—to change my identity, my life-style, to become someone completely different from the person I was during my last cycle."

Caroline sounded as if something was caught in her throat. I looked at our speed. We were going seventy, in blinding rain, nearing the interchange with I-75, the way home to Sky Valley. I took a deep breath. There had been some hard years, but I was going to miss the beauty, the orderly pace of life in Sky Valley.

"Do you want me to go on, Caroline? It's an opportunity for me, actually. I've never been able to explain this to any of my wives. Maybe you'll understand."

"I understand that you—need help." I couldn't tell, looking at her reflection in the windshield, if she was crying. There was so much rain streaming down the glass.

"I was married to Roxanne Sullivan. Everything she said was true. Becoming a shitheel named Frederick Sullivan was an experiment in altering my personality, adopting a totally different exterior from that of Barnaby Wilde, who taught fifth-form English at a girls' school in New England during the thirties and forties, and wrote poetry for little magazines. But Frederick exhausted me; it isn't easy to be primitive, even in a raw, primitive place like New Lost River. So I went back to what was closer to my true nature: someone contemplative, religious, no one of great importance, just a man who earns a decent living, and values his wife, his home, his family. That's the man you married, Caroline. The name doesn't mean anything."

"You're—making this up. It's a sick, crazy—"

"Caroline, I can't die. I'm immortal, as long as I observe the protocol of the 19-year eclipse cycle that saw me into this world one hundred and ninety-three years ago. My cycle as Greg Walker expires next February. It didn't expire when I was shot in the head by Ricky Gene Kindor, because almost nothing short of beheading or exsanguination will kill me. I was gassed in the trenches in World War I. Run through my liver in an *affaire d'honeur* many years before that. I've been trampled by wild horses in Australia, fallen from the roof of a ten-story building. I mended quickly; all scars disappeared. There is no foreseeable end for me. I can live as long as I choose. I'm not alone, either. There are others like me. Men and women totally in control of their destinies. As long as they are willing to pay the small cost involved."

"Insane. Insane. Oh, God. I'm afraid."

She was frozen to the steering wheel, guiding us by instinct alone through the slashing rain. We were still going very fast for the conditions, passing everyone else on the interstate.

"Isn't it better to know what you already suspected, Caroline?"

"I wanted to believe—in a miracle! That God saved you. I wanted you to—grow old with me. Oh how I wanted that! But you never aged a day. I tried not to think about it."

"Maybe it is a miracle. I don't know why I have immortality, and others don't."

"But you don't have to leave, do you, Greg? I'm sorry. I'm really sorry I called you a liar. I believe you now. You've been a wonderful husband, a loving father. Think of us. Think of Sharissa. Stay with us, that's all I ask! Won't you go on being Greg Walker, for my sake?"

"I can't, Caroline."

"You were planning to—walk away, disappear, always leave us wondering—"

"That's the hard part."

"And—turn into someone else, marry another woman? But you can't—can't just say you *love me*, and do a horrible, treacherous, despicable thing like that! That isn't love. It's selfish. It's monstrous!"

"Caroline!" I shouted. "Watch—"

I don't know. Maybe if I hadn't tried to grab the wheel, we wouldn't have run into the concrete divider. Caroline had excellent reflexes, even under stress. It was just instinct on my part. But we were going much too fast, and after rebounding from the disintegrating divider the car flipped. We were both wearing seat belts and shoulder harnesses, of course. The restraints probably would have saved Caroline's life, but the eighteen-wheeler coming along behind us in the second lane couldn't avoid the tumbling sedan in its path. The big transport struck us on the driver's side and knocked the car clear off the road, down into a gully. Thinking back, I don't even remember the impact. What I see in my mind's eye is Caroline's face lit up by the lights behind us. Sometimes I imagine I can hear her scream. But I'm human, aren't I? And not immune to guilt.

* * *

"A most tragic end to a fruitful period of your development," Francisco Colon said to me. He sipped dense black coffee from a small eggshell china cup. We were at breakfast on the terrace of the hotel Villa Mayapan, which he had inherited from his late father. "I hope you were not seriously injured in the accident."

"A dislocated shoulder. I was cut by flying glass. No, nothing serious," I told him. "And your father?"

Francisco looked momentarily at a man with a tier of birdcages, containing cardinals and keel-billed toucans, which was strapped to the top of his head. Francisco gave directions to the peddler, who then walked, with a graceful swaying gait, down a winding stone path into the tropical gardens of the Colonial-style hotel, where it had been my good fortune to spend several pleasant winters preceding the station of my eclipse cycle.

"Papa passed on peacefully in his sleep at the winter solstice," Francisco said, and turned back to me with a contented smile: contentment for his beloved father, and his own, newly elevated position. "He had 121 years." He sipped coffee again, gazing frankly at me with obsidian eyes. He was a broad brown man with a neat oval of mustache and beard and long hair which he brushed straight back from his forehead. His face, his build, were classically Mayan. I glanced at the jade of prestige which he wore on a gold chain around his neck. It was a carved owl, perhaps as old as two millennia. It would be the same jade which Francisco's father, and his father's father, whom I also had counted as a friend, had worn before him. "His instructions to me before his death were incomplete."

"They were meant to be," I said. In the gardens, among the charming thatched-roof cabanas, a howler monkey screamed in its cage. On the terrace a tethered quetzal spread magnificent wings. The quetzal was the exact blue color of the flawless Yucatan sky.

Francisco dropped his eyes. "I realize I may not enjoy the longevity of the immortals. Still—whatever extension of my life is available to me will of course be welcome."

"How old are you now?"

"I have forty years, sir."

"Then you are barely in the springtime of the long life that will be my gift to you."

His face was immobile, but his chest swelled with relief and happiness. "Thank you, sir."

I looked out over the extensive garden to the pyramids in the shimmering distance, the pre-classic Mayan city of the Rising Sun. Excavations had been underway for almost a hundred years. There was still much to be discovered in the forest, and under it. And much that would never be discovered, as long as the chattals of the Owl and the Harpy, Keepers of the Underworld like Francisco Colon, were faithful to their trust.

"Your time is near?" Francisco asked me.

"On the 9th of February. Three days from now."

"And what will you require?"

"The chert dagger. The jaguarundi cup. On the day before the metonic station you will guide me to the cenote, so I may be sure—"

He nodded. "I know the way."

"Of course." I had no reason to remind him that if for any reason he was attempting to deceive me as to the rightfulness of his succession, the penalty would be severe. The Villa Mayapan would be in the market for a new owner.

The *Xate* palms on the spacious grounds of the old but immaculate hotel rattled in a strong breeze. He glanced at me as if expecting more.

"And—the sacrifice?" he murmured.

"That does not involve you. You will be there only to receive the blood annointment that prolongs your life."

He nodded. "And it is done—in the old way?"

"You know how sharp the dagger is. I remove the heart from the breast with a few strokes at the culmination of the eclipse."

"The—the matter of the virgin has troubled me. The authorities ask many questions when a local girl vanishes. Even in my grandfather's day—"

"There were problems in obtaining a virgin. I know. But I resolved that dilemma a long time ago. I raise my own."

Looking out at the garden, I saw her now on the path to the terrace, coming from our cabana, her hair the color of a jaguarundi's coat flashing in the sun as she hurried in walk shorts and a shirt of colorful Mayan weave toward the hotel. She saw me watching, waved, lengthened her stride, bounded up to the terrace past the appreciative eyes of Francisco Colon and draped her slim tanned arms around my neck. My face was tilted to receive the kiss she gave me on my forehead. I smiled and tingled at her touch, thinking of all the happiness she had brought me, the love in her heart that would live refreshed in me for a thousand years to come.

"Good morning, daddy," Sharissa said.

Interlude: Folk-Naif: 1942

The Lobby of the Central Hotel is furnished with square, oxblood leather Chairs. Each Chair has a standing Ashtray beside it. The Floor is a checkerboard, squares of black and white. Black and white. A Man in a gray pin-striped Suit with a floral Tie has fallen asleep over his Newspaper, snoring gently in the quiet desuetude of the Lobby on a Saturday afternoon. A Saturday afternoon between spring and summer. One notices the unfanned air, the coarse linger of Cigars. There are three high Windows on one side of the Lobby. The green Shades are up.

This is after Pearl Harbor. There is an American Flag in one Window, as large as the Window itself, the Sun shining through it. The light around the Window is fiercely rose, with bars of indigo. And Stars that swarm like Flies in the blasé sunning.

A young Woman is waiting for the Elevator. She is wearing an organdy summer Dress. White Pumps. White Gloves. A close-fitting Hat. She is slender, with good legs, and standing very still, a flat, white, square Purse under one arm.

In the Barbershop
off the Lobby my Father is having his hair cut in the middle Chair.
My Father is a handsome Man. He wears his hair combed straight
back, and parted on the left; uses plenty of rose oil Hairdressing. I'm
next. Looking up, I see Myself in the Barbershop Mirror, and also
the Woman waiting for the Elevator. Waiting. The Woman with
gloved hands, and interesting calves. I look down at *Field and
Stream*, at the short-haired pointer Dog on the cover and the Men
in leather shooting vests. I wish I had a Comic Book.

                        Some
of my Father's cut-off hair drifts down from his draped shoulders to
the checkerboard Floor. There is an Animal of hair on the black-
and-white Floor, no head, no tail, but an Animal. I sit on my feet.
The Elevator comes. The brass Gate snaps open. The Woman gets
on. The Elevator Man is an old Negro with red Suspenders who sits
on a Stool inside, never getting up, never getting off. Lives in the
Elevator. He was born before the Civil War. My Father is laughing
at a whispered joke of the Barber's. Loud laughter after whispers.
The Elevator

                    rises

conveying the Woman upstairs. To the unimaginable upstairs of the
Central Hotel.

More Than Mischief

The little man with the Indian head tattoo on his left bicep walked into the convenience store and called out his name to the proprietor.

"I'm Poolie Mayhap, and I could use a job of work."

He was shabbily dressed, but clean. He had with him a homemade dobro in a ponyskin case, and a knapsack. His boyish lack of stature was in his runty legs, but he had good shoulders, and a large man's head, with waves of gray hair curling back from his temples like the horns of a wild old ram.

"That's well and good," said the sad-eyed proprietor, whose own name was Tobias Frost. "But there ain't no work for you here. It's a fact that I'm a poor man, and getting poorer every day."

Poolie Mayhap looked around. The convenience store occupied the plot of ground at the southeast corner of two intersecting country highways. Behind the store, at a distance of seventy yards, was a three-room house with a front porch. Midway there stood an old, barren peach tree, all that remained, except for stumps, of a once fruitful orchard. Before Poolie spoke again, two cars passed on the highway, and a third pulled in for gas.

"How could you be poor, with so many cars passing, and no competition in the neighborhood?"

"Didn't say I had no business. There's a right smart of folks stopping by. But them that come at nightfall like as not have guns; and it's their kind has scared the heart out of me and my wife, and made us poor."

"No help from the high sheriff?"

"Sheriff's miles from here; and his deputies can't spare all their time just to watch my store. I'm telling you, Mr. Mayhap, the robbers that come up from the city will be after putting me out of business in another month!"

"That's why you should hire me," said Poolie Mayhap, with a no-nonsense grin. "I'm just the man to put a stop to it."

Tobias Frost looked skeptically at him. "Can't be more'n five feet tall, if you don't mind my saying so."

There was a glitter in the little man's eyes that made Tobias wish he hadn't spoken. But he was weary from standing on his feet all day, and here was help, just walked in the door. From the looks of Poolie Mayhap three square meals and a place to sleep would do him.

"I'm four feet nine and a half inches. But there's no method in size; I don't use force, only persuasion, to get my way."

"Uh-huh. Reckon since robbers took nine hundred dollars from my till just the night before last, I can't afford to pay you more than room and board. Until things get a heap better, that is."

"You may depend on it," said Poolie Mayhap with another exuberant grin, and he clapped his hands sharply. The Indian's head tattooed on his left arm, a sinister-looking thing with long braids that drooped nearly to the elbow, and a top knot holding a feather, quivered with the rippling of muscle and seemed almost to come to life. Tobias felt momentarily queer and faint, as if there had been a sudden change in the air to snatch his breath away. He pulled his corncob pipe from a pocket of his apron and tapped the mouthpiece against his front teeth. "Done," the little man said. "As for pay, I have only a single request that I hope you won't deny me."

"Hm?" Tobias murmured cautiously.

"I want all the peaches from the tree standing in your yard between the store and house."

"Well, now—let me be fair about this—that old tree ain't bloomed nor bore fruit since we had us the four-year drought."

"It will bloom again; and the peaches are mine. If we have a bargain?"

"Done," Tobias said, and turned his attention to the farmer who had come in to pay for his gas. Keeping one eye mildly cocked as Poolie Mayhap wandered up and down the aisles of his store, opening and closing the refrigerator units, squaring loaves of bread in their racks, cheerfully making himself useful.

He spent a fair amount of time looking up at the old calendar on the wall behind the counter that moved fitfully whenever the head of the ugly black fan on the shelf turned toward it. There was a red tractor pictured on the calendar, and a smiling girl posed beside the tractor. She had shoulder-length hair that looked as thick and fragrant as Tupelo honey, turquoise eyes the size of pigeon's eggs, and a royal-red mouth. Such girls were born to be on calendars. She wore very little clothing, and wore it as if it were a necessary nuisance: a gingham blouse tied off below her ample breasts, a very short pleated skirt, and high-heeled shoes. There were fly specks on the calendar, which was lacking all but the torn fringe of its monthly leaves, and dated 1959; apparently the dust and excreta of decades had not dimmed the pleasure Tobias took in the convenience-store madonna's musty but forever-youthful presence.

"A lovely girl," Poolie Mayhap said, extolling her with a rolling of the eyes and a not-too-obvious smacking of his lips. "Does she have a name?"

"She was just the Ferguson Tractor Company calendar girl," Tobias said, with a certain gruffness of voice, resisting a backward glance at his treasure.

"'Bout time you hung yourself a new calendar," the customer said with a wink at Poolie. "And brung yourself up to date, Tobias."

"'59 was a good enough year," Tobias said. "I had me a new tractor. I had peaches. Had all of my hair, and plenty of pep. What do I want with a new calendar? All the years are alike to me now."

When the customer had driven away Poolie returned to the check-out counter with a plastic milk box. Standing on it, he was eye-to-eye with Tobias. He placed his knapsack on the counter and from it withdrew a plain quart mason jar with a brass-colored screwtop lid. This he placed on the counter in front of square display jars filled with lollipops and bubblegum.

"What's that for?"

"Bait," Poolie said.

Tobias blinked and stared. As far as he could tell, the mason jar was empty.

Poolie hopped down from the milk box. "Follow me."

Tobias went outside in the mild early-spring sunshine. He glanced at the sapless branches of the peach tree that had afforded no shade during the past summer, then looked around at Poolie, who was drawing a line in the red clay dooryard with the toe of a desert boot.

"Why're you doing that?"

"It's the threshhold," Poolie said, intent on his work. He stared at the line, and made a fist, several times, pumping his bicep, causing the tattooed Indian to jump and wriggle and sneer with his inky-dark mouth. Then he smiled at Tobias.

"You and the missus will want to stock up from your shelves and freezer," he said.

"Stock up? What for?"

"I forgot to tell you. While I'm minding the store, you and your wife are to stay inside your house for seven days and seven nights, with the shades drawn. Don't come out for any reason until you hear me knock three times on your door."

"Well, now, mister—"

"At the end of seven days, all the money that has been stolen from you will be returned, sevenfold. There will never be another robbery at your store. But you have to follow my instructions exactly. *Don't come out.*"

Tobias looked sternly at Poolie Mayhap. "Do you think I'm an old fool? What kind of mischief are you up to?"

"More than mischief," Poolie said, and winked at him.

With that wink Tobias Frost felt as if his feet were no longer touching the ground; as if his head were floating several inches above his shoulders.

He said, nodding, "Seven days and seven nights? Reckon Mrs. Frost and I can deal with that. Particularly as how she hardly goes out any more since she was stricken with the lupus."

His wife was not sanguine about the arrangement. "Seven days? Our money back, sevenfold? Now you've done it, mister! Took leave of your senses, have you? He's here to clean us out, that be all there is to it!"

Tobias knew better than to answer her back, while she hobbled all around him, waving her gnarly fists under his chin.

But before she could get a reasonable start at venting her pique, they heard the plucky high-steel music of the dobro coming from the convenience store. Poolie Mayhap played nothing but danceable tunes, and soon they were both dancing; for the first time since he could remember, the wife of Tobias Frost smiled at him.

MORE THAN MISCHIEF

When he awoke refreshed from an afternoon nap, there was a hub-bub on the highway. Tobias cautiously peeked around a drawn shade and saw what he mistook for a parade outside his convenience store. Cars and pickup trucks as far as the eye could see. Men, women, and children were lined up patiently waiting their turns to get into the store. Despite the crowding, everyone seemed to be in a fine humor. There were picnickers beneath the leafless peach tree. Someone played a mouth organ. But the real music was the sound of Tobias's old cash register, ringing up sale after sale.

His wife took her turn peeking out the window, then fell back wide-eyed into her rocking chair and fanned herself.

By nightfall the crowds were gone. Poolie Mayhap resumed playing danceable tunes on his dobro. Tobias and his wife danced in the parlor until they wore their socks out.

Near midnight Tobias woke from a dreamless sleep on the couch. His wife snored heartily in the bedroom. He heard a car door and went quickly to the parlor window, pulled back the shade.

There were three of them, emerging from a lacklustre sedan with fenders of different colors. They looked stealthily around, and Tobias saw light reflected from the oily barrel of a sawed-off shotgun.

He reached instinctively for the doorknob, thinking of all the business they'd done that day. But what could he do? For that matter, what could Poolie Mayhap do to prevent all the money from being stolen? Tobias drew back from the door and took up his station at the window, watching, barely breathing in his anxiety.

Ten minutes passed; fifteen. The robbers did not reappear. Tobias heard nothing except the midnight songs from pond and woodlot.

Then the lights of the convenience store winked off, as if Poolie was closing up.

Tobias could see, from his place beside the window, the front of the store with its island of gasoline pumps, and the wooden steps leading up to the front door. He could not see inside the store.

Presently the screen door opened, and someone stepped out. Someone invisible to Tobias. All he clearly saw was a pair of desert boots—Poolie Mayhap's boots. But there was none of Poolie to be seen.

One of the boots tapped, heel and toe, on the top step. Then the boots walked nonchalantly down to the dooryard and over to the dark sedan with the mismatched fenders.

Paused there. After a few moments a boot lifted off the ground and gently kicked a tire.

Tobias heard the sound of the engine turning over, the husky burbling of twin exhaust pipes. The headlights flashed on.

The bodiless boots walked around to the front of the car and proceeded briskly away from the convenience store onto the highway. The sedan followed until all Tobias could see of it in the darkness were slits of taillights. The sound of the engine faded beneath the nightlong croak of tree frogs, the bristly sawing of cicadas.

Tobias put cold cloths on his head and rocked in the parlor, and then, less feverish and heartshocked, he began to laugh.

The first thing he saw in the morning when he looked out was the peach tree blooming against the rosy sky. Tobias's wife awakened, with fresh color in her ravaged cheeks, to an irresistible hoe-down tune.

This day proceeded very like the day before, although the picnickers now enjoyed shade where they sat beneath the widespreading peach tree.

The night brought another gang of robbers, in a dusty van that was eventually led away by the empty boots of Poolie Mayhap.

Tobias applied more cold cloths to his brow and reckoned that he would be a rich man by the end of the week.

On the third day the tree in the yard showed thick clusters of green peaches.

On the third day, and the fourth day, the cash register in the store made so much music there was little time for Poolie to play danceable tunes on his dobro.

Once, when the flow of customers slackened and Poolie stepped out into a glamorous sunset to mop his brow with a bandana, Tobias Frost had the temerity to call to him through the opened window.

"How are you, Mr. Mayhap?"

"Hanging in like Gunga Din!" Poolie called back cheerfully, and returned to his duties.

The peaches ripened on the fifth day.

"I want one," said the wife of Tobias Frost, hungering behind the parlor window. "Why don't you fetch me one of those luscious peaches, Mr. Frost?"

"They ain't belonging to us, missus. I done give them all to Mr.

Mayhap, in lieu of wages."

"The fruit of our beautiful tree? How could you do such a thing?"

"For one thing, there weren't no fruit in sight when I struck the bargain."

"Well, there's peaches a-plenty now, mister, bushels of choice fruit, and it would seem to me you struck a pitiful poor bargain for a week's wages. And him with all he can eat besides, helping himself to sweet cakes from the Dolly Madison rack in the store!"

Tobias Frost thought of the empty boots of midnight, leading away the vehicles of would-be holdup men to some uncertain doom, and wondered if he ought to say something placating, or cautionary. But his wife's attention was devoted to the flourishing, newly gilded peach tree. Its radiance awakened the starving graces of her old eyes; she shuddered blissfully, her mouth working. There could be no talking to her while she remained in this state.

On the parlor couch he slept uncommonly profound that night. Once, just out of range of his peaceful dreams, yet intrusive, he heard the stealthy turning of the key in the lock of the front door, the creak of porch boards. But, far from the antiquity of his flesh, drenched in supernal light and drinking the wine of yesteryear with cherished companions, Tobias failed to be alarmed, to awaken.

In the morning there was no trace of his wife in the house except for her morose teeth in the bedside glass. The front door was, as he'd feared, unlocked. Beneath the dense, cloud-high green tree a single enormous peach, shaken down from a weighty bough, blushed and twinkled in dew. Mrs. Tobias Frost was not in sight. He was afraid to call to her. Afraid not to be answered. He thought of strolling desert boots, leading her dumbly away from beneath the tree to a spectral place no living, breathing mortal could enter, and from which there was no return. Trembling, he sat in the rocking chair. The daylong din of commerce at the convenience store was for once without charm for him. His heart pumped dryly, blood barren as sand.

Only one more day to go. Then Poolie Mayhap would take his leave with all the peaches he could haul, and there would be nothing for Tobias to do but open the drawer of his cash register and gasp at the sight of the packed-down greenbacks within. Or so he imagined. But he did not find the marrow-tickling pleasure in his imaginings that he'd come to depend on.

Seven days and seven nights. Poolie Mayhap's rule; but what was the sense of it? Tobias's missus had gone out, and not returned. If some harm had come to her, then he must find out about it, without delay.

At one minute past eleven o'clock the lights of the convenience store went out. Tobias Frost raised the front window of the parlor a few inches and called to Poolie Mayhap. The little man with the home-made dobro did not reply.

The fallen peach on the ground beneath the fruitful boughs was silvery with dew, a beacon of sorts.

The night was unnaturally quiet; a solemn kind of silence, like that of an empty church.

Tobias sidled to the front door, shoulders hunched, and contemplated the antique key in the lock. His fingers itched; his better instincts bridled. So much conflict of body and mind, he was soon a mass of nerves. His mouth was very dry. He longed for a soda. Mrs. Frost had drunk most of the cartons laid by for their enforced retreat.

I'll just creep into the store, and out again with a sody, Tobias argued silently, as if he were arguing with an unseen devil. *Poolie Mayhap must be sound asleep after his long day. He'll never know. It's not a-going against our bargain to want a drink of sody, is it?*

Before he reached a conscious conclusion the key had turned in his fingers, the door opened. Tobias went out onto the porch, hunched and clinging to his suspenders with both hands, peering this way and that with considerable alarm. He saw nothing but his own faint shadow, and the dark trunk of the peach tree with its radiant crown. The glow of the single fallen peach.

He walked one yard past it, turned and stared. That peach would go good with his soda, he thought. He bent trembling toward the ground, then retracted his hand, a flood of virtue warming his breast. No, he wouldn't touch it. He'd promised all the peaches, and that was that. Let Poolie Mayhap come to collect it himself.

Tobias held his breath and took cat-steps up to the screen door, listening with his ears, his skin. He heard a satisfying snore from somewhere inside. So the little man was sound asleep, as he'd figured.

He opened the screen door just enough to slip inside. He knew which of the old floorboards creaked, and avoided them. The lights were out in the refrigerator cases, but the moon shone on the glass doors. It shone as well on the empty quart mason jar on the front counter near the cash register.

Bait, Poolie Mayhap had said, placing the jar there. It had been empty then as well. Tobias shrugged uneasily, listening for any sort of disturbance in the sawing rhythm of the sleeping man's snores. But Poolie Mayhap was deep in slumber. Tobias advanced down the aisle toward the refrigerator cases, paused to draw a deep breath, and opened one.

The light came on in the case, startling him.

Amid the rows of cans and bottles, something stirred in a shadowy way inside one of the quart mason jars stored with the soda and juice. The jars hadn't been there the last time Tobias was in the store. Poolie must have put them there. Tobias pushed a dark two-liter container of Coke aside to see better, his head in the swirling nimbus of cold air breathed by the tall case, not quite able to make out—and then he thought he saw—and at the same time heard her crying, a voice as tiny as the tick of a watch:

"Tobias!"

It was Mrs. Frost, or at least an image of her, in the quart jar, her head coming not even half way to the inside of the brass lid. She was sitting on a big peach like a plush dark red chair, a peach that had been bitten, but only once.

"Tobias!"

In the jars surrounding the one in which the missus waved frantically there were other stirrings, shadows evolving into full-fleshed tiny men, some with weapons so ridiculously small they could have no impact on the thick green-tinted glass that enclosed them. They waved and called too, frantically, all of them making no more noise than bees in a hive across the road.

The loudest sound Tobias heard in the convenience store was the imperious jangling of the cash register on the counter as the cash drawer slammed open.

Tobias, freezing from the neck up, his heart dropping to his socks, closed the refrigerator door and crouched trembling in the aisle.

He was going to die. He'd called it down on himself, and now he was going to die!

By and by he heard floorboards creaking. Looking toward the screen door, he saw empty desert boots appear. The door opened, the boots walked out and down the steps. The screen door closed.

Ten minutes passed before Tobias had the nerve to rise. But he was unable to bring himself to look into the refrigerator again.

Instead he crept around to the counter and stared at the rifled cash register, the sticking-out, emptied drawer.

The biggest thief of all had turned out to be Poolie Mayhap. But who, after all, was to blame?

There were tears in Tobias's eyes as he looked around.

And spied, on the counter, the mason drawer with the brass lid.

Something gleamed on the bottom of the jar. Gold—six gold coins.

Poolie Mayhap hadn't left him penniless after all.

The lid unscrewed easily. He thought he heard peaches thudding down from the tree behind the store but his mind was on the gold. *There should be more*, he thought, feeling cheated as he tried to dump the coins into his palm. They wouldn't come out. He would have to reach into the jar and—

But in a flash of freezing terror he recognized, before he could make that fatal mistake, that this was the trap of thieves, and of his own greedy wife: pieces of gold, a lovely piece of fruit—they were nothing but bait. Should he reach down into the jar, he was sure to be shrunk to the size of his own forefinger by Poolie Mayhap's mischief.

So he set the mason jar back on the counter and walked numbly outside, going down the store steps like a blind man. Behind him there was a muffled sound of combustion, he felt heat on the back of his neck. The night sky around him glowed orange but he wouldn't look back. He walked beneath the newly barren limbs of his peach tree, scuffling through the fall of leaves. They slithered dryly over his bare feet. There was not a ripe peach anywhere. He dripped tears. Everything had been taken from him, everything . . .

The screen door of his cramped little house flipped open when he was only a few feet away, and she came striding out onto the porch with a smile for him. He felt a critical electric tingle at the nape of his neck; his mouth was jarred open. Tobias had often tried to imagine her like this, in the flesh, not just riffling in a mime of aliveness every time the head of the electric fan swiveled her way. But the poverty of his imagination, the limitations of calendar-art photography, were obvious to him as he gaped: he had never seen anything so outrageously beautiful. The way her golden hair flowed in the hot wind from the burning store across a provocatively bared shoulder, the lascivious heights of her barely concealed breasts. The waistline of her short pleated skirt dropped to an almost indecent level, and all, yes, almost all, of her long legs—he didn't know where to look, there was an unbearable libidinous treat at every twitch of his eyeballs. When she exhaled, the power of her breath seemed to flow into his own lungs, refreshing them. When she gestured, his arthritic joints loosened, he felt a youthful freedom to bound up those few steps to the porch and sweep The Ferguson Tractor Company calendar girl into his arms.

But a part of his brain contracted darkly; his mind screeched *madness*.

"No such thing," she said, as if his doubts were written in flame across his brow. "Poolie Mayhap's a hard man, but fair." She gestured again, in a flighty, tantalizing manner, and springs long since dried up and forgotten flowed like champagne through Tobias's veins. His scalp contracted, then expanded thrillingly, and he ran his fingers through a new growth of wavy dark hair.

Only his voice remained aged, a husk of suspicion as she came jauntily down the steps to take him by the hand.

"What mischief—is this?"

"More than mischief," promised the calendar girl; and she blew lovingly into his ear, a breath of warmth and lightness. He was bouyant, he felt himself beginning to soar in her musky wind. "But really, Tobias; what do you care?"

Postlude:

Revenge

Rosiebays a /dea/d one
  sheare/d hea/dless by the ol/d Gimp
    cut /down with the cattails
      in mamas gar/den
        so hows a boy to fall asleep
          May   June   the bo/diless
            moons shining on black patent
              /danceshoes next to her be/d
                but Rosiebay'll never wake up
                  snipsnap her hea/d rolle/d into
                    the gol/dfish pon/d an/d they   ate
                      it
                        serves her right
                          but I cant sleep
                            MayJune   its the hea/dache moon
                              Rosiebays not in the next   room
                          Uh-uh
                              shes
                          /dea/d

Stephen Gallagher

The Back of His Hand

Billy had done a lot of walking and pacing that morning, mainly to keep himself warm. He'd marked out a stretch of the pavement across the road from the tattoo parlour, and by now he knew it like . . . well, like the back of his hand. As long as he kept to this same piece of ground, he'd know the minute that anybody came along and went inside. He'd tried the door several times already.

But it *was* still early.

There was a greasy spoon cafe almost opposite the parlour. It opened at eight, and Billy was on the doorstep when the proprietor came down and drew back the bolts. The proprietor was a stocky man, dark-haired and not so tall, and he seemed to be in sole charge with no help. He made no comment as Billy shouldered past him, leading with his well-stuffed kitbag. The cafe interior was basic, to say the least, but it was clean. The warmth of the place folded itself around him like a blanket. He let himself relax a little, almost as if he'd been wound up tight by the cold.

He picked out a table that was close to the cafe's paraffin heater but which also was near to the window. The window was already beginning to mist up on the inside. He could still see the tattoo parlour from here.

When the man came over to take his order, Billy kept his gloves on and his hands under the table. The man seemed not to notice. Billy ordered the full breakfast with nothing spared.

Though Billy had his problems, lack of money wasn't one of them.

The man went around into the back where he had a radio playing, and Billy could hear kitchenware being moved around on a range. It was a reassuring, almost homely combination of sounds. He yawned, and stretched his back. He'd been hitching all through the night, and had landed here in this seaside town at some utterly godforsaken hour of darkness. He'd zigzagged the country, leaving a trail that he was pretty sure would be hard to follow, and he'd kept his gloves on all of the time apart from when he'd needed to pee, and that he'd done only in locked cubicles on motorway service areas. Two gloves weren't necessary, but one glove would have looked odd. It might have attracted attention to him.

And attention was the last thing that Billy needed right now.

He'd never been here before. But the name of the place had stuck in his mind from just a couple of years ago when about a thousand bikers had descended on the place and settled in for a long Bank Holiday weekend. The bikers had been able to protest to the TV cameras about how misunderstood they were, the police had picked up plenty of overtime and had the chance to wear all their spiffy new Darth Vader riot gear, and the local traders had made a mint out of everybody; in fact, just about everyone had gone home happy although not one of them would ever have wanted to admit as much.

The town looked different now. The dawn sea battered at an empty promenade, and the wind howled through the deserted spaces of the new shopping centre. Most of the guest houses had hung out their *No Vacancy* signs and roped off the two-car parking spaces that had once been their front gardens. He might find a place here tonight where he could go to ground for a while, but it might be better to move on. It depended on whether he could face another night in transit. He'd never thought of himself as a soft case, but the last few hours had been the most miserable of his life. He'd waited out the time before daylight in the town's bus station, sitting with his bag and drinking weak piss-flavoured tea from a machine and trying to look like a legitimate traveller between destinations. A soldier on his way home, maybe; he reckoned that he could look the part and he carried a genuine forces kitbag as well, bought from Mac's Army Surplus Store. He'd watched a total of three buses come and go, all almost empty. In the phone booth he'd found a Yellow Pages with most of its yellow pages ripped away (there was no paper in the squalid toilet, and it didn't take a genius to put two and two together) but there had been enough of the directory left to tell him what he wanted to know.

He looked out through the fogging window again. No action over on the far side of the road. According to the listing, the tattoo parlour was the only place of its kind in town. The whole biker scene had led him to expect more but, what the hell, one was all that he'd need as long as it was the right kind of a place.

It looked like the right kind of a place.

There was no shop window. The entire facade apart from the entrance had been boarded up and painted white, and this had become a background for a riot of hand-drawn lettering by someone who clearly had an eye for colour and design, but who equally clearly wasn't a trained signwriter. The style fell somewhere between 'sixties psychedelia and freehand baroque; across the top it read STEVE, 'PROFESSIONAL' TATTOO ARTIST, and the rest of it crowded out the frontage completely. From here it was almost as if the building itself had been extensively tattooed, as an example of the owner's craft. It was the inverted commas around 'PROFESSIONAL' that had impressed Billy the most. That showed an education.

Breakfast came.

Billy realised almost too late that he'd pulled his gloves off without thinking, and his hands were on the table. He quickly drew them back and slid them underneath as the proprietor set a huge plate before him. "It's hot," he said, and the stuff on the plate was still sizzling.

Billy waited until he'd walked away, and then he rearranged the sauce bottle and the cruet set and propped up the plastic menu wallet so that it would screen his hands from the counter.

He kept an eye on the parlour as he ate. It was his first genuine meal in more than twenty-four hours, not counting grabbed snacks and chocolate bars along the way. A couple of transport drivers came into the cafe shortly after he'd started, but they didn't sit close. On the pavement opposite a few people walked by the parlour, but no-one went in.

He'd finished. He ordered something else. It was starting to feel as if this was an open-ended situation that could last indefinitely. His attention began to wander, so that after a while he only belatedly realised that he was actually watching someone over at the door who had stopped and seemed to be about to enter.

He sat up, and paid attention.

It was a man. A youngish man, tall and skinny, with an unkempt thatch of hair and some kind of a beard. He wore thrift shop clothing and carried a plastic Sainsburys bag. Billy didn't get the chance to see much more because then the man was inside, the darkness of whatever lay beyond swallowing him up as the door swung shut to keep out the rest of the world.

He finished, and went over to the counter to pay. He held the canvas handles of the kitbag with his gloved hand and paid with the other, so that nothing looked suspicious.

Then he crossed the street to the tattoo parlour.

There had been a padlock on the door, now there was none. The hasp and staple, both new-looking, hung open; the hasp had been crookedly fitted and secured, not with screws, but with nails. One of them had been bent over and hammered flat—either the work of an amateur, or the world's least 'PROFESSIONAL' carpenter. As before, there was nothing in the frosted glass of the door to say whether the place was open for business, or what its hours were, or anything. Billy pushed, and it opened. He went inside.

There were no lights on downstairs, but a door stood open to the daylight of a grimy kitchen beyond the main room in which he stood. Billy could hear somebody moving up above.

"Hey," he called out. "Anyone around?" and he heard the movement stop. A moment later there was the sound of a hurried tread on an uncarpeted stairway, coming down. As Billy waited, he looked about him in the gloom. The walls showed the signs of bad plaster under too many layers of cheap redecoration, none of them recent. There were signs in the same flamboyant, spidery lettering as the frontage outside *(Strictly over 18s only—proof of age may be required*, and, somewhat less tactfully, *Not having a tattoo? Then Fuck Off)* and then poster after poster showing about a hundred different designs. He saw cats, dragons, jaguars, skulls, women, swords, daggers, scrolls . . .

"What is it?"

The man stood in the kitchen doorway. Seen from closer-to, he had the look of an aged juvenile. His eyes were of a blue so pale that he would probably always seem to stare no matter what he might actually be thinking, and his hair had a coarse, faded texture like curtains left hanging for too long in the sunlight. He seemed a sensitive type.

Unlike Billy.

"Look," Billy said, "before anything else, I'm talking five hundred quid and no questions asked. If that interests you, then we'll take it from there. If it doesn't, then I'm walking out now and I *don't* want to be followed. Is that understood?"

And the man said, "Five hundred quid? For real?"

"I can show it to you if you don't want to believe me."

"I'm interested," the man said.

And Billy, looking at him, thought *Yeah, I reckon you are . . .* because he knew a junkie when he saw one, and this starved-looking specimen had to be one of the classic examples. So then he looked around and said, "Well then, how about some light?" And the Junkie, suddenly spurred into nervous action as if being jerked out of a trance, turned around and seemed confused for a moment as if he was so overcome by the idea that he'd forgotten where the switches were.

The overhead tubes flashed once or twice, and then one of them came on. The other just glowed orange at both ends, as if in resentment of its brighter neighbour.

The room didn't look any better. Quite the opposite. There were old grey vinyl tiles on the floor, the self-stick kind that often don't. A few of these had lifted and shifted, exposing the grimy wood flooring underneath. There were four straight-backed chairs over against the wall, and in the middle of the room a single padded chair with a headrest that was somewhere between the kind that you'd find in a hairdresser's and the kind that you'd find in a dentist's. The dentistry image was continued in the form of the tattooist's hanging system of long rubber drivebelts and gear-wheels running all the way back to the motor at its base. On the table alongside the chair were a rack of needles, some dyes, and a bottle of Savlon antiseptic.

Billy said, "Show me your hands."

The man frowned, puzzled.

Billy said, "If I'm going to pay you that kind of money, I want to see steady hands first."

"I've got steadier hands than you," the Junkie said, offended, and held them out; they weren't exactly rock steady, but they weren't unusually shaky either.

Billy said, "You shoot up already this morning?"

And the Junkie said, "That's none of your damned business.

Now show me the money."

Billy put the kitbag on the padded chair, and unzipped it a little of the way. It was enough to show some of the bundles of used notes, most of them still in cashiers' paper bands, that were inside. The man stared.

Billy said, "You haven't even asked me what I want you to do, yet."

And the man shrugged.

"For five hundred, who gives a shit?"

This was going to work out.

So Billy zipped up the kitbag again and then removed his glove and rolled back his sleeve and he held out his clenched fist, knuckles upward to show the dragon tattoo.

"I want this taken off," he said.

The man looked at it. Billy guessed that he had to be casting a professional eye over the design. It had cost Billy a lot of money, some ten years before; his friends at the time had told him that the man they were taking him to was the best in Europe. He'd been a big fat slob who hadn't looked like the best anything of anywhere, but Billy had been interested enough in the designs he'd been shown. They made the ones on the walls around here look like fingerpaintings.

The Junkie looked up at him. "Taken off?" he said.

"Completely off," Billy said. "You can do that? I mean, you can do it here and I don't have to go into a hospital or anything?"

"I can do anything you want," the man said. "But am I allowed to ask why?"

"No, you aren't," Billy said. "Lock the door, and let's get down to it."

The man looked again, and shook his head in disbelief. And then he made a little shrugging gesture as if to say *Well, it's your tattoo and it's your five hundred, so what does it matter to me?*

And he went to bolt the door from the inside.

Billy looked at the chair. It had a padded arm support at right angles to the seat, and the armrest had worn right away to the dirty-grey foam at its end. He felt his heart sink. Much as he knew he needed this, he hadn't been looking forward to it. Billy hated physical discomfort, not least his own. That ten years before he'd almost fainted when, after much more than an hour with his eyes screwed shut and his teeth gritted and his insides scrunched up

THE BACK OF HIS HAND

tighter than a washleather, he'd finally looked at the new pattern on the back of his inflamed hand and seen the tiny beads of blood that had been welling up from every needle strike. This was why he'd only had the one hand tattooed, instead of the matching pair that he'd intended. Much as he'd wanted the dragon design in the first place, he'd never been able to bring himself to go through the experience again.

And now he was sorry that he'd ever had it done at all . . . now that it was *that* close to landing him in jail.

"Shall I sit here?" Billy said as the Junkie turned from the door.

"Wherever you like," the Junkie said.

"Will it take long?"

"I shouldn't think so."

Billy took off his coat and climbed into the chair, and laid his arm on the rest. It was at right angles to his body, and raised as if to fend off a blow. As he was doing this the Junkie was scratching at his beard, looking down at the tattoo needles and other implements on the table.

"Is this going to hurt?" Billy said.

"Oh, definitely," the Junkie said, nodding absently.

"What about blood?"

"Lots of it," the Junkie said. "You don't make an omelette without breaking eggs."

"Oh, shit," said Billy, and turned his face away.

The Junkie said, "If it was me sitting there, I'd take something for it. Painkiller. You know what I mean?"

Billy turned his head back again and looked at him suspiciously. "You mean smack," he said.

"Not necessarily. There's other things you've never heard of. You wouldn't feel a thing and, even if you did, you wouldn't much care."

"These other things. Do they have to go in through a needle?"

"For something like this, yeah."

"Oh, shit," said Billy, "I hate needles."

"It's okay," said the Junkie. "I think I've got a clean one."

"Oh, *shit*," said Billy.

So the Junkie asked for another fifty and Billy offered another ten, and they finally settled on the fifty because Billy hadn't got a clue how much the stuff was really worth and, besides, a hard light seemed to come into the Junkie's eyes which suggested that he'd conducted this kind of negotiation a thousand times before.

And, besides, Billy was getting scared.

"Wait here," the Junkie said finally, and disappeared upstairs.

Billy slumped back in the chair with a feeling of miserable resignation. He wished that he didn't have to do this. He liked his dragon tattoo, and would be sorry to see it go; he'd had it for so long that it was like a part of him, and he was hardly even conscious of it for most of the time. That, in a way, had been his downfall. When he'd been standing there at the Building Society counter with the replica Luger and the open shopping bag and the ski mask (courtesy of Mac's, once again), the last thing on his mind had been the chance of his tattoo being picked up by the cameras. He'd been wearing his gloves, but the glove had ridden down the back of his hand and uncovered almost all of the design.

And then two nights ago there he'd been, sitting at home with a few cans of Draught Guinness in front of the TV while his mother pottered around upstairs, when up had come one of those *Crimewatch* shows where they asked for help with real-life cases and all the TV people who wished they were working in movies got the chance to ham it up doing crime reconstructions. He'd been watching it all with a sense of professional interest when, in a segment that they called *Rogues' Gallery*, he'd found himself looking at his own last job from an unexpected angle. He hadn't recognised himself straight away, but then he'd felt an inner leap of joy at the realisation that here he was, making the big time at last.

But then the joy had turned to ice as they'd taken a part of the picture and blown it right up and there was his one-of-a-kind tattoo, filling the screen from side to side and clear enough to be recognisable.

He'd packed his kitbag and been out of the house without any explanation that same night, almost within the hour. They were saying that the police had linked him with a string of other jobs. There was even a reward. Some of the people that Billy knew, they'd have sold their own parents for medical experiments if there was a drink in it for them. And the worst of it was that the people whom Billy knew, also knew Billy.

Millions of people watched that show. The people who made it crowed about their successes every week, and Billy sure as hell didn't want to become one of them. Even if his own friends didn't turn him in for the reward money, he'd inadvertently given the police a gift that they couldn't ignore. Small-time though he was they'd stay after him, like a man scratching around in his own behind until he dug out the peanut.

Somewhere upstairs, coming down to him through the ceiling, there was the sound of a floorboard being lifted.

Less than a minute later the Junkie was coming back down the stairs, and when he appeared in the doorway he was holding the same supermarket carrier bag that he'd had in his hand when Billy had first spotted him. In his other hand, he held an ordinary kitchen plate. On the plate lay a hypodermic syringe, an unlit candle, and a soot-marked spoon.

"Oh, shit," said Billy, and looked away again.

"I told you, it's clean," the Junkie insisted, setting everything down on the worktop. "It's a brand-new needle. I take the old ones down to the clinic, and they do me a trade."

"Wait a minute," Billy said, and even in his own ears it sounded like the beginnings of a whine. "I'm not so sure this is a good idea. I don't want to get hurt but I don't want to get hooked on anything, either."

"Nah," said the Junkie, undoing Billy's cuff button and starting to push back his sleeve. "That whole thing's just a myth."

"Really?"

"Really," said the Junkie. "I've been using this stuff every day for the past four and a half years. If there was anything to it believe me, I'd know."

"I'm just gonna look over here," said Billy.

The Junkie seemed amused. "You really that scared of needles?" he said.

And Billy said, "I'm not scared of anything, I'm just gonna look over here."

A couple of minutes later, he said, "Was that it?"

"That was it."

"You're pretty good at this."

"Thank you. Just relax and let it start to work on you. I've got to find a few things in the kitchen."

Billy lay back and closed his eyes. Maybe he could feel something already, he wasn't sure. He thought you were supposed to get a rush all at once like you were coming your brains out, but it wasn't happening that way. He wondered what would be next.

He knew even less about the art of tattoo removal than he did about the art of tattooing. Some people said it simply couldn't be done with any success, others that you had to go to a really expensive clinic and maybe even have skin grafts and everything. But then he'd heard that what they did was to use needles to hammer bleach down into the skin, deeper even than the inks that they were being used to eradicate, and he'd thought Well, it doesn't sound pleasant but it doesn't sound too complicated, either.

And then he thought, the *kitchen?*

And he thought Oh my God, he's going to use ordinary household bleach, and he started to sit up with the intention of getting out of the chair and heading for the door without a single look back; he could maybe just wear a bandage and tell people that he'd been burned and his hand was taking a long time to heal, and then he could settle in a new town and meet new people and he wouldn't have to go through anything like this at all . . .

And then a great sense of warmth and well-being hit him all at once, and it was better than coming his brains out because, to be honest, he'd always had this little problem of self-control that he never liked to talk about and always had to apologise for, and he sank back into the padded seat and, hey, wasn't it just the best and most comfortable chair in the history of mass-produced furniture?

"Getting any effect yet?" the Junkie said as he laid a few things out on the table alongside, and Billy said, "I dunno. Maybe."

He let his head fall back. It felt as if it was sinking into the padding about a foot deep or more. He smiled stupidly.

"Last chance to change your mind," the Junkie said.

And Billy said, "Do it."

The Junkie asked him to flex his fingers and he did, and then he had to ask the Junkie if anything was happening because he couldn't feel any feedback at all. The Junkie told him that was fine, and so Billy turned his face to the sweat-scented vinyl in the knowledge that when he sat up again, it would be over. He could move on, start again; and if anyone came looking, he could hold up his hands and say Who, *me?* with total confidence.

Move on. That was about what it entailed, because with or without the tattoo there was no going home. Thought about in the abstract, back when he hadn't actually been obliged to make the break, the notion had even held certain attractions; there was a lot of shit in his life that he'd always reckoned he could happily leave behind, a lot of arguments and all kinds of resentments, but somehow he couldn't see it that way any more. He kept thinking about his video collection. Every Saturday afternoon he liked to hang around street markets and car boot sales, looking for old stuff that the video libraries were selling off. He had all the *Halloweens* except for the first one, every one of the *Friday the 13th* movies, and almost a complete set of the *Police Academies* except for the one that was too new to have made it through the system yet. All lost. His mother would probably give them away or even just throw them out, the way she had with his comics all those years ago. Some of those comics would have been worth real money today. If he'd still had them, he'd never have needed to turn to crime at all.

Obviously, his troubles were all her fault.

He winced. Something hurt.

"Sorry," the Junkie said. "This isn't quite as sharp as I would have liked."

He'd been drifting. That wouldn't do. The last thing he needed would be to fall asleep and then wake up with the job half-done and the Junkie gone and his bagful of money gone with him. Even worse . . . what if the Junkie followed *Crimewatch*? Stranger things had happened. He'd know that the reward was more than the five hundred that Billy had offered, and he could wake up surrounded by police.

But if the Junkie had ever owned a TV, Billy reckoned that he'd probably sold or hocked it long ago. Not much danger there. But as far as the security of his kitbag was concerned, he'd already shown the Junkie what was inside.

Better to stay awake.

Concentrating his attention as best he could, Billy searched around for a conversational opener and then said, "How long have you been doing this?"

"About ten minutes now," the Junkie said. "It's not quite as easy as I thought. I'm trying to do it neat and there's all kinds of stuff in the way."

"I meant, how long have you been doing tattoos?"

"I don't do tattoos," the Junkie said.

This struck Billy as not a bad joke at all. He said, "So what's the big sign over the door and all the needles and stuff?"

"Oh, they're Steve's. *He's* the tattooist. But he doesn't open the shop on Wednesdays."

Billy frowned in his stupor. "So, who are you?"

"I'm Kevin. I just rent the upstairs from Steve. The roof leaks and it's a dump, but he lets me have it cheap as long as I pay him cash. I think it's a tax dodge. But I owe him more than a hundred in rent and he was going to throw me out; this means I can pay him off and have some left over."

Billy let his mind work on this one for a while, to no great effect.

And then he said, "But if you're not a tattooist, how come you know how to do a tattoo removal?"

There was a long silence.

And then the Junkie, his voice sounding as if it was coming from a long way away, said, "You wanted someone who could take off the *tattoo?*"

Billy sat up. He could only manage about halfway.

He looked.

The Junkie was sitting there on one of the hard chairs from by the wall, looking politely puzzled. He was spattered with red from the chin down, as if he'd been mixing up something nasty in a blender and had forgotten to put the lid on. In one hand there was a big, none-too-sharp looking kitchen knife; in the other, a towel that he'd been using to dab his working area clean. On the padded support before him, Billy's wrist had been tied down with a length of bandage that appeared also to be serving as a tourniquet.

But the most curious thing about the entire scene was the clear piece of daylight that was showing between Billy's hand and arm.

The Junkie said, "Don't judge it by what you see right now. It'll look much better when it's finished."

Billy gawped at the sight. Couldn't take it in. Still he felt no pain, no sensation at all from the shoulder down. The Junkie was watching his face, trying to guess his mood.

He was lost for words. Except, perhaps, for the phrase *Hanging by a thread*, which dropped into his mind unbidden and wouldn't go away.

He didn't dare move.

Not an inch.

He looked at the Junkie.

And the Junkie said hopefully, "Do I still get the five hundred?"

Comparative Anatomy

There was a pall of late-evening mist out over the harbour, and no-one to be seen in the ferry service waiting room. The ticket office alongside it was closed-down and dark; somebody had left a jacket on a chairback in there but, unless I was misreading all the signs, he was unlikely to be returning for it tonight.

I could see a handwritten notice propped up by an old brass paperweight on the other side of the ticket window. I couldn't even begin to translate what it said, although the indication seemed to be that the office had closed down at five. But the waiting room had been left unlocked, and the lights were still on, and inside I'd found timetables in three languages that showed a once-hourly service running on almost until midnight. I walked back to the car and, as I drew level with the open window on the passenger's side, I stopped for a moment.

"I think it's going to work out," I said. "If I've got it right, there should be a boat along in about twenty minutes."

Deborah was looking up at me; not apprehensive, not even tense.

"Can you be sure the information's up to date?" she said. "I don't see much happening around here."

"I don't know. Just keep your fingers crossed."

"Well," she said, "if it doesn't happen, it'll be no great disaster. We passed a few decent-looking inns on the road coming down."

I kind of smiled. But I don't think I said anything.

You'd have to see Deborah to know what I mean. Right then I'd say that I was still in the last part of that happy, stupid phase of a relationship where you can hardly feel the ground that you're walking on. Until she'd come along I'd almost forgotten the sensation; I'd been assuming that I'd grown out of it, I suppose, but then all in the space of a couple of weeks I'd discovered that one never really does. It simply lies there within you, dulled by habit until some major personal upheaval opens its way to the surface; and then all you need is the kind of luck that makes you want to check on your soul in case you've unwittingly put it in hock to Satan, and you're away.

Deborah was—is—quite something to see. A great-looking, intelligent blonde, and neither a juvenile nor a bimbo; nature had been getting more than a little help when it came to the hair colouring, but she made it no big secret and the effect wasn't cheap. Well, I never thought so, anyway, although I know that there was all kinds of stuff being said behind our backs once our secret had started to leak out. I really didn't care, and you'd have to have been in my shoes to understand why. We were a long way from home and all of home's problems and, as far as I was concerned, in a state damned close to paradise. I'd managed to get a last-minute rental on a summer house on the northernmost point of the biggest island in the group, and we'd gone there together. The summer was over and the autumn had set in, and it was a time of deserted beaches, shuttered cafes, long empty roads . . .

And—I have to say it—a set of increasing charges on my credit cards like you wouldn't *believe.*

I went around and got into the car. The loading area had been marked out into lanes, but mine was the only vehicle in it. I'd owned it for less than a year, and it was fast and sleek and red—your basic male midlife crisis car. It had pop-up headlamps and everything. Dark grey cloud seemed to be pressing down over masts of the fishing boats in the harbour, but that was mostly because it was getting late. I'd seen some empty fish boxes on the quays, but nobody working.

Deborah was looking through the dozen or so cassettes in the rack that was a part of the dashboard.

"I can't find a single one that we haven't played to death already," she said.

"Give the radio another try," I suggested. "See what it comes up with."

COMPARATIVE ANATOMY

"Right."

She worked the auto-search button as I cranked my seat back a couple of notches and tried to relax. It would be all right. It was all going to work out. We'd make it across this short hop and then on to the last big scheduled boat of the evening that would take us back to the island and our rented cabin. Which was just as well, because I was so close to broke by now that a night in a hotel would have sunk me completely.

"I really thought we'd had it with that big lorry," she said, for no apparent reason and without taking her eyes off the rapidly-changing frequency numbers in the radio's LCD.

"We had a few yards to spare," I said.

"He was going too fast."

I didn't comment. But she was saying it to make me feel better, that much I could tell. If anyone had been going too fast it had been me, and I think we both knew it.

And as for how it had all come about . . .

Well, it had started that morning when we'd set out in the car for a two-hour boat trip to a part of the mainland from which we could drive to the capital. This wasn't a big country, but it was broken up and had so much coastline that there was no straightforward way of covering any distance. We'd ventured little further than the house and the beach in the past ten days, unless you count the odd trip into the nearest town for supplies, and I think that both of us were feeling ready for a change.

It was almost a mistake. Almost. The capital was downbeat and crowded and a total waste of time, and it threatened to disrupt the mood of the entire trip. But then we'd altered our plans and driven north to what the guidebook seemed to feature as the only other attraction in the area, which turned out to be a fairytale castle in a perfect state of preservation and with its atmosphere undimmed by the handful of late-season tourists who, like us, had fallen across the place almost by accident. It had everything—courtyards, chambers, dungeons—and it as good as saved the day for us. Afterwards we'd dined in a small restaurant in the shadow of the castle's walls, tables aglow from the shaded lamps that stood on each; and as I looked at Deborah across the table I was beginning to think that life couldn't get any better than this, that everything had magically come together and that my child's bright vision of the future, which had been so painfully dismantled on the route to maturity, had been returned to me complete . . .

And then I happened to look at my watch, and I began to panic.

Time had been slipping by us like a well-trained, silent army. We now had less than two hours to make it back to catch the last island ferry of the day. Two hours; there was no way that we could cover the distance and still make it. Even if the car was fast, the roads weren't; but I had to do it somehow, and I had to do it without knuckling down and admitting that the only reason for my haste was financial. The cost of the meal I could manage, just; Deborah tried for the bill but, fool that I was and so eager to keep up the illusion of the effortless high life, I got to it first.

But then it was Deborah who, back at the car, had spotted an alternative route on the map that had a chance of getting us to the quayside with only minutes to spare. It was a short dotted line linking two horns of land, a small local ferry service that, if it was still running, would cut a big piece out of the journey.

"Great," I'd said, "let's go for it," and I only hoped that it wouldn't be an expensive crossing. According to the figure on the map, it would take about twenty-five minutes. How costly could that be? I pointed the car's nose in the right direction and put my foot down, and as we came out of the car park I checked the traffic on the wrong side and sailed out almost under the wheels of one of those huge articulated trucks. Haste, pure haste, and it almost got us killed. I don't know how we made it through, and I can hardly believe how our luck held; Deborah sat and said nothing for a long time, and her remark of a couple of minutes before had been her first reference to the incident.

She found a signal on the radio, and leaned back. I don't know what it was, perhaps one of the stations in Eastern Europe. She sighed. Out over the water, a couple of gulls hung and turned against the evening sky.

"I don't want this to end," she said simply.

"Me neither," I said.

But both of us knew that it would and, no matter how we eventually sorted out the problems that we'd left behind us, that no time would ever be quite like this again. Magic always stops at midnight. Understanding this, neither of us said anything more; because I think we both knew that talking about it too much would carry the risk of killing it stone dead before its time.

COMPARATIVE ANATOMY

The boat was coming in.

It slowed and came to at the harbour's tiny quay, dropping its metal ramp with a crash. A couple of battered old cars, shapes that I recognised with European marques that I didn't, came rolling off and scooted away through the docks as if glad to hit land again, their drivers indistinct shadows at the wheels. I started my own engine and backed around to face the ramp. A solitary figure, muffled against the evening's chill, waited with a book of tickets and a well-worn leather money pouch. Mine was still the only car in the line, and I wondered if they'd stick to the timetable or wait around for latecomers before setting off.

Being kind of in a hurry, I hoped they'd just go.

I drew level with the ticket-taker. When I asked him how much, he held up the fingers of his cut-off gloves by way of reply. Well-wrapped was hardly the way to describe him; there was a scarf around his head that was held in place by his peaked seaman's cap and, apart from his fingers, only the tip of his nose was on show. All that I could think was that it must be pretty damned cold, out there beyond the harbour.

He waved us aboard with a big flashlight and as I was driving us forward onto the car deck, Deborah said, "Was there somebody inside of all that?"

"Yeah," I said. "Popeye the sailorman with an embarrassing case of herpes."

Nobody waited to direct us any further, so I stopped in the middle of the deck and we got out. There was room for a couple of dozen cars, at the most. The deck itself was of wood, oil-stained and worn, and it ran through the middle of the ship like an open-ended tunnel. Drive on at one end, drive off at the other. There were doors to either side of us, a couple of them open but most of them bearing *No Entry* symbols; only one of them carried an image of a stick figure ascending a stairway in the direction of an upward-pointing arrow and that one, I guessed, would take us to the passenger deck.

Deborah shivered slightly as I locked the car. I didn't know what kind of facilities to expect on a boat like this, but I wasn't expecting much. It looked really old, a real warhorse of a vessel that had probably been chugging back and forth across this same part of the seaways since God was in short trousers. If the noise coming up through one of the open doorways was anything to go by, the engines were of a pure vintage rustbucket type; the sound was like that of a couple of dozen three-year-olds having a good time with frying pans and hammers.

"Looks like we're going to have it all to ourselves," I said to Deborah and she shrugged as if to say, *Fine*. As we were crossing to the stairway, I glanced back at the car. Sitting there in the middle of the open deck, it looked as if it had been set up for an ad agency's photo session for one of the glossy Sunday colour supplements. The sky beyond the deck was now the colour of new lead, with all the yellow shore lights beginning to show up in the dusk. Everything else was turning to shades of blue and grey as the air grew noticeably sharper.

Life could be worse than this, I thought, and I followed Deborah inside.

The stairway was narrow and steep, and it led us to the passenger deck. What we found up there reminded me of the kind of no-space, ingenious, squeeze-it-in kind of carpentry that you used to find in wooden caravans and steam-age railway sleeping cars . . . all deep brown varnish and brass-headed screws, a real museum-piece of a vessel. There were three lounges at slightly different levels, none of them a regular shape and all linked by tiny passageways where two people could pass face-to-face, but only just. I hit my head on something as we moved to look into the first of the lounges, a squarish, low-ceilinged room set out with chairs and half a dozen card tables. On the nearest of these had been left three packs of playing cards, each held together by a rubber band and all looking as if they'd been handled by someone who was taking a break while draining oil sumps. The second room was hardly more than a cupboard, and had a couple of benches and no legroom. It ended in a narrow doorway with another of the *No Entry* symbols. The third ran almost the length of one side of the boat and was, apart from the underside of a stairway that cut down on the headroom at one end, the least claustrophobic. There was a table under each porthole, and at the far end were two coin-operated drinks machines and a plastic crate for the empty bottles.

Basic? The word seemed to flatter it.

"This'll do us," Deborah said, and started to shed her coat. It was pretty warm once you were inside, probably from the surplus steam heat being piped around. "For half an hour, anyway."

I couldn't help smiling as I looked about us. The ferry that had brought us out from the island, and which would soon be waiting to

COMPARATIVE ANATOMY

take us back, had been huge and modern and like a floating hotel. This was more like a cafeteria at a dog track, but Deborah hardly seemed to mind.

I said, "How about a drink?" and she looked toward the machines. One was a big chilled-bottle dispenser—I wondered how they'd managed to manoeuvre it up the stairs—and the other was for hot coffee and soup.

"Dare we risk it?" she said; but the machines were more modern than the boat, and they were all lit up and humming, so I reckoned that it was probably worth a try. Having said which, we couldn't make up enough change between us; and so, leaving Deborah to wait in the lounge, I went back down to the car to see if there was anything in the meter money that I'd been keeping in one of the door pockets.

I saw no crew along the way. And then when I got to the car deck, I was surprised to see that we'd already cast off and were moving away from the shore; I'd heard no change in the engine's note, and even now I'd no sense of movement. I stood for a moment, looking out over the raised metal ramp that now formed a part of the ship's rail, and watched as the shore lights receded.

I think that I wanted to feel elated. I wanted to feel satisfied, at peace, content . . . all of those things that cluster around happiness and yet vanish the moment you try to give it the name.

But when I listened to the echoes inside, all that I could detect was a far-off note of regret; and I'm not sure that it was entirely because I was taking in a sunset.

I went back up to the passenger deck. She was by one of the portholes, looking out, and I went over and stood close behind her.

"How are you doing?" I said.

"Fine." She'd relaxed back against me a little, but she was still looking out. The land was receding from sight, and we were passing an orange marker buoy. We seemed to be heading into deeper and deeper shadow as we steamed out toward the open sea.

She said, "I've been watching for the crew."

"See anyone?"

"No."

"Me neither. They probably like to stay out of the way."

"In that case, they're experts. I've been watching the bridge, and I've seen nobody moving around."

"I can't see the bridge from here."

She led me through to the smallest of the three passenger areas, the compartment with no legroom and a no-access door. The door itself had a porthole window, and I squeezed in alongside her to look through it.

We were looking forward. Just outside was a short exposed gangway, with a pitted safety rail on the seaward side and part of a davit from which, I assumed, would be slung one end of a lifeboat just beyond my line of sight. Jutting out ahead of us was a corner of the ship's bridge. I could see inside, but I couldn't see much.

"They've got lights," I said.

"Those have been on since we boarded."

"Still nothing for us to worry about."

We went back into the section with the dispensing machines, and I banged my head again on the way through. We used up my change and took the drinks over to one of the tables, which vibrated slightly with the beat of the engines as they drove us onward. I was wondering if we shouldn't have been able to see land, or at least the lights of land, ahead of us already; but the whole area was pretty remote, and so perhaps there was nothing to see. My impressions of the countryside so far had consisted of rolling fields, some of them of burned-off straw, and the occasional hi-tech windmill like a marker set down on the high ground by some alien civilisation—very few buildings at all, and these mostly modern and standing in isolation. I'd look at places like that as we drove by, and I'd try to imagine the lives of the people inside. But I never could, not convincingly, because I didn't even know how to begin; and yet I'm sure that as far as they were concerned, they probably reckoned that they were looking out at the world from its centre.

"What are you thinking about?" Deborah said.

"You," I told her automatically, even though it wasn't true.

"You mean about how I'm plain and half a stone overweight?"

"I can't see any of that."

"Then keep on thinking." She reached across the table and took my hand. Something inside me still leapt at her touch.

She said, "We're on our own, there's nobody waiting. So why's it so important to you that we get back tonight?"

"No reason," I said. "I just like where we're staying." And then I turned my wrist slightly so that I could see my watch again. "Less than ten minutes to go. We should be landing pretty soon. What do you say we go back to the car and get ready to roll?"

She shrugged, and I could see that I hadn't exactly convinced her. But what more could I have said? That our time together had been bleeding me dry, and that now it was starting to hurt? Perhaps I should have told her exactly that, I don't know. I only know that the best that I could manage was this lame-sounding excuse.

The car deck looked strange and unreal, the yellow deck lighting in contrast to the black square of night at its end. There was an edge to the sea breeze that was being drawn through, and it was tainted with the smells of oil and something else that I couldn't quite identify. The bulkhead lights were undiffused, and all of the deck's fittings—the pipes, the joints, the rivets, the cabling—were thrown into sharp detail like the bones and sinews on a dried-out butcher's carcase. Against this, the lines of the car were less harsh, more welcoming. The car was home on wheels, here in the belly of the whale.

As I was turning the key to pop all the locks, I looked forward into the night. I saw no moon, no stars, no suggestion even of the line between sea and sky.

"I still can't see any land," I said.

Deborah paused as she was opening the passenger door, and she looked for a while. I saw her eyes narrow slightly, as if the lack of expected detail bothered her.

But she said, "There's probably mist over the water. We have to be closer than it looks."

And she got into the car.

Mist over the water. That sounded reasonable to me. The sailing time was nearly over, there couldn't have been more than a few hundred yards left to cover to the far shore. The pilot wouldn't need much in the way of visual information if he had radar. And these kinds of ships always had to have radar these days, didn't they? There was probably some kind of regulation on it.

I heard the rumble of the automatic aerial as it telescoped up out of the bodywork somewhere behind me. Deborah was trying the radio. Where there had previously been at least a faint signal, now there was nothing. She tried all the preselects, and then she hit the *search* button again.

"It'll work better when we're out in the open," I said.

Deborah said nothing.

With only a couple of minutes left to go, I started the engine. It was a more reassuring sound than that of the dead radio; the automatic search was stopping at certain frequencies, but no signal was coming out. She tried it on the FM band, the AM, the longwave. There was a hint of something at one point on the longwave, a man's voice speaking emphatically in some strange language. It sounded as if it was coming from about a million miles away, and it faded quickly and didn't come up again.

After a while, she switched off and sat back. The aerial telescoped itself back into the bodywork again. She didn't look entirely happy.

"I think we're going to miss the connection," she said.

"We can just about make it."

"So you can nearly get us killed again? No thanks."

And in that moment I looked across at her and I thought, You know, you're right; maybe you *are* about half a stone overweight.

I switched off the engine and got out of the car. The throughbreeze was clearing the exhaust fumes, but slowly. She had a point. We'd been out on the water now for nearly fifteen minutes longer than we should have. I went forward to the rail, and looked for some indication of what lay ahead.

Away from the glare of the deck lighting, my eyes began to adjust. It wasn't quite as dark out there as it had seemed; now I could make out the last streaks of day in the form of a few fading grey bands across the sky, not much in the way of illumination but enough to counteract the impression of a featureless void.

Whichever way I looked, I could see the moving surface of the sea.

Nothing else.

So then I turned and walked the length of the deck to the other end, thinking that perhaps there was some fancy manoeuvering going on which would involve some kind of a reverse approach, but I think I knew the likely outcome of *that* particular line of speculation even before I'd reached the stern rail.

As I walked back to the car, I tried to tell myself that my anxiety came entirely from the need to meet a schedule while having no control over the means. But it was too late anyway, wasn't it? I'd already been working on the basis of my best estimate, with no margin. Now that I hadn't even the slightest chance of making it, I ought to be able to relax at least a little.

I got inside. Deborah had been trying the radio again. She

looked up at me, and made a weak smile.

"Look, I'm sorry," she said.

"No," I said, "you were right. I was pushing it too hard. I got careless for a minute. I won't make the same mistake again."

"I think I can guess what was worrying you."

"Nothing was worrying me."

"We're still going to have to find a hotel for tonight, but it's going to be on me. That was always my intention. And before you start to object, can I point out that you've hardly let me pay for *anything* yet?"

"You think I was worried about *money?*" I said, sounding suitably astonished.

"Come the end of the trip, we'll settle accounts. Fifty-fifty, all down the line."

"Forget it," I said.

"We came into this together, and it's got to be fair."

"I don't even want to talk about it," I said.

"Hey," she said, "wait a minute. What does that make me?"

I didn't exactly know how to answer. The whole money thing was so sensitive, and I'd been brooding over it for a while now. I suppose I'd become like a wounded dog that bares its teeth at anyone trying to help.

"It's . . . it's not an issue," I said. "All right?"

"Fine," she said. "You go broke, but at least you can keep your pride."

She grabbed up a tape, and banged it into the cassette slot without even looking to see what it was. She probably didn't care, as long as it was noise and it filled up what otherwise would have been a stony silence. We both of us sat there, looking out of the car in different directions.

And when the tape finally ran out we both looked at it in the same moment, and I expect that we probably shared the same thought.

Because it meant that an entire half-hour had passed, and there was still no sign of us making a landing.

"Something's wrong," she said. And she didn't sound angry anymore, she sounded sick and scared.

"There must have been a misprint on the map."

She turned to me. "What did the timetable say?"

But I dodged the question, because the timetables back in the harbour waiting room had indicated exactly the same thing; a twenty-five minute journey, made at hourly intervals throughout the day. No other boats were shown, no other sailings listed.

"I'll see if I can find out what's going on," I said.

I got out and went down to the rail and looked again. The sky was completely dark now and I saw no shore lights, no stars, nothing —just the ferryboat's own navigation lights and their limited spread across the near surface of the water. The sea around the vessel was cold and dense and unwelcoming. Where the lights were caught and reflected, they plated the waves in yellow and silver.

I looked back at the car. Deborah had climbed out and was standing alongside it, watching me, waiting for me to do something. So then I tried walking to the nearest of the ship's doors and knocking on it. It was like the door on a meat safe, solid metal and with a big lever handle. I hurt my knuckles on the paintwork but I don't think I made any sound that could be heard on the other side, especially not over the steady beat of the engines. When I tried the handle, it wouldn't move. The next door opened for me, but only to reveal the inside of an unlit deck locker full of mops and rags and other cleaning stuff.

I don't know what was making me more nervous, our increasingly belated arrival or the thought of being caught like a prowler in some area that I shouldn't have entered. The door to the engine room was still open and I stuck my head into the vertical shaft and looked down. The noise enveloped me and drowned out everything else, a raucous hammering like the heartbeat of a beast; I couldn't see a thing apart from the first few rungs of an iron ladder that was bolted to the side directly beneath me, and the indication seemed to be that whatever lay below, it lay in total darkness. I didn't get it. As far as my limited knowledge went, ship's engines didn't run unattended; not on a vessel of this size, anyway, and not for the length of time that we'd already been at sea. Perhaps there was a second door down below somewhere, and there were working lights and people beyond it.

But I really didn't feel like climbing down into the darkness to find out.

When I pulled myself out and turned back to face the deck, Deborah was waiting for me. She'd brought the road map over from the car, and for the moment it seemed that the spark of our near-argument had been forgotten.

"Look at this," she said. "I've been comparing some of the distances. There's only one direction we could have been going in, and that's due North. Any other way, and we'd have reached some kind of land before now."

"Unless we've been circling."

"The wind direction's pretty much the same as it was when we set out. I don't think so."

There seemed to be only one course left for us to take; to the bridge, and I led the way up the narrow stairs. The only explanation that I could think of was that perhaps the man at the helm had suffered an attack of some kind and that he was lying there now, unconscious—dead, even—while the boat continued to drift away from its regular course. But surely he wouldn't be out there alone, I was thinking as we entered the smallest of the three passenger lounges and I reached to open the forbidden door at its end; others had to be there with him, and *someone* ought to have been able to step in and take over. I'd heard of big modern ships that ran almost entirely on automatics, but even they were supposed to have a minimum bridge crew to keep an eye on everything. And this wasn't a modern ship, not by anybody's standards.

The crosswind hit me as I stepped out, and I reached for the safety rail. We'd been sheltered down on the car deck; this wind was bitter and cold, and it tasted of salt. It was just a couple of strides across the open to the bridge, and we didn't wait around. We went in through another one of those big watertight bulkhead doors, and even before we'd got it closed behind us we'd been able to gather that my heart-attack theory had been wrong.

Nobody lay slumped over the wheel.

Nobody was up here at all.

There were all the signs of life. Just no life itself. Most of the illumination came from the green nightlighting of the instruments, apart from a single downward-pointing spotlight over the chart table. The chart was recognisable from our road map by its land shapes, but all the concentration of detail was reversed from land to sea. Grease pencil lines showed our supposed course from quay to quay; they'd scuffed almost to nothing, as if they'd been drawn a long time before and went more or less unchecked by the crew on what had become a familiar route. Close to this was the radar screen, which I wouldn't have known how to read; there was this sweeping line and a couple of repeating blips just like in every submarine movie you've ever seen. At each crew position there was a swivel chair bolted to the floor. I checked, but none was even warm.

"Someone has to have taken us out of the harbour," I said. I was moving by the helm to look at the ship's compass, one of those gimbal-mounted affairs designed to stay more or less stable in a rough and stormy sea. "We didn't just drift out."

As far as I could tell, the compass was reading due West. But if we'd actually been heading due West, then it was as Deborah had said; we'd have reached land long before now, and probably not too far away from our original destination. I gave it a push. It swung easily on its bearings—it hadn't jammed at all, that was for sure. And when it settled down again, its reading was unchanged.

"Try the radio," Deborah said.

I tried the radio. Try was about all that I could do, because nothing about it made any sense to me at all. There were little dymo-printed labels over some of the switches, but they were all in the local language and I couldn't understand what they were saying. I found the switch that turned up the volume on the loudspeaker, but all that I could get out of it was static.

"There's got to be someone around," Deborah said with rising desperation in her voice. "Where's the man who took the money?"

I turned on her.

"How the *fuck* would I know?" I roared. "Have I got X-ray eyes?"

Her mouth dropped open. I've never seen such blank, uncomprehending shock.

And I quickly said, "I'm sorry, I didn't mean that. But I don't know anything more than you do. So don't ride me as if I'm your father or something, all right? I mean it, I'm sorry."

But I wasn't. Not entirely. If anything, I felt slightly better. I don't blow off like that often, but I've sometimes wondered if people wouldn't treat me better if I did.

There was another exit at the back of the bridge, one that led down into the part of the ship that couldn't be reached directly from the passenger areas. Crew quarters, at a guess. Just before I led the way down, I took another glance at the radar; the picture had changed slightly from what it had been, the distance between the centre and the most significant blip having narrowed. And then I tried a half-turn of the ship's helm. The wheel moved with almost no resistance; and then when I took my hand away, it slowly began to move back. It took about thirty seconds altogether and, when we finally left the bridge, it had reset itself with the same silent efficiency as the ship's compass.

Down below we found a small common-room for the crew, a galley with every surface so covered in burned grease that it looked as if it had been painted with tar, and beyond that three double-bunked cabins that all smelled stale and sour, like unchanged sickroom linen. I was thinking about the radar, and wondering about the significance of the blip. The problem was that I didn't know how to interpret the screen; the most obvious explanation was that it was a much larger vessel catching up on us from behind, but it could just as easily have been some stationary object lying somewhere ahead just off our course. If it was another ship, then perhaps we could signal it; and I was just beginning to wonder how when Deborah called me along to another of the cabins.

"I recognise these," she said.

Hanging on a hook behind the door were an overcoat, a scarf, and a battered leather pouch. I raised the pouch and shook it, but it made no sound.

"The ticket money's gone," I said. "But he still could be somewhere on board."

"Or maybe there was nobody inside the coat after all," Deborah said. I suppose she meant it as a joke, but somehow after a moment it didn't seem to strike either of us as being too funny.

In one pocket of the coat I found a pair of gloves, in the other the flashlight with which the ticket-seller had beckoned us on board. It was an old flashlight, its handle taped to give a better grip. I tried switching it on and off, and the batteries seemed well up to strength.

Perhaps when we'd looked everywhere else, then I might even be able to raise the nerve to climb down to check the engine room with it.

But now I was moving with a little more confidence. Finding the ticket-seller's coat had given an extra little kick to my determination. It confirmed that someone had been around here after all, and it rooted the entire, increasingly strange experience in a kind of reality. The rest of the crew-only area took no more than a few minutes to investigate, and turned up nothing. There were upright lockers, but no corpses toppled out when I opened the doors. There was a washroom with shower cubicle, but no body lay curled-up behind the curtain. No severed head glowered up from the toilet pan, no hanged man swung on a creaking chain from the overhead pipes as we descended a different stairway that would take us back down to the car deck. We came out on the opposite side to the passenger stairs, and I swung the heavy door shut behind us. The slam echoed across the deck.

I said, "There's only the engine room left to check out. You want to wait in the car for me, or what?"

She wanted to wait in the car. I can remember how, when I was a child, climbing into a wardrobe and pulling all the heavy coats around me in the corner had produced a tremendous sense of security; I could see the increasing uncertainty in her eyes and I guessed that being in the car might give her the same kind of primitive reassurance now. I was nervous and confused, I'll admit it, but she was actually scared; it almost made me want to shake her, but I didn't. Instead I gave her the keys, and I took the flashlight across to the engine room access shaft.

The door to the shaft appeared to be kept permanently open; someone had fixed its handle back against the bulkhead by winding several turns of stiff wire between it and some bracket. I switched on the flashlight and aimed it down the shaft. It ended about twenty-five feet below me, in a grey metal gridiron floor. Beneath the floor I could see a reflected glint of water. Bilgewater, probably, backed-up from some blockage.

Oh, great, I thought resignedly, and I swung myself in and started to climb down the ladder.

I wasn't exactly good at this. The flashlight beam was swinging about all over the place and my feet kept missing the rungs. Every now and again I'd stop and check below me, just in case something was coming up. Not that I was irrationally nervous, you understand. But you know how it is.

At the bottom I was expecting a door of some kind, not an open doorway with a warehouse-sized sense of dark space beyond it. I shone the light through and it hit grey-painted metal, all pipes and angles and dials exactly like you'd expect from a ship's engine room. The noise was terrific. I moved inside, shining the light around so that the machinery threw big, hulking shadows across the ceiling. There was no mistaking that this was a working area; no panelling, no attempt to conceal the wiring, not much in the layout to accommodate the human form. This was the machines' home territory, and anyone who entered it had to enter on their terms.

And I, it seemed, was the only one to have done so. At least on this trip.

A mistake has been made, was all that I could think. A major mistake. The equivalent, perhaps, of leaving your car on a hill with its dodgy handbrake applied and then finding it gone when you returned. I swung the light; the shadows zoomed. And then I swung the light back, because I'd caught something in the beam that hadn't registered until after I'd passed it by. Targeting in, I felt my way across. The entire floor was of the same kind of grating as the bottom of the shaft outside but instead of waste water underneath, there were conduits and dusty runs of cable.

What I'd seen was a coffee mug, perched on the flat upper surface of something like a flywheel cover. It wasn't much, but it *was* a sign of life and worth a closer look. The mug was full, and the surface of the coffee was quivering in a series of rings from the vibration of the housing on which it stood. I checked all around for spanners, rags, any sign of someone who might have been working close to the spot, and then I looked at the mug again and reached out to touch it.

The coffee was still hot. Too hot to drink, if anything.

So then, very tentatively, I touched the flywheel housing on which it stood. I was expecting to find the metal of the housing to be at the same fierce temperature, which would have explained it.

But the metal surface was barely warm.

It was exactly the kind of sign that I'd been looking for.

And suddenly, I didn't want to be here any more.

An empty ship, adrift, was one thing. But this hinted at something else, almost as if the vessel was being run by ghosts who popped out of existence the moment that one of us looked their way, and then faded back and quietly went about their jobs when our backs were turned. I shone the flashlight all around from where I stood and I was pretty sure that nobody was hiding, although I couldn't be absolutely certain; but who would work away in the dark like a troll, and then hide from the light so completely?

If there was an answer to that one, I no longer wanted to know it. All I wanted was to get back up to the car deck, preferably as quickly as possible and with nothing hanging onto my leg in an attempt to drag me back down. The manner in which I climbed up wasn't any more efficient than my earlier descent.

But I *did* manage it in about half the time.

I could hear the music the moment I stepped out. It came across the deck like the distant sound of a loud party and for a moment, I wondered how she was standing it. She'd switched on the car's interior light and I could see her there, looking straight ahead like some pale sketch in a badly-illuminated display case. I didn't know what I was going to do next. Search the place, find somebody, find out exactly what was going on; that had been the total of my strategy, and all that I'd found was a series of meaningless details that had built up to an unsettling and inexplicable effect.

I went to the stern rail. I was thinking about that blip on the radar screen, and wondering again at its significance. I could only guess at the horizon now, an indistinguishable line where one profound darkness met another. I could see nothing.

So I went back to the car and got in.

The music was so loud that it hurt; she'd got it cranked up even louder than the noise of the engine room, and I could hear the door speakers beginning to bend and tear under the pressure of being driven so hard. She didn't look at me as I turned it down to a level where I could make myself heard.

"Look," I said. "We're going to be all right."

"Are we?"

The way she said it, she was obviously throwing it down as a challenge. I said, "We're in no danger. The ship isn't sinking or anything. And unless I'm wrong, there's something going to be passing close by to us sometime soon. I've got the flashlight, I can give them a signal."

Now she turned her head to look at me. I looked into her eyes and saw a total stranger.

She said, "You don't understand anything, do you?"

"What's to understand?"

"It's wrong. It's all wrong. And it's just getting worse and worse."

"Now you're being stupid."

"Don't you call me stupid," she said, her cheeks afire with irrational fury. "You're not bright enough to call *anybody* stupid."

And then when she cranked the music back up to its earlier level, I reckoned that this was effectively the end of that particular conversation.

I left her to it. I couldn't talk to her, I didn't even want to sit with her and have that kind of mood in the air. Maybe it was unfair but I was thinking that everything good about the last few days was being blown away. I'd really believed that everything was going to be different this time. And it wasn't.

I think it was the biggest disappointment I'd ever known.

Going up through the passenger deck again—the thought of returning via the crew's quarters gave me a lingering, haunted feeling that I was no longer ready to confront—I went out onto the open walkway and so back onto the bridge. Nothing here had changed. I planned to try every setting on the radio, to study the charts and compare them to anything that I could find on the radar screen, to see if I could knock out whatever automatic pilot we were running on and turn us right around . . . the one thing that I *wasn't* going to do was sit in the car and listen to the fucking Beach Boys.

I looked at the radar screen. That second blip was still showing, only now it was much closer. It was so close to the centre of the image that in a minute or so it would have passed by.

I dived out onto the walkway again, and held onto the rail as I looked out. A few more seconds, and I'd have been able to see it from inside the bridge anyway. It was coming up from behind and closing fast; huge in comparison to our own humble little ferry, and moving in silence. For one panicky moment I thought that it was on a collision course, but then I realised that it was going to pass with little room to spare, a matter of a hundred metres or less. Its bow was cutting through the waves like a guillotine through so much paper.

Some kind of an inshore freighter, I suppose you'd call it; too big for the kind of run that we were supposed to have been doing, but hardly world cargo class either. Its plates were streaked with slime and rust, no paint left visible at all; chains and lines were trailing from its sides as if it had simply broken free from the shore and struck out on its own. Where there were portholes, they were the same opaque, muddy colour as the rest of the ship.

From the deckrail down, it resembled a salvage job. From the deck up, it blazed like the day.

The best way that I can try to describe it is to say, think of a football field at night; all of the overhead floodlights on but with no players, no crowd, none of the usual signs of life at all. Just this well-lighted container deck without a single freight container on it, nothing at all other than the squared-off hulk of a big sixteen-wheeler truck that had been roped down in the middle of the open space as if in anticipation of rough seas. Behind the cargo deck rose the main superstructure, and every one of its windows was as blank as camouflage paint. The closer this semi-derelict came, the more I was in its shadow and the less I could see.

I can't say that I recognised the truck. And I can't say that I didn't, either.

As the ship came level, shaving it about as close as it was possible to get without the risk of taking a piece of us along, I looked up and saw that there was a man standing at the rail. He was holding on with both hands and he was looking down. All the light was behind him, so he was nothing more than a silhouette. He didn't wave, he didn't move, I couldn't see anything of his face or his expression. He stood there with his hands on the rail, and he looked down as if in judgement. He might have turned his head to keep his eyes on me as the two of us passed, I don't know. The whole thing was going to be over in less than a minute.

The flashlight was still back inside, on the map table by the radar. I didn't run to get it.

The cargo vessel ploughed on past, still in silence until the regular chopping of its engines came by with the stern. Its wake was a river of foam that rocked the deck under my feet as the swell hit us. I tried to see if there was any name across the back, but all that I could make out was the place where a name had once been.

Wherever it was going, both of our ships appeared to have the same destination. Maybe it was just my imagination, but I was beginning to think that I could make out a faint glow of some kind on the horizon ahead.

I watched it for a while longer. And then when it was almost out of sight, I went inside and watched it on the radar.

And then I went back down to the car deck.

The same tape was still playing. She must have had it going around and around on the auto-reverse. Both doors were locked, and she didn't look up at me when I tried to open one. I knocked on the glass and called to her, but she stared straight ahead and didn't respond in any way at all.

So then I went to the car deck's forward rail.

I hadn't been imagining it. I was looking at the horizon ahead to where a greenish light was beginning to show in a thin band like the lights of a drowned city. I knew that I ought to have been feeling that this was something promising and I wished that I could, but all that I felt was a growing sense of dread.

Now I'm waiting for an education that I know I'd prefer not to receive. Below me the engines beat their steady beat, and around me the cold sea rushes by. Deborah can't be planning to stay in the car forever. The horizon's drawing nearer, and the light just beyond it is becoming more intense.

What's coming? God only knows. But if hell's the place where you get what you want only to find that it all turns sour on you, then I suppose that it's as good a name as any.

That big truck. I was so sure we'd made it through.

What a killer.

Dead Man's Handle

I can tell you exactly when it happened, because it was late in the summer of 'seventy-four and I was nineteen years old. When I say late I mean sometime around September, getting almost to the end. Why do I remember it so well?

Probably because I've been having bad dreams about it ever since.

It was the year that I got a summer job working for the council, and they sent me to a place down by the seafront called—honest to God, I'm not making this up—Happymount Park. I was the park supervisor's assistant, which meant that I had to help out wherever an extra pair of unskilled hands was needed. The park supervisor was about my father's age and a decent type, which was just as well because I had to have been one of the least able workers that he'd ever been assigned. I hardly knew one end of a wheelbarrow from the other, and my hands were so soft that after that first bruising week I took to wearing heavy work gloves almost all of the time. I don't know what some of the others must have made of me; I'd half-expected resentment, but I think they looked upon me as some kind of a pet or a mascot. I was a student, I always had some impressive-looking Penguin Classic stuck down the side of my lunchbag, I always seemed to know the hardest clues in the *Daily Mirror* crossword . . . and the first time that I sank a shovel into the ground, it stuck there and I had to look for help to get it out again. When I painted railings, I always managed to spatter the asphalt underneath. To keep me out of harm's way I was sent to feed the ducks in the Japanese garden, and two of them actually died.

Personally, I think that was just coincidence.

But by then, my reputation was set.

Most of the other park employees had been hardened by decades of all-weather outdoor work, and seemed to have been knocked together out of tougher material than me—even Vince, and he couldn't have been much older than I was. He already had two years in the Navy, and a set of the most amateurishly-executed forearm tattoos that I'd ever seen. There was him, there was Old Jack, there was Irish Michael who hardly ever spoke and who, when he did, revealed teeth like broken liquorice. Let's face it, the bunch of them could have eaten me alive.

But . . . they didn't.

Only in retrospect can I see how they must have felt. I was so useless, it was reassuring; with hardly a paper qualification amongst them, it must have seemed as if I'd been sent over from the other side of some great intellectual divide to show that the rarified creatures who lived there were actually no great shakes, and nothing to fear. After those near-disasters of the early weeks I found my level, which mostly consisted of general gofering, picking up litter, and changing the dud bulbs in the park's illuminations.

The illuminations. Now, they were what the park was mostly about in the summertime, and they were the feature that drew the evening crowds. Every year the same old canvas and hardboard flats would be trundled out of a council warehouse somewhere, patched and touched-up, and then brought to the park and erected on scaffolding to make larger-than-life nursery rhyme scenes at various points around the gardens. The artwork was kind of homely and unprofessional but the little kids all loved it, even the horrendous attempt at Mickey Mouse that looked like Dustin Hoffman with bats' ears. Copyright? Don't even ask. But set them amidst the greenery and floodlight them at the dying of the day, and even a hardened cynic of nineteen wasn't immune to the magic. If you wanted loud noise and white-knuckle rides, you went to the big amusement park at the far end of the promenade. But if you'd only just learned to walk and talk, and loud noises scared you, and a sure sign of a good time was that you had to be picked up and carried home on somebody's shoulder afterwards, then your parents brought you to Happymount.

It was an old-fashioned kind of a park. I mean, how many of

them these days still have deckchairs for rent? Or a special terrace just for the elderly? Or a cafeteria that actually opens every now and again, with ice cream and home-made cakes and not a hint of fast food on the menu? Happymount had them, along with a Crazy Golf course, and a miniature roundabout on a trailer whenever the owner turned up with it, and the Japanese gardens that I already mentioned. They also had a petting zoo at one time, until the goat died. I plead not guilty, I never went anywhere near the damned thing.

And at the far end of the park, on an oval track of maybe five hundred yards or less, ran the Happymount Express.

The Happymount Express was one of those miniature trains consisting of a diesel engine and a half-dozen open carriages, the entire thing being scaled for the under-fives. You walked down the main central boulevard of the park and there it was at the end, just before you turned off into the gardens. There was even a little station with a concrete platform, and benches for parents to wait. In the evenings there were coloured lights strung all along the boulevard, and a line of them followed the track out through the woodland right up to the outer perimeter of the park. Beyond that was a fence and then a golf course, a real one this time, but in the evenings this would be in darkness.

The train's driver, ticket-taker, and general maintenance engineer was a man called Len Cunningham. I knew him only as a distant figure, because when he wasn't actually running the train he tended to not to emerge from the long, shanty-style engine shed at the far end of the woodland. The shed opened at both ends and the track ran straight through it, so it doubled as a tunnel. It had been built in a haphazard manner out of wood and corrugated iron, and it looked as if a good fart would blow it all down.

Len Cunningham was middle-aged and overweight. He wore overalls and a railway engineer's cap and he always perched on the back of the tiny diesel engine looking as if he'd rather be somewhere, *anywhere* else. Each ride consisted of three circuits of the track and at the end of each he'd pull into the little station and sit there waiting for the toddlers to disembark and load up. The little ones would fuss around like chickens in a yard, and occasionally some of their parents would be dragged along to squeeze themselves into the carriages as well. They'd look like daytrippers in Lilliput. When everyone was aboard, Len would go along and take the money and give out the tickets, and then he'd walk back up the line to his engine with all the eagerness of a man on the way to his own hanging. Then off around again, going *put-put-put* through the shadows of the trees.

And that was more or less it, all through his working day.

For my part, I liked the evenings best. Not least because there wasn't so much to do. The gardeners all stopped working at five and we tried to get all the rest of the general maintenance done in daylight, so by switching-on time it was usually just me and the boss in our little brew hut that was tucked away in the no-man's-land behind the Mad Hatter's Tea Party, killing time until shutdown at nine.

We didn't have much in common, but we seemed to have no problem finding things to talk about.

One night, I asked him about Len Cunningham.

"You don't want to mess with him," he told me. His name, I remember, was Brian, although everyone called him Big Brian except for Irish Michael, who called him Action Man. He said, "Len Cunningham is an obstacle course in human relations."

"I wasn't planning on messing with him," I said. "I just wondered what makes him tick, that's all."

"Fuck knows," Big Brian said. "But I'll tell you a story that set up my ideas about him for life." At this he craned back and took a look through the hut's little window, as if he was getting himself ready for a story with some point to it. This window gave us a narrow angle on the park's main gate, glimpsed through a crisscross of scaffolding and a gap between two of the flats. Big Brian was always on the lookout for what he called 'the yob element', usually local boys of around thirteen or fourteen who'd come in and mess around on the under-fives playground. When he saw them, he'd warn them off. When I did, I'd usually think of a reason for being somewhere else.

And then he said, "There used to be a kid came in the park about two years ago, Keith I think his name was. He was a big lad but he wasn't very bright, you know what I mean? There could have been something wrong with him. Dropped on his head in the

delivery room or something like that, I don't know."

"Retarded?" I said, and he frowned at me not entirely seriously.

"Now, don't get all educated on me," he said. "I thought we were getting along fine."

I made an overly-contrite face. "Sorry."

"Anyway, this boy Keith . . . Look what you've done, I've forgotten what the point of the story was, now!"

"I don't know. It was something to do with Len."

"Right. This boy Keith, he was the kind who used to play with kids half his age. I think *simple* is the word I'm looking for because, you'd look at him and you'd see no harm in him at all. He used to come in the park a lot, and he *loved* that train. Now if it was me, I'd have taken his money for the first couple of rides and then I'd have looked the other way. I mean, nobody gives a toss, really. But not Len. He took the lad's pennies until he had none left, and then he ordered him off. This was still early in the day, it wasn't even busy. So the next thing is, Len's going around and around on his little train and this lad's running alongside the track, making all the noises. You've seen the speed it goes at."

We were talking here of a maximum of around eight or nine miles an hour. "Not exactly hard to keep up with," I said.

"Well, Len didn't go for this. He didn't like it at all. I was up on a ladder stringing fairylights, and I could see the whole thing. Len's face was starting to look like a bucket of thunder and this lad, he looked as if he was all set to go on following the train around till he dropped. He was getting really giddy and when the train came to a stop, he was jumping around and waving his arms and shouting. So Len got off his little engine and went over to him. He didn't lay a hand on him—I'd have shopped him if he did, I wouldn't have cared if he lost his job for it—but the way he carried on, it made me really sick."

"What did he say?"

"I can't remember all of it. But it was something like if this boy didn't stop messing around, Len was going to drag him into the tunnel and stick him in an oildrum and boil him down till there was nothing left but bones. Now, you could say that kind of thing to some kids and they'd shrug it off, no problem; they'd know it was a warning and that the rest of it was just, you know . . ."

"Rhetoric?" I offered, but Big Brian had a better word of his own.

"Bollocks," he said. "But this Keith, it was like he was on top of the world one second and it was all knocked out of him the next. He just kind of deflated. I couldn't do something like that to *anyone*. So he's walking away and he's bright red and he's as good as crying, and as he's going past my ladder I call down to him and say, Hey, call him fatsod and then run away, he really hates that. So the boy brightens up a bit and looks back and shouts at the top of his voice, *Fat sod! Fat sod!* And then he turns and runs off out of the park."

"Did he ever come back again?"

"No, but not because of that. He was seen getting into some stranger's car out along the front, one day. The car drove off, and he was never seen again. Made all the papers. Then most people forgot. Next to that kind of behaviour I suppose Len's is just sheer bad manners. But it tells you something about him."

So, that was Len Cunningham.

Whenever I saw him after that, whether he was walking across the park to his work or perched on the back of his engine like a gorilla on a roller skate, I always thought of him as the Fat Sod. He looked the part and, if Big Brian's story was anything to go by, he'd certainly earned the name.

But I didn't give the matter a lot of thought until about a week later, when I got in one morning to find Big Brian in the brew hut reading a handwritten note. He really needed glasses to read but he wouldn't admit it, and so there was a lot of frowning and peering and holding the note around to find the best light.

Throwing down my lunch bag and picking up the kettle, I said, "Love letters?"

"You cheeky bugger," Big Brian said, lowering the note which appeared to have been written on a page torn out of those Challenger account books, the ones with the numbered pages that you can buy cheaply by the dozen on the market. "Just for that, you can have the job."

"What job?"

"To put a new lamp in the engine shed for Len. I'm surprised we've lasted this long. He did all his own wiring and they're always burning out."

"After what you told me last week? No thanks."

"Go on, stop moaning. He's not even in yet. Take the spare key from the board."

I'll admit it, I was curious to get a look inside the engine shed as long as I could do it in the absence of the permanent tenant, and this was probably the best opportunity that I was going to get. You know the kind of feeling. It's like getting the chance to read someone else's mail. So I took the key from its hook on the board—I was the first to be using it in ages, if the layer of dust around it was anything to go by—and went around to the next hut to pick up a spare lamp. Then I set out down the boulevard.

The park was almost empty at this hour. I counted about three dog-walkers, one jogger (they were rarer, in those days), and a tramp checking the litter bins for clean newspapers. By the time that I reached the railway tracks, there was nobody at all.

There was a sheen of dew on the grass, making it look as if it had been covered in a fine gauze. I cut across it, through the trees toward the engine shed. There was a chill in the morning, but nothing serious or off-putting. It was the kind of day where you *knew* that it was going to be fine later on.

Life seemed about as good as it could get, right then.

The engine shed had a kind of hillbilly look about it considering the way that it had been thrown together out of sheet iron and timber and then patched, shored up, extended and extended again. It was long and low and it had no windows at all. Down at the far end, there was a stovepipe poking up out of the roof. Even that wasn't straight.

I had to walk all the way around, because the nearest of the double-doors was bolted on the inside. Later on when the train was running these would be pinned all the way back to make the tunnel opening, and I could see the arcs scored in the gravel where their lower edges had dragged. Right now the trackbed simply went on under them. It reminded me of those Roadrunner cartoons where the Coyote paints a white line around into a bogus tunnel on a rockface.

There was a big padlock securing the doors at the other end. I had a difficult time opening it, and at one point I thought I was going to have to give up . . . but then I got the angle just right and the key turned easily, and I pulled back one of the doors to go in. The door was in a bad way; a single sheet of corrugated iron, it had dropped on its hinges and screeched loudly as it caught on one of the rails. The iron along the edge was all bent and ripped and rusted, as if this happened every time.

I stepped inside.

STEPHEN GALLAGHER

* * *

The darkness wasn't total. Anything but. I could see a maze of chinks and needles of light as if I was in a closed barn. I could just about make out the train, filling the shed from one end to the other, but otherwise I had to reach around inside the doorway looking for a switchbox so that I could turn on some lights.

I found one. It made some difference, but not much.

I'd never been in here before. Not in years, anyway, not since I'd have been too small to remember, and then I'd only have been riding through. There was a second spur of track running alongside the main one and connected at either end by a set of points, presumably so that carriages could be run off the main track for servicing and repair. Nothing stood on it now. There was a lot of junk in there; iron, timber, sheet ply, all of it mildewed-looking and stacked against one of the walls. Screened from the track by a makeshift curtain were the stove, a brown table with a teapot, a mug and a half-bottle of rancid milk standing on it, and alongside the stove an oilstained easy chair worn right down to the stuffing in places.

Len's little haven. Further along there was a workbench, and a big drum of diesel oil whose smell was pervading the place. And that wasn't all; because there was also Len's concession to showbusiness.

Whether he'd made it or inherited it, I really couldn't tell. But there was a little tableau in the corner of the engine shed that you'd see from the train as you were leaving the tunnel. I might have been startled by the figure if it hadn't been so patently unlifelike; it was posed like the worst Frankenstein monster ever, with a pick in one hand and a hurricane lamp in the other and a shapeless little hat on its head. It was supposed to be a gold miner. My guess was that it had been made by sticking some thrift shop clothing on a crude frame and then stuffing in some newspaper to give it bulk. The clothing had been daubed with two colours of fluorescent paint, rather like a tar-and-feather job. The figure leaned forward alarmingly, as if the weight of the pick were about to pull it over; at its feet were a heap of gravel, a dirty map with a big X on it, and a few more rusty and broken tools. All that I could see of its face under the hat was a bunch of whiskers that looked suspiciously like the bristles from a yard brush.

And how did I know that it was supposed to be a gold miner? Because there was a handpainted picket sign that said *Laredo Gold Mine*, jammed at an angle into the tailings pile. I was glad that it was there, because otherwise I would never have known.

"What are you doing in here?" a voice from behind me said.

I turned around, startled and unaccountably guilty.

Len Cunningham was standing framed in the open doorway. I couldn't see much more than his dark silhouette, but even that was unmistakable.

I swallowed hard.

"I brought the new lamp you asked for," I said, hoping that my voice would keep steady. "If you'll show me where it's to go, I can put it in for you."

He said nothing right away. Just stood there, unreadable.

And then he seemed to decide that, even if he didn't like it, I'd given him an explanation that he couldn't do much other than to accept.

"Just put it on the table," he said. "I'll see to it."

"It wouldn't be any trouble. And it's what I'm here for."

"I said put it down."

I put the box down so fast, I almost cracked the glass inside.

Of all the days that he could have come in early, he had to pick this one. Wasn't it just my luck? I stood there fidgeting like a schoolboy in the headmaster's study as he walked past me. Bear in mind that I hadn't been so long out of school, and the habits hadn't yet died. As he lumbered by, I kind of shrank back. I felt like an injured bird being stepped over by a dog, and hoping not to be noticed.

Perhaps he picked some of that up, I don't know. But he glanced back at me, and he seemed to relent a little.

"There's only me knows where everything is," he said by way of explanation.

"Fine," I said.

He set his duffel bag down on the table alongside the teapot, took a folded newspaper out of his pocket and dropped it alongside, and then looked at me again.

"Who are you working with?" he said.

And so I told him that I was with Big Brian, and Len snorted with obvious contempt.

"Yeah," I said, beginning to get some of my nerve back. "He said you were old mates."

"Him?" Len said. "I've got no time for him. He wouldn't give you the pickings from his arse." And he started to unload the duffel bag. Lunchbox, chocolate, packet of biscuits, a well-worn T-piece of brass which I recognised as the Dead Man's Handle, the speed control without which the train couldn't be run . . .

I needed an exit line, and I didn't have one.

Instead, I heard myself blurt out, "I wasn't nosing around."

"There'd be nothing to find if you did," Len said, and then he pulled out a big handkerchief and blew his nose. The way that he did it, it sounded as if he was shifting about a pint of mucous. He glanced at me over the handkerchief, as if he was beginning to get puzzled as to why I was still here.

"Well?"

"I've got a suggestion," I said. "If you get one of those UV tubes and set it on the ground in front of that figure, all that fluorescent paint would glow. They use it in the ghost train down at the other end of the shore. It doesn't cost anything and it's really effective."

He looked past me, to the tableau behind. But it was only for a second.

"It's only for kids," he said dismissively.

"We've got spares in the stores. You'd only need the one tube, and you could hide it behind the gravel heap."

"Nah," he said, and turned his back.

Which, with nothing further being said, I took as my cue to leave.

A couple of days later, when Irish Michael and I were brushing away some of the dead leaves and litter that always seemed to pile up in front of Tom, Tom, the Piper's Son—a wind trap, that corner, if ever there was one—Big Brian stopped by and said to me, "What exactly happened between you and Len the other morning?"

"I told him he was the nicest man I'd ever met," I said. "And he spoke very highly of you."

"You didn't talk about doing up the tunnel?"

"I suggested one of those black light tubes, that's all. The way he's got it now, the lights just show up how cheap and crappy everything is."

"Well, I wish you'd keep your ideas to yourself. He's asking for all sorts of stuff, here."

Big Brian handed me another of those torn-off Challenger sheets, and I set down my brush and took a look at it. Irish Michael carried on working, just as if he hadn't seen or heard any interruption. The writing on the paper was spiky and childish, the spelling barely literate; it was the writing of someone to whom penmanship had never been much of a skill even when first learned, and it had rusted unused ever since.

"Yeah," I conceded, reading down the list. "Some of this could be my fault."

"Oh, *could* it?" Big Brian said. "Well, when you're finished here you can go and chase all of this stuff down and take it over. Whatever you use, make sure you note it down in the big book. And then the next time you get one of these brilliant ideas, perhaps you'll try keeping quiet about it, eh?"

"Yes, massa," I said.

If the intention was to make me sorry that I'd opened my mouth, it worked. Len hadn't simply stopped at the thought of a UV tube and a fitting and some cable to wire it in. He wanted more paint, he wanted some timber, he wanted chicken wire, he wanted a tannoy loudspeaker. It took me most of the rest of the day to get it all together, chasing around the various council stores in different parts of the town, and then I had to borrow the gardeners' pickup truck to bring it all back. There was no road out into the woods, but there was a dirt track. Mostly this was used for taking out grass cuttings and dead branches, which were then heaped up and burned in the furthest corner of the park. And I'm pretty sure that Old Jack always waited until the wind direction was right before he had a bonfire day, because he got so much satisfaction out of hearing the golfers choke and splutter as the smoke billowed out across the ninth hole on the adjacent course.

I stopped the truck by the open tunnel, and went around the back to drop the tailgate. The train was working, the doors at either end of the shed wide open. As I was unloading, I heard the Happymount Express coming around; I looked back and saw it approaching on the curve with about a half-load of passengers.

I waved as it passed. If Len saw me, he didn't acknowledge it.

Now, I'm not pretending that I'd suddenly seen the light back there when we'd talked in the shed. But I *had* gone in with a pretty one-dimensional attitude to his character based entirely on Big Brian's account, and seeing that inept little tableau had forced me to rethink. All right, so it was crap. But he'd taken the trouble to set it up. The man had a creative urge, even if he had no talent; and the point was that I could no longer despise him in quite the way that I had when I'd known nothing about him.

And I suppose there was a vanity angle to it as well. Here was this obstacle course in human relations, as Big Brian had described him, and yet my simple little suggestion had broken through. I was like the teacher of the Wild Boy of Aveyron, except that my success had been with the Fat Sod of Happymount. Thorns and lions' paws would be as nothing to me after this. As I was stacking everything by Len's workbench inside, the train came through again and I stepped back into darkness until it had passed by.

I had to walk past the figure of the miner to get out, and it was only when I reached the open air that I could identify the unease I'd been feeling.

I'd assumed that it was something territorial, a sense of being less than welcome in someone else's place.

But it wasn't.

Crap or not, and no matter how unlifelike, it was more as if the figure had been waiting for me to leave.

"Get a gallon can of that grey undercoat and meet me up behind the Mister Men," Big Brian ordered me one day, and there was something in his voice that made me get up off my seat in the brew hut without a smart remark.

The Mister Men were a series of figures up at the highest point in the park, set around a crescent that itself was built around an ornamental flower bed. The figures all had names, but I couldn't tell you what any of them were. They were basically just different-coloured blobs with faces. Behind them were bushes, and behind the bushes was the perimeter fence.

Big Brian was waiting there for me, his face filled with troubled fury at the latest doings of the Yob Element.

"Look at this," he said to me. "Is this a sign of a tiny mind, or what?"

I looked.

The tiny mind in question had set itself to the task of writing the words *Toe Cap Ted* along with a few more notions of even deeper mystery on the back of one of the flats. I think it was magic marker. Down at the bottom of the flat there was evidence of a halfhearted attempt to set it alight, but the flame-retardant paint had barely charred. Spent matches were scattered all around, along with a few empty Woodpecker Cider cans that had been crushed and bent double. It didn't look like it had been much of a party.

Big Brian said, "They write their own names as if they're something special, but they have to hide before they can feel big enough to do it. They make me sick. Get it all painted out."

"Is it worth it? They can always come back."

"I'll be watching for them if they do," he said darkly, and clambered out through the scaffolding as I set down my can of undercoat and levered off the top.

The job didn't take more than ten minutes but I didn't enjoy doing it, any more than I enjoyed picking up the litter. It was too much like being a lackey for whoever had made the mess, with me being stuck here while they moved on to other, equally trivial pleasures. I could take a guess at who'd done it, although it *was* only a guess; there were three only-just teenagers who came into the park every now and again, plug-ugly and each with the dress sense of a circus geek, laughing and shoving each other and swearing out loud to shock anyone who might be listening. There was nothing here for them, so they never stayed long; the park was basically just somewhere to go. Even if they weren't the ones responsible, they were close enough to type for it not to matter. Kids with nothing to say, saying it loud.

The reason that I'm making so much of this is that I saw the three of them again the next evening, and they were down by the railway. I'd been walking by and wondering what kind of progress Len had been making, thinking that maybe I could wait until he was collecting the ticket money over on the far side of the track and then take a quick peek inside the shed without his knowledge, when I spotted them on the path that ran alongside the track for a way.

One shoved another, the other bawled *Fuck off, spunkface* and attempted one of those aimless kung-fu kicks that was always a sure sign of having sneaked into too many Bruce Lee movies, the first one dodged, the third one laughed like an emptying drain.

And then around came Len, the big man on the little engine with his toddlers all riding behind. If you've ever seen one of those circus cycling acts where they bring out a tiny tricycle and one of the acrobats hunkers down with his knees up alongside his ears and pedals it along for a few yards . . . well, that was almost how he looked as the Happymount Express came around the bend.

I was more than a hundred yards away but I stopped and watched, fascinated, almost like an astronomer watching a couple of stars on their way toward an imminent collision. The boys heard the train coming and glanced back; I couldn't see Len's face but I could imagine that it would be set like stone, staring dead ahead.

They all started making train noises. One of them tried to sing *Casey Junior's comin' down the track*, which I think was in *Dumbo*, but he messed up the words.

And another one jumped in front of the train, waving his arms.

I'm sure that if it had been at all possible to put on a burst of acceleration, Len would have done it and run the boy down. As it was, the Express chugged along at its regular speed and the boy jumped off the track after a fraction of a second, walking away with about twenty-five yards to spare. As a feat of daring, it basically wasn't; and then the three of them had all turned their backs and were drifting off in a careful piece of timing that said *look at me, I'm not running*, while dodging the prospect of a direct confrontation.

The Express slowed, and then it stopped.

I'd never before seen Len stop the train anywhere other than in the shed or at the station platform. The boys heard it, but they didn't turn; even so, I saw them tense with apprehension as events began to move in a direction they hadn't expected.

Len stood up on the engine. Behind him one or two of the smallest children tried to get out thinking that the ride was over, only to be restrained by their parents.

"Boys!" Len called. "Oh, *boys!* Yes, I'm talking to *you!*"

I wouldn't have called it a friendly tone. That's how it sounded on the surface but underneath, it was anything but.

They could hardly pretend not to have heard, and there was no-one else in the immediate area. They turned, cowed and caught-out looking.

"I'm just about to close down for the night," Len said, and if I hadn't known better I'd have said that he sounded downright genial. "One more run, and then that's it. Now, I see you're quite interested in the railway. So how about one last ride? On the house?"

They all hesitated. Their faces were drained and slack. If I can say it without being too unkind, these boys were not Nobel Prize contenders and were unlikely ever to become such; Len's irony was wasted on them.

And so they puffed themselves up in an attempt to recover some trace of their stolen bravado, swallowed the bait and, rather selfconsciously, climbed into the last empty carriages at the end of the train.

I watched as the Happymount chugged past me and away. The three of them were sitting with their knees up in the tiny carriages and trying to look cool and at their ease, already laughing again; Hey, a free ride from the fat man, are we the bee's nuts or what? But they couldn't see that, even as they'd climbed aboard, they'd been conceding victory to Len without even being aware of it.

I didn't see the train as it reached the platform. But when it reappeared, moving along track through the most distant part of the woodland, I could see that everyone else had disembarked save Len and, right at the end of the carriages, the three boys.

I watched them as the Express chugged through the trees and then on into the tunnel.

And then I waited, but it didn't come out.

So I waited a while longer.

And *still* nothing came out.

Oh, shit.

By now I was seriously beginning to wonder whether I ought to go and tell Big Brian. I couldn't imagine what might be going on in there . . . or rather, I could, and it owed rather more to Hammer Films and the Chamber of Horrors than to any likely version of reality. There were no screams, no noises, nothing. All that I could hear were the faint strains of taped music from the kiddies' carousel, all the way back across the park alongside the cafeteria. Perhaps, I started to think nervously, I ought to go over there and take a look. And if I found the shed doors closed then I'd . . . I'd . . .

Well, afterwards I could imagine all of the heroic and responsible things that I surely would have done, because at that moment I saw the first of the boys emerging from the far end of the shed. I couldn't see his face, but his entire attitude was that of a beaten dog in a state of shock. The others skulked after. One of them looked back, and I've never seen anyone quite so pale. They all looked as if they were walking on hot sand, in shoes that were too thin.

I couldn't help it. I had to go over to the engine shed.

By the time that I got there, Len was almost ready to leave. I stood by the tracks just inside the open doorway, hesitating to walk any further uninvited; he was over at the table, packing his empty lunchbox and the rest of his stuff into his duffel bag, but he looked up and saw me. For a second his face was dull and ugly, but then he smiled. It wasn't much of an improvement.

And it wasn't a pleased-to-see-you smile, either. I said, "What happened?"

If he was pleased with anybody, it was with himself. "I only did what their parents should have done a long time ago," he said, picking up the duffel bag and moving over to the engine. There he unscrewed the brass operating handle and put it into the bag to take home with him, effectively immobilising the train. Maybe you could have done something with a spanner to get around it, I really don't know, but for all practical purposes it was like taking the gas pedal out of a car. "I explained a few things to them and rubbed their snotty little noses in the facts of life. Showed them what they'd get if they crossed me again. They won't be back in a hurry."

As he walked past me and out into the daylight, I could smell diesel oil and corruption. I hadn't gone any way towards liking the man, not at all, but I *had* begun to think that perhaps he couldn't be as bad as Big Brian had had described him. But not any more. I'd no reason to feel anything for those three boys; but somehow, I was desperately glad that I hadn't had to share any of the last few minutes with them.

I glanced around before I followed Len out. I was wondering what exactly he might have said to them; somehow the old bones-and-oildrum routine didn't seem enough to explain their reaction. I could see where he'd been working on the goldmine tableau, although he hadn't made much in the way of progress at all. The figure had changed position slightly and had been daubed with even more fluorescent paint, and Len had added some chickenwire and newspaper boulders and a couple of crates with *Dinermite* stencilled onto the sides. He'd painted skulls on the walls. He'd dug out a shallow trench to hide the UV tube—or the dandruff light, as they called them in the local discos, because they showed up every fleck and fibre and made your teeth glow like Liberace's—and he'd made a start at burying the tannoy wiring, which I almost tripped over because he'd threaded it under the tracks and hung the loudspeaker alongside the door. The wiring ran all the way back to the workshop area, but didn't seem to have been connected to anything yet.

Above the workbench hung three dead rats, dangling by their tails in a bunch.

Suddenly I wanted to be out of it, now. It was like a small child's nightmare of the Batcave in there. The crudity of it all made it worse. They say that artists reveal themselves through their work, whether they mean to or not; and if this was a peek into Len's head, then I preferred not to dwell on the details. It was like seeing a fish cut open, and its insides found to be teeming with parasitic worms.

He was waiting as I emerged. As soon as I was out, he closed and padlocked the big doors after me.

And I said I had to be somewhere, so that I wouldn't have to stay in his company as the two of us walked away.

Here's what happened then.

It was a Monday, about two weeks later. The preceding weekend had been the last to feature the illuminations, and the final switchoff had taken place on the previous night. Big Brian had gone around and taken out all of the fuses, and wouldn't be putting them back. This was the day that we were due to start taking everything apart to go back into storage until next year.

I knew as soon as I got in that something was wrong, because there was a police car alongside the Mad Hatter's Tea Party and a uniformed man inside talking to Big Brian. I hung back, not wanting to walk in and interrupt but wondering if there might be some way that I could just, kind of, *sidle* in at the back and pick up on what was going on without actually getting involved, when another police van went past behind me at rather more than the park regulation speed of ten miles per hour. It carried on down the boulevard, and I followed it.

There was quite a crowd building up. Well, when I say quite a crowd, I mean quite a crowd for Happymount Park on a dull Monday morning; two or three dozen people, at least, and they were all craning for a better look at whatever was going on around Len's engine shed. More police vehicles had been driven off the pathways and into the woodland, and they'd been parked—probably deliberately—in a way that screened the main doors from view. And just in case anyone got any ideas about getting closer, there was a man in uniform standing with his arms folded and his beady eyes daring them to try it. Behind him, two more men were staking out the area with plastic tape.

I spotted somebody I knew.

His name was Simon and he'd been at school around the same time as me, although in a different class. When he'd left he'd been taken on by the local newspaper as tea-maker and general office-boy, and after a while he'd progressed to coverage of all the wedding anniversaries. But that hardly seemed to be his purpose here.

He came up alongside me and said, "What's your angle on all of this, then?"

And I said, "I haven't got an angle. What's supposed to have happened?"

But instead of telling me, he lost interest and wandered off. I don't think he actually knew, at least not yet. I think they'd sent him out to the scene without any guidance on how to tackle the job. From Silver Weddings to suspicious death, in one uneasy leap. I actually found out the details from Big Brian later on, when the police had finished and a big lorry had come to take away the engine of the Happymount Express to be stripped down and checked.

Len Cunningham had been discovered by one of the gardeners that morning, face-down on the track about ten yards outside the engine shed. The train was half-out of its tunnel like a snake emerging from a hole in the ground. The way they reconstructed it, he'd been crouched on the track inside doing something with the tannoy wire when the train had somehow rolled forward and caught him. He must have had his head right down, and hadn't seen or heard it coming at all; it was almost like being sucked into a blender. It pushed him out of the shed while dragging him under at the same time, so that his head and arm had finished up about halfway along under the engine. They weren't clean off, but apparently nobody had dared to pull too hard when they'd been lifting him from the track. And he hadn't died straight away, either, if the signs of clawing all the way alongside the trackbed were anything to go by.

All of this had happened late the previous evening, probably when the park lights had been out and the rest of us were going home. They reckoned that he might not even have been able to make a sound. He'd been lying there all night, and his torn coat was heavy with dew. Someone who'd seen him told me what he'd looked like, and I don't care to think about it too much. The police were interested because, without a driver's hand on the Dead Man's Handle, the train shouldn't have been able to move.

But somehow, it would seem, it had done exactly that.

I'll tell you my first reaction, and that was to think about the three boys who'd been given that one last ride of their childhood; but they'd all been somewhere else for the biggest part of the evening, and there were witnesses who could prove it. They were at a pantomime, no less. The one with a goose in it.

Taking it all together, it was one of the park's more interesting days. The rest of us tried to work around the activity, but inevitably very little got done. I spent most of the day just trying to believe what I'd heard. Even though I saw Old Jack being let in to spread sand on the trackbed where it had happened, I still had trouble making the story connect with reality.

Late on in the day, I saw Old Jack talking to one of the policemen. When they'd finished, Old Jack came over to me and said, "They're all done here. You can lock the shed up, now."

Me? Old Jack went mooching off, and I went looking for Big Brian. He was up on a scaffolding, taking down the skyline of Toytown with the help of a couple of council electricians who'd come along to put it all up at the beginning of the season.

"The police are all finished," I called up to him. "They want us to lock up the shed."

He looked down at me, and I could see that the two hundred pounds of painted board that he was supporting made this an inconvenient moment. I could already guess what he was going to say.

"See to it, will you?"

"It ought to be someone in charge," I offered lamely.

"Did anyone say that?"

But nobody had.

"Go on, then," he said. "Nothing's going to bite you."

And so I went to get the key.

The tapes were down, but a couple of scraps of it were still blowing about. The park gates had been closed, and no-one was hanging around now. The engine shed hadn't exactly been Sleeping Beauty's palace before, but now it had all the appeal of an abattoir.

Both ends were open. I was going to have to bolt one set of doors from the inside, and then walk the length of it in the dark. When I went to switch on the few available lights, I saw the scattered sand and I saw the marks where Len Cunningham had scrabbled at the trackbed in the last few seconds of his life. So its end hadn't been quick, and it hadn't been painless, and here was the proof.

The bolts squealed like gallows chains. That's the kind of mood the place had put me in.

As I was walking back up the track, I could see along the engineless carriages to the tableau at the far end. I wasn't looking forward to having to pass it. Len appeared to have rearranged everything a little more, moving the figure again and changing the lights, and I wished that he hadn't; as before the figure was unnatural and astonishingly ugly, and the effect now was as if it had moved when I hadn't been looking. The only way that I can describe my feelings as I approached it would be to go back to a number of years before and the first time that I'd ever been into a waxworks, a really cheesy one in New Brighton where the figures all looked like painted death-masks and none of them taken from the people that they were supposed to represent. The building itself had been run-down and damp, its timbers so rotten that all of the floors creaked when you walked over them . . . and with certain boards, in certain places, you could walk over a spot on the floor and, in some totally different part of the room, one or other of the figures would slowly begin to lean forward.

Well, this one didn't really move. At least, not while I was looking. But it gave me exactly that same, slow-burning scare as I approached it, and as soon as I got to the end of the carriages I crossed over the tracks so that I'd pass by it on the other side.

I must have tripped a switch down on the trackbed, intended to be kicked over by the train itself. The tannoy speaker crackled into life and I looked around wildly for a moment before I realised what was happening; the sound of a pick rang out on stone, a shovel plunged into gravel, and I realised that I'd triggered Len's over-amplified cassette tape of atmospheric mine effects. A faint voice cried out, *Look out, it's all gonna fall,* and there was an avalanche effect that sounded like a few rocks being emptied out of a zinc bucket. The voice was unmistakably Len Cunningham's.

It was all so utterly fucking spooky.

And now the lurching, falling-forward figure of the gold miner was grinning at me.

It took a moment to register exactly what I was seeing. The shapeless hat and the bristles that had concealed his features were gone. He was grinning because he had no choice; because his face was a day-glo painted skull and his eyes were two pitted golfballs, probably boosted from the Crazy Golf hut at the far end of the gardens. Dark pupils had been drawn onto them like cartoon eyes. Two teeth were missing. And in the gaps between his coatsleeves and his heavy workman's gloves, I could see not the broomhandles that I'd have expected but a slender inch of bone.

Look out, it's all gonna fall, the dead man cried as the tape loop went around again.

It stood there, almost daring me to come closer.

I was looking at what I would later learn were the remains of a teenager named Keith Mills, slightly retarded, missing presumed dead. Tests on the bones showed that they'd been boiled for several hours. Of all the people who'd been in and out of the engine shed in the course of the day, not one of them could have given the figure more than a passing glance.

I was out of there faster than a cat out of a bonfire.

I don't know how long it took before Big Brian was able to get any sense out of me. But when the police came back again and wanted me to walk over to the shed with them, I'm told that they couldn't get me to go. I was in a state. To be perfectly honest, I don't remember very much of the next couple of hours until my father arrived to take me home. And every time I tried to talk to anyone about it, I stopped making sense. This lasted for more than a week.

And, as I said, I've been getting bad dreams about it ever since.

The police gave me a hard time. They were sure I'd been messing around. I think a lot of it was to cover their own embarrassment at the way they'd trudged through their procedures and yet missed something so obvious. They said that I'd tampered with the figure. Which, of course, I hadn't.

But I can see why they'd think that I had.

I'd only stared at it for a matter of seconds, but the picture's still vivid in my mind after all these years. That unreal glow of blue and orange in the UV light. That grin. Those golfball eyes. How that shapeless old hat was now missing from the figure's head; and how in its place there now sat an engine driver's cap.

The big shadows on the wall behind it. The sense of triumph in its attitude.

The presence of Death.

With a well-worn brass handle in its hand.

Hunter Killer

Frank waited until the patrol had gone by, and then he ran for the wire.

Patrol? From what he'd been able to see, it had hardly warranted the name. More like goons in badly-fitting uniforms taking a stroll around the perimeter, the three of them bearing more than a passing resemblance to Curly, Larry and Moe; if the official word was that security around here was supposed to be as good as it could ever get, the reality seemed to be more a matter of the lowest bidder and the crappiest service. There was supposed to be a vehicle check every fifteen minutes and a foot patrol of the fencing every hour, but Frank seemed to have been waiting for an awfully long time with nothing happening. And then when they'd finally arrived, they'd ambled on by without even shining a light in his direction.

He felt almost let down. Here he was, high on his own adrenalin, and they couldn't even make a stab at discovery. He'd heard a rumour that at least twelve people had made it past them in the last two years; he'd thought it impossible, but with security like this he was beginning to see how it could have happened.

The fence was even less of a problem than he'd expected. It stood ten feet high but it had been thrown up in a hurry, by men who had been looking over their shoulders constantly as they worked. No cutting would be required; he could simply prise out some of the staples that held the wire to the post and then roll it up far enough to squeeze under. Crouched at the foot of it, he took a crowbar from his tote bag. It clinked against the sawn-off barrel of the shotgun and he froze, but nothing happened. Nobody seemed to have heard.

Dogs would have made a difference, of course. But dogs couldn't be worked so close to the complex; within a few hundred yards they began to panic, and at this distance they'd be uncontrollable. It was as if they sensed the unseen presence in the building, and had to respond. So instead it all fell on the shoulders of the night shift, and the night shift obviously shrugged a little under the weight and looked around for some way to make life easier. Frank had done security work himself, somewhere in amongst the dozens of jobs that he'd held down for varying lengths of time, and he reckoned he knew the score; in his own brief stint as nightwatchman with an engineering firm he'd counted on getting at least four hours' sleep on an average shift in order to keep his energies up for the day job. He couldn't remember what his day job had been at the time, but it was probably something best forgotten.

Yes, he knew the score. But given the circumstances here, he'd expected better. These people had contracts on power stations and air bases, after all, and yet they couldn't stuff the holes around one piece of industrial plant.

Not even when the general understanding was that almost certain death awaited anyone who got in.

But not me, he told himself as he levered on his screwdriver and felt the staple easing out of the wood. Not you, Frank.

It sprang free, and flew off into the darkness.

He began to work on the next.

The so-called lucky ones had been the three who'd been spotted and pulled out before they'd covered any distance. None of the others had ever been seen again. But they were losers, this much Frank understood; they'd gone walking in with the mark upon their foreheads and simply collected whatever destiny they'd been assigned. Frank was up for more than that. Ever since he'd been a child, he'd sensed that he was special. He was going to be *somebody*.

And he was starting to get a little tired of waiting.

The wire came up, and he pushed his tote bag through. Then after it he slid the plank with the nails, and then he put his face down into the dirt and started to crawl. The ground was cold, colder than the night itself. And the space wasn't as big as he'd thought, so that the links along the bottom of the wire plucked at his back. He felt the material of his jacket catch, and then spring free.

And then he was through.

He scrambled to his knees. He was inside the perimeter now, but he'd hardly begun. Across the fifty yards of cleared space ahead of him was an eight-foot wall topped with razor wire, the actual boundary of the complex itself. He slung the tote bag over his shoulder, picked up the plank, and headed across.

He didn't want to waste any time. He was too exposed, here, and even the Three Stooges couldn't miss him if they decided to turn and come around again. This had been part of a road, once; when the authorities had thrown up the containment fence, they'd gone ahead and taken a measurement and hadn't paid too much attention to where it had run. Like the old Berlin Wall which it so much resembled, the new perimeter crossed roads and pavements and parking lots and the gardens of a few nearby houses, and on the side by the old docks at least one entire warehouse block had been bulldozed to take it through.

The wall looked so much higher close-to. And the razor wire . . . the razor wire was positively frightening. Even the name made him want to pucker up inside. He laid the plank at an angle against the wall, and he wished it was a ladder. It would have been, if the man who'd promised him one hadn't messed him around and asked for more money. He'd hocked everything that he owned for the gun, so what did the bastard expect? Blood? He'd taken the plank from a fence over a derelict railway siding, and he'd pounded in nails to form makeshift treads. He'd had to carry it through the streets, hoping that he wouldn't be stopped and wondering how he'd explain it if he was. Now, as it leaned against the outer wall of the newspaper printing plant, he could see that it really needed to be about a foot longer.

Well, tough, he told himself, and pulled the fire blanket out of his tote bag and unrolled it.

He wondered if they'd miss it, back in the hostel kitchen. He wondered, but he didn't exactly care very much. The hostel was a dismal place, full of old unshaven men who'd lost all of their teeth and whose faces seemed to fold in on themselves, and of younger men with glazed eyes and permanent facial displays of half-healed scabs that might equally have come from drunken fights or drunken falls. They lived on soup and handouts, they slept in tiny fleabag rooms subdivided from what had once been an assembly hall. For half a year now he'd lived amongst them in a permanent state of dismay, studying his face in every mirror that he passed for the signs that he might be coming to resemble them. All right, say there *was* a fire, and there was no blanket to put it out. Who'd mourn any of them?

Who'd mourn him?

The plank bowed in the middle as he climbed it. He was scared that it would break, and that he'd fall onto the nails; he couldn't windmill his arms for balance because he had the fire blanket in both hands, and the tote bag across his back didn't help his sense of stability. It only held the gun and a flashlight and the few tools for the fence that he'd been able to gather, but it was enough to worry him. He could feel himself starting to overbalance sideways even as he threw the blanket over the wire, but then the blanket caught and he was able to hold on.

He clung there for a few moments, almost poised for a drop. Another inch or so, and the plank was going to slide away from underneath him.

But then, moving slowly and deliberately, he was able to reach up and get a footing on the wall.

The plank fell. He heard it go. But never mind, there was all kinds of crap down there. They wouldn't spot it before morning.

The fire blanket was of a heavy weave with some kind of a metallised coating on one side, and the razor wire didn't pierce it. He felt it bounce under his weight as he scrambled over, felt the points through the thickness of the material, but none of them broke through. Once on the inside, the idea was to lower himself down until he'd only have two or three feet to drop, and then to kind of jiggle around in the hope of tearing the blanket free so that he could pull it down after.

But so much for forward planning. He couldn't keep a hold on the material, and he fell like a sack of shit.

Landed like one, too.

All that he could think of as he lay there on the asphalt gasping for wind, was that he was going to have to leave the blanket up there flapping away like a flag. It was an unmistakable sign of entry. Once they found it, they'd send in one of the armoured cars that was the only safe way to manoeuvre around inside the more accessible areas of the plant. Without knowing the layout, he didn't know how much of the complex that would cover. They might catch him. They might drag him out.

Just like one of the losers.

For a while, now, this day had been all that he'd had to look forward to. And if they took this away from him, what then?

He started to get to his feet. He'd been winded, but that was all. He unzipped the tote bag, and he took out the gun and the flashlight; they were all that he'd need now, and the rest he could leave behind. As he was crouched over the bag, busily sorting himself out, the realisation hit him. He was inside; this was the danger zone, right here, it had already started and he was fussing around with his bits and pieces like some halfwitted old gimmer. He looked about him quickly, wildly, but he saw nothing. He didn't know what he ought to be expecting, but of one thing he was certain—when it came it would come fast, and it would take no prisoners.

The gun in his right hand, the flashlight in his left, he straightened with the wall at his back. He'd no experience with firearms but the gun felt balanced and secure, and he knew that he'd been right to saw it down. Anything longer would have been too awkward; he'd have caught the barrel in every doorway, and probably blown off his own foot in a panic when the time came to swing around and take aim. As it was he could rely on an operating distance of about ten yards, according to the man who'd sold it to him. Beyond that, the shot would quickly lose its pattern and become far too dispersed.

Ten yards. Ten strides. He had to hit it within ten strides of it reaching him.

And he didn't even know what it would look like.

He did what he always did when the thought of the danger threatened to overwhelm him. He thought of the rewards, instead. Not just the cash that had been offered by the proprietor and by the developers of the adjoining docklands—an offer which had enraged the authorities and been opposed by the police, amounting as it did to an inducement to suicide—but also the prospect of seeing the boy again. It had been nearly a year, and Frank couldn't even imagine what he'd look like by now. But as soon as he was rich, his ex would almost certainly come out of hiding and bring their kid with her. After that, they'd see. Let her try to pass him off as nothing *then*, when he was famous.

He was in a yard of some kind. It looked like a prison yard, or the back of a modern brewery. The wall of the complex had no doors or windows around here, just a blank facade of brick and then an upper storey of some kind of moulded cladding. Some way further on down the yard was lit, but here it was dark. His choice was deliberate; the lights came from hastily-erected watchtowers outside the perimeter and covered areas that were supposedly under constant observation, but their coverage was patchy and seemed to be distributed without much sense of purpose. He'd heard a rumour that certain of the entrances to the complex were continually spotlit with infra-red and targeted by automatic machine guns that would fire as soon as anything moved within their field of view. This was in case of an escape attempt by whatever still roamed inside; for it to break through into the outside world . . .

(Was something moving over there, on the edge between the light and the shadows?)

 . . . would be a true disaster on an epic scale. No survivor had ever actually seen it in action—or seen it at all, in fact, unless you counted what were probably the most famous eight seconds of out-of-focus home video in history, retrieved from a still-running Panasonic camcorder amidst the bloody remains of what had been the paper's assistant features editor—but it had left plenty of mess behind it to give everyone a fair idea. In the days that it had taken to seal off the entire plant, close to a million people had grabbed their essentials and jammed the roads in an attempt to be somewhere else. They'd been filtering back ever since as it had gradually become clear that the apocalypse had been postponed even if it hadn't altogether been cancelled, but most of the property in the immediate area stood empty and was likely to remain that way. Finding buyers? A sick joke. The docklands redevelopment boom of the decade had suddenly become a financial disaster; housing inside a leper colony would have been easier to move. Apartments that had carried a six-figure premium now couldn't even be rented off as warehouse space—which was an irony, since most of them had been exactly that before conversion.

Nothing was moving along the edge of the lit area. It was his imagination. He'd always had a vivid imagination. He'd read hundreds of comics, dozens of books; but that had all been a long time ago.

He started to move, following the wall away from the light.

Not knowing, that was what made it so scary. The video had been so blurry that it had shown movement and nothing more; he'd seen on TV how they'd run it through space computers that were supposed to bring out the picture better, but it was like starting with a smudge of exhaust smoke and trying to work up a detailed image of the car that had made it. Frank trusted the reality of most things that he'd seen on TV, but even he couldn't swallow *that*. His personal opinion was that the camera had simply been pointing at furniture as it fell. He'd seen some ugly furniture in his time, but none of it had ever killed anybody.

He turned a corner.

A big articulated flatbed truck stood in the yard, its trailer half-unloaded of its newsprint. The paper was on big spools like toilet rolls, each of which probably weighed a ton or more; they'd been out here in the weather ever since the day of shutdown, and would almost certainly be ruined by now. The forklift that was presumably meant to have unloaded them appeared to have careered off on its own and run points-first into the wall some way down. Frank shone his flashlight around but there was no evidence of the truck's driver, or of the forklift's operator. The loading bay stood open and Frank, nervously hefting the weight of his sawn-off shotgun, went inside.

The feeling of danger intensified. He shone the light around into every corner of the bay. The most commonplace objects cast looming shadows like gargoyles. Around the sides of the bay was a platform about four feet above ground level. At the back was a door, which stood open. He climbed a short iron stairway to the platform's level, and then he crossed to the door. There was no light at all beyond it.

He went in.

He could hear his own breathing, feel the beat of his heart like a demented prisoner in his chest. But as far as he could tell, he moved in silence. He went through one set of fire doors and then another, easing through and holding onto the doors so that they closed without noise behind him. The loading bay had been bare and functional, but he emerged into something quite different. He'd come through the back way into the building's entrance foyer.

There was some light coming in from the towers outside, but not enough. The power supply to the complex hadn't been cut—he'd been able to study its lights from a distance for several nights running, ultimately learning nothing—but the supply in certain areas seemed to have failed, and this was one of them.

He ran his beam around. The entranceway was a glass revolving door, with push-doors to either side for the nervous and obese. The palms around the visitors' seating area had died in their pots, now resembling limp dune grasses with no green in them at all. At the unmanned security point, a telephone hung abandoned on its wire. There was a big modern-art mural on the wall beyond the desk.

Frank stopped. It looked pretty weird, even by modern art standards. It was a big airbrushed stain covering half the wall, and it had a stencil-cut silhouette of a running man at its centre. The image was intensely realistic, everything in his outline being charged with energy. You could read the terror in him.

And then Frank realised.

It was no mural. The spray wasn't paint. It was a preserved image, not unlike those blast shadows that they'd found on a wall at Hiroshima. What he was seeing was the last moment of a man's life, flash-photographed onto the white plaster in the violently exploding bodily fluids of another.

He swallowed hard, and looked at the floor.

There were stains, the contract carpeting all ripped-up and burned in one spot. That was all. No signs of anything arriving, no signs of anything leaving. Even a slime trail would have been better than nothing, because it would at least have been a starting-point for some picture in his mind; the sheer unknowability of the enemy was probably its worst and most terrifying feature. So far, he now realised, he'd been tending to think of it like a big dog or a bear. In the scenarios that he ran in his mind, a big dog or a bear fell easily before the blast of his shotgun; but the image would no longer hold up in the light of this first evidence that he'd found, and he had nothing to put in its place.

For the first time seriously, he began to think about backing out.

And then he closed his eyes. He knew that he shouldn't, but he closed his eyes just for one moment and tried to summon it all up before him. The pattern of his life. The depth of his loss, and the awesome zero of his achievements.

Then he went on.

He could see lights here and there, ahead of him down the main corridor. He could hear the constant background whisper of air conditioning. Apart from the dead plants, the place could have been deserted only ten minutes ago instead of two years before. At least he'd now passed the point at which he could have been pulled out against his will; they couldn't get their armoured carrier this far inside the building, and they sure as hell were unlikely to venture in without it. The corridor looked familiar. This had been on the TV news as well, back when they'd sent in one of those little robots that looked like an anglepoise lamp mounted on a toy tractor. They'd borrowed it from a bomb disposal unit, and the unit had been mightily pissed off when they didn't get it back. Everything had been fine until it had reached the big newsroom at the corridor's end, at which point it had passed beyond the range of the operator's radio signals and ploughed onward alone. TV pictures had faded with the on-board batteries a few hours later.

On the way, they'd featured nothing that was at all unusual.

Frank checked each office as he passed. Jackets still hung on the backs of chairs. Cups of long-congealed tea and coffee stood untouched on a number of desks; it had all happened just after eleven in the morning. One room was empty apart from a big Xerox machine with its lid raised and a last, forgotten page still in place on the glass.

And on just about every desk stood little framed photographs of the yet-to-be-bereaved.

The corridor's end opened into the big, empty newsroom, just the way that he'd seen it. This was where the lights still burned, bright as day and, for a moment, painful to his dark-attuned eyes. He turned off the flashlight to save the batteries, and stuck it inside his jacket. Then he switched the shotgun from one hand to the other, wiped his palm on his pants, and switched it back as he moved through the double-doors.

He'd never been in a newsroom before. It was no big deal. It was like a big modern barn with about a hundred desks and a computer on every one of them, and more mess than he'd ever seen in his life. Books and papers and old newspapers were piled everywhere, hanging from the tables like so much foliage and overflowing the wastebins like popcorn. The computer screens flickered like sentinels, just a few of them darkened like the dead spots in a honeycomb.

There was the robot that they'd sent in, slewed nose-first into a filing cabinet. It gave him a slight buzz, having seen it on TV and now seeing it—well, not in the flesh, perhaps, but in the hardware. The video camera sat on top of the arm like a single eye, staring fixedly at the teak-effect front of the drawer as if studying it for defects.

Frank prowled the length of the room, tensed for anything that might pop up from behind one of the desks. He glanced at one of the screens in passing. There was a half-written piece on the display, frozen in time and never to be finished. He didn't stop to read it all, but he flickered a smile at the headline. Bros. Talk about yesterday's news . . .

He stepped around a chair that had been flung back as if in panic. Had it prowled through here, sweeping them all before it? If it had, then it had allowed none of them to get away in the end. God, it had to be fast.

Well, he thought . . . I'm fast, too. He'd been running every day, and he'd practiced his gunplay in the bathroom of the hostel at dead of night after studying the greats. Alan Ladd, in *Shane*. And the Duke, when he'd played Rooster Cogburn. Not to mention Peter Weller in *Robocop*. He could do the fast draws and trigger spins and everything. When it came for him, he'd be ready.

It hadn't come for him by the time he got to the end of the newsroom.

As before, the corridor beyond the newsroom was dark. But again as before, there was light further along. He pulled out the flashlight again and clicked on the beam.

And then, staying close to the wall, he started to make his way down.

He wondered how many of the other wire-jumpers had been along this way. And of course, he wondered what had happened to them. From what he'd heard about the first ones, back in the days when an intruder was still big enough news to be worth the coverage, they sounded like the kinds of people who'd have been leaping off bridges anyway if this more spectacular opportunity hadn't presented itself. Breaking into the plant was almost like Russian Roulette for the already-committed, with five loaded chambers and the last, longest-odds chamber primed with a jackpot big enough to make you forget why you'd ever considered suicide in the first place. Frank had never considered suicide, ever; it simply wasn't an option. But he *was* bright enough to acknowledge that he was down and dropping fast, and the scale of the reward had grown more and more attractive as his days had grown darker. In the end it had all come down to one straight question; how much did he have left to lose?

He carried on with his tour of the floor. He'd once held down a job with a firm of City windowcleaners, during which he'd looked in on places like this every day. They'd let him go in the end, because he couldn't take the heights in the outside cradle. But this was more than any of those places, because along with the hi-tech offices there was just about everything needed to produce a major national newspaper under the one roof. Editorial, archives, financial, typesetting and design, the whole works in a single integrated plant. It hadn't been running for more than six months when disaster had struck.

At first—and this could only be pieced together from the immediate reactions of those who'd been in mid-conversation on the telephone when it happened, since none of them had survived to write their memoirs—it had been assumed that a light aircraft had crashed onto the plant on its way to an emergency landing at the new City airport some way down river. But the fact was, nobody really knew *what* had hit the place. Police and striking print workers on the picket line outside the gates said that they'd heard a shriek and a bang like one of those pistol-launched distress flares, but they'd actually seen nothing. Aerial photographs had later shown a hole punched into the roof at one end of the complex, and that was it.

The police had gone in, and hadn't come out. After hearing the screams over their radios a Tactical Support Unit had gone in, and they hadn't come out either. So then the army had been called and a crack, battle-hardened team went in, and . . . for a while there it had been like Flanders fields, wave after wave of men being sent to their deaths while their commanders puzzled over how this could be, until finally someone had conceded that the only reasonable bet for safety would be to make limited forays from a heavily-armed and protected vehicle. It lacked glamour, but it might actually work. Even then two more men had been lost, and nobody was quite sure how . . . but enough had been learned for everyone to realise that something unprecedented was on the loose, something that moved fast, struck hard, and was devoid of mercy.

The decision had been taken to close the place down, sealing in whatever roamed there until a more definite plan of action could be formed. In the course of planning the shutdown, it had taken another three men.

That had been enough.

They'd pulled back, they'd locked the gates, they'd thrown up the outer perimeter fence for a further level of containment and then they'd backed off to consider the problem. Considering would cost nothing. Everything else had seemed to cost lives by the bucketful, plummeting straight down into the well without even the sound of a splash.

The proprietor, of course, was furious. He'd have started a campaign over it, if he'd still had a newspaper in which to conduct one. From his point of view the timing couldn't have been worse. He'd just emerged as the victor-by-default in a labour dispute over new technology after locking out his printworkers at the old city-centre plant and then telling them that no jobs waited for them at the new. It had been ugly for a while, and he'd been ready for it; hence the walls, hence the razor wire . . . those same features that had been so useful in holding-in the presence before its dangers had been fully realised. In the preceding weeks there had been a near-riot every night outside with police on horseback, water cannon, TV crews getting beaten up, the whole works. Meanwhile the proprietor, secure in the success of his coup, had been—in the words of informed sources—happier than a dog with two dicks. He couldn't have been slapping himself any harder on the back if he'd taken a course in yoga.

But then, quite literally, the roof had fallen in on his triumph.

It was the news story of the decade, and all his rivals had the best of it; at least until after a few more weeks had passed and seen a humiliating climbdown and a renegotiation with the unions to open up the old plant and resume production. By which time the containment had been in place, and the surrounding area had spontaneously cleared of much of its population, and the writs had been starting to fly in earnest.

The man was rich. He'd survive. But others, mostly tied into local waterfront development, had found themselves facing losses on the scale of the Nicaraguan national debt. The various interests had put their heads together, and the reward had been announced. It gave no consideration to the indecisiveness of the authorities, or to those who called for isolation and a programme of intensive scientific study; it simply meant that whoever could sneak into the danger zone and come out with the intruder's head—whatever it might happen to look like—could begin to number his or her assets in the millions.

Millions.

Frank could hardly even begin to imagine a million of anything. All that he could think of were big cars and huge houses and yachts moored in places where the trash weren't allowed. There on the yacht were Frank and his boy, best pals. Frank was drinking champagne. The boy had a Coke. They were talking about football.

She wouldn't even tell him the boy's legal name.

He'd thought about this venture for weeks. In his mind's eye, he always went in like Bruce Willis or Big Arnie and the worst thing that could ever happen was that he'd be seen entering and the armoured squad would dive in and bring him out before he'd managed to get anywhere. That would be too much. Beneath dignity. And if his failure were to make it onto the TV news then he might as well put the gun to his head right there and then, because she'd see it and there he'd be, confirmed in her opinion as the flop of the century. The way she talked about him, he'd never done a thing right in his life. Sometimes he wished that he'd strangled her when he'd had the chance, instead of exercising restraint and just knocking her backwards over the sofa. Even then she'd blown it up out of all proportion in court, as if she hadn't been asking for it.

He stopped, holding the flashlight beam steady.

Here was the first real evidence of damage.

The false ceiling had buckled down and all of the doors along this small side-passageway had sprung open. He wasn't exactly sure where he was. One room was full of office stationery and the rest of them comprised some kind of library or storage area, at a guess. He could see rows and rows of shelves, and more boxes than he could count. Those on the uppermost shelves had burst under the downward pressure of the dropped ceiling, spewing out clippings and cuttings and, in one of the rooms, sleeves of microfiche like so many playing cards. Ahead of him the passageway made a right-angled turn, with no clue of what might lie beyond.

He stopped, and listened.

Nothing.

So then, cautiously, he went on.

He sensed it before he saw it. A feeling of open space, of walls breached and the outside world let in. The torchbeam tracked along the floor and then suddenly it was shooting off down into nowhere.

He shone the beam upward. The entire ceiling had been punched down like the roof of a straw hut under the impact of a falling safe which had then carried on, taking the floor with it. He was looking up at the stars. Trailing wires and burned insulation hung around the edges like tatters of flesh around an exit wound.

Testing the floor with each step, he inched forward to the edge and looked down. The hole wasn't as big as he might have expected. Twenty feet across, not much more; the passageway continued over on the far side. He was looking down through at least two more floors, and there were probably more of them beyond the range of the flashlight. The falling object had crashed on as if through so many layers in a Pavlova, leaving the bared and bent ends of steel reinforcing rods to stick out of the concrete on every level. Two floors down he could see the wreckage of half a car, chomped neatly in two because it had stood in the way. So the basement levels were a parking garage.

What was that? He spun around.

Nothing there.

Maybe it had died. From its performance just after its arrival, it appeared to have chomped through a mountain of living flesh like the Tasmanian Devil in the Bugs Bunny cartoons, leaving nothing but scraps and stains. Since then, almost nothing. Only nine intruders in all this time, barely a snack by those early standards. It might have starved.

In which case, he'd claim it anyway. The best scenario would be to find it alive but too enfeebled to attack, in which case he could simply put it down like a mad dog. No-one need ever know. He sure as hell wouldn't let them barter him down on the reward, just because he hadn't had quite the tussle that they had in mind.

It might be weak.

Or equally, just very, very hungry.

He looked into the hole again. He'd checked out nearly all of this floor, but he'd found nothing. So the chances were that it was lurking down below. Weakened, dead, whatever, he was going to have to go down into the parking basement and find out.

He went back, looking for stairs.

Frank was wishing that he could have more faith in his own theory. But he couldn't help thinking of that sequence of holes, and how tough anything would have to be in order to survive that kind of impact. There was a special kind of ammunition that he'd been offered but hadn't been able to afford. French-made, his supplier had said, and very hard to get hold of. The round consisted of a number of buckshot pellets threaded onto a wire; it was called a necklace round and, discharged at close range, was supposedly devastating in its effect. It had been tested on beef carcasses, and had cut them in two. Frank had weighed it up and thought about it, but the decision in the end had been one purely of economy. This was before he'd known about the impending problems with the man who was supposed to be selling him a ladder. In retrospect he wished he'd gone out and stolen a ladder from someone's backyard, which was probably what the man had been planning to do anyway, and then gone ahead and bought the necklace rounds . . . even only as insurance. The phrase *out of one's depth* came up into his mind as he pushed open the stairway door on its pneumatic damper, but he turned it aside.

He edged through, tensed for any surprise. The stairway was bare and functional. The walls were of painted cinderblock and the stairs of cast concrete. Frank shone his light down the centre of the well, probing around the limited area that he was able to cover and watching for any response—a flinch, a darting shape, any flicker of movement at all. He kept at it for quite a while, even though it had quickly become clear that he was going to learn nothing this way. The fact of it was, he was putting off the moment of descent; and as soon as he'd realised this and admitted it to himself, he'd no further excuse for delay.

You're a hunter, he told himself. *A killer. So get the fuck down those stairs and start acting like one.*

He started to descend.

First turning, no problem.

Second turning . . .

He missed his footing as something leapt up into the air before him. It was bone-white and knobbly, that was all he could tell; he was scrambling back and trying to get it all together the way he'd rehearsed it in his mind a hundred times over, but somehow it wouldn't fall into place. He was panicking. A part of him knew it, and that part of him also knew with utter certainty that he was done for already. He was swinging up the shotgun but he was also losing his balance, and he was *slow* . . . his mind was firing off these commands in every direction, and his limbs were responding like so much ballast. The shotgun caught on something as he tried to bring it to bear. The flashlight was gone, spinning away across the landing between flights. He was falling. His finger was pulling on the shotgun trigger . . .

Oh, Christ, he thought, not that, not *yet* . . .

And there was a kick like a car door being thrown back against him, and an explosion in the stairwell that made the delicate structures of his ears feel as if they'd been turned to so much pulp, and a hot and bitter wind fanned his leg as an entire chunk of the balustrade was taken away in a single bite . . .

And when he hit the floor, he immediately scrabbled backwards into the angle where the walls met, and he stayed there.

The echoes seemed to go on for a long time, all the way up the stairwell and then back down again. The flashlight came to rest.

Frank was still in the corner. And still, as far as he was able to tell, in one piece.

Nothing moved.

Gingerly, he looked at the gun. His finger was still white on the trigger. He'd given it both barrels and he hadn't even got it up level, let alone taken aim; in fact, he'd come pretty close to blowing the front of his own leg off. His ammunition wasn't unlimited. He could reload, and then he could reload again; and then after that he could maybe think of using the shotgun as a club, because he'd be out of cartridges.

So, what had he seen?

Stiffly, he levered himself out of his corner and got to his feet. He was feeling stupid, the way he'd once felt when he'd come home late one night and a neighbour's cat had jumped out of the doorway and made him yell out loud. First he reloaded, leaving the spent cartridges where they fell. Then he picked up the flashlight and moved to the top of the stairs to look down. The beam appeared weaker than before. He didn't think that it was just his imagination.

There it was, lying at the bottom. He'd kicked a stick. A white, carved, knobbly stick that had been lying on the second stair and which had flipped up into the air when he'd stepped onto the end of it.

But no. Not a stick, exactly.

A human bone.

He went down to where it lay, and crouched before it with a sick kind of fascination. It was definitely a bone, and it wasn't spotless. There was old black meat sticking to it like shreds of pasted-on leather, the way it might look if it had been buried in somebody's garden for a month or so. One of the few quiz questions that he could answer concerned the longest bone in the human body; and here it was, the thighbone, looking like some elegant piece of ivory carving. He didn't touch it. Once had been enough. But he looked all around that small area of the stairwell, and he found nothing more.

It must have heard him. Surely, wherever it was, it must have heard the shotgun blast. If it hadn't known of his presence before, it would know of him now.

Think positive, he told himself. Look for the bonuses.

Well, the dress rehearsal was out of the way. He didn't think that he'd react quite so blindly a second time.

And that was about it.

He was half-expecting to see more human traces further down the stairwell, but there were none. Maybe there was something unspeakable right down at the bottom, but he didn't plan to descend that far. What he did find was a big grey electrical junction box behind the car park's upper-level access door, and when he opened up the box he found that it carried the fuses for no less than twenty circuits and that every one of the breaker switches had popped out. He started to push them back in, and with the third of them the stairwell lights came on.

When he put his nose out into the parking area, the place seemed almost to have been returned to life again.

Parked cars shone under the striplighting, looking as if they'd been abandoned only for hours instead of months. He saw Mercedes, BMWs, a scattering of Saabs and Volvos; these were in the reserved spaces closest to the elevator and beyond them, in the unreserved slots, stood a scattering of mid-market family saloons and the odd, halfheartedly-restored old banger. Way down at the far end of the level was the big hole; he could have gone along to it and looked up to the spot where he'd been standing only a few minutes before, but he didn't. The ceiling was low, the aisles narrow, and just across the way he could see a car ramp which angled down to the next level. Down there a striplight was flickering, spasming, trying to ignite but not quite making it. Frank eased out onto the parking floor, and held onto the door behind him so that it closed without noise.

It didn't matter where you were, these places always looked the same. A ramp at either end, painted arrows on the floor, oilstains, yellow zones, all the usual fire hazard notices, and all the atmosphere of a freightyard. He moved out as quickly as he could, scanning all around him; the malfunctioning light was putting out a zizz and crackle that made the silence less than total.

Now, he thought, come for me now. Now, when I'm ready; now, when I can see you coming; now, before my nerve finally deserts me for good and I turn to run into the arms of the pickup squad.

But nothing came.

He walked down the ramp, in the direction of the strobing light. Close to the foot of the ramp lay a motorcycle, keys in and looking as if its rider had laid it down on its side and then walked away as if from a fallen horse. It was a big Honda, its expensive-looking paintwork the colour of crushed berries and its brightwork shining through a layer of dust like liquid mercury. The mirror down against the ground was broken, otherwise it appeared to be undamaged. After looking it over, he looked around. Elsewhere on this level there were other signs of attempted flight; a couple of cars that had been run out of their spaces only to crash in the middle of the aisle, and one that had simply run along a wall for a number of yards and then stopped, one complete side ripped and destroyed while the other was untouched.

Frank moved on. He gave a start at one point, thinking that he'd seen something out of the corner of his eye. But it was only a fire hose, coiled over against the wall. He saw no signs of any living presence, except for the complete handful of human hair that he spied trapped in the closed rear door of a Microbus.

He dropped another level. He stayed out in the middle of the ramps and the aisles, keeping space around him all the time. *Now*, he kept thinking, *Come now*, but still nothing came.

Maybe it was afraid of the gun. Or maybe it liked a waiting game. If that was the case, its patience had to be phenomenal.

Perhaps he was right. Perhaps it had starved and was dead, after all.

At the furthest point of the very lowest level, he found the resting-place of the object that had rammed its way down through the layers of the building like so much paper.

Rock bottom.

Even after punching through a roof and four reinforced floors, it had still carried enough energy to make a hole of about twenty feet deep or more. He had to get the flashlight out and shine it down into the crater. What he saw didn't impress him much.

It looked like nothing more than a big rubber ball with its outside layers flaked and scorched away. And there was no way of telling whether it had happened because of the impact or afterwards, but somewhere along the line it had split from one side to the other and the contents had oozed from the gap in the manner of matter from a septic wound. Now the ooze seemed to have hardened, like candlewax or lava. He directed the torchbeam onto the inside, as well as he could, but the ball seemed to be empty. The inner surface might have been scaly, it was hard to say.

And that was it.

As far as Frank was concerned, the whole thing was a big letdown. He'd been hyping himself up for weeks, and for what? Nothing. Now even this was unimpressive. He'd been expecting a chunk of a flying saucer or maybe a Star Wars-type escape pod. It just looked like a shitball.

A sound echoed down from somewhere above. Not an animal sound, nor the sound of anything that might be stalking him, but an engine. He listened for a while longer, and he heard it again. He knew what it had to be; it was the pickup squad, on its way down to round him up and drag him out.

He turned to face the rest of the empty parking level.

"What's the matter with you?" he yelled, and his voice sounded shockingly loud in his own ears. "Scared to come out? What is it, you only like to pick on them when they're running away?" He stopped for a moment and listened, but all that he could hear was the distant revving of the armoured truck's engine. It sounded as if it was stuck somewhere, or at the very least having to attempt some kind of a tight manoeuvre.

"Well," he said, "I'll tell you what I think of that. I'll tell you what I think of *you*, and it isn't much. Are you listening? You're FULL OF SHIT!"

Silence.

He spun around now and looked behind him. He'd suddenly had the premonition of something rising out of the hole, rearing up over him as it spread itself wide and then falling on him like a tidal wave.

But there was nothing.

Frank turned from the hole again. He used his sleeve to rub the tears from his face. He couldn't have said whether they were of disappointment, or of rage, or relief. There had been no beast. There would be no reward. There would be no glory. The dreary downward spiral of his life would continue unchanged.

Or would it?

Could life really be the same, when you'd almost literally been to hell and back? Could it? The experience had to count for something in terms of self-respect, if nothing else. To have been tested, and to have gone the course without ever once turning to run . . . he'd at least done that, hadn't he?

He felt his heart beginning to lift, as the realisation came over him. Frank was no deep thinker, and had never pretended to be. But something important had happened to him down here, and he knew that he would leave this place like one reborn. He'd raised the nerve to face this demon, and he'd held on without flinching. Perhaps now, he might have the strength to face his own.

Although he'd still have preferred to get his hands on the money.

It was time to go. All that was left for him now was to get away from the complex without being caught, and he'd an idea of how he might do it. Dropping low so that he had less chance of being seen over the waist-high concrete barriers, he scampered up to the level above and then doubled back up the next ramp to the one above that. The revving of the security wagon's engine grew louder and more immediate as he ascended, and on the second level from the top he was able to see it.

He stayed low, watching. It was a big, heavily-armoured transit van of the kind used to move around large amounts of cash. There was wire over the windows and about half a ton extra of add-on plating, with bumpers and vent covers. The glass was tinted so that he couldn't see inside; and it was a fair bet that those inside couldn't see much of the world beyond the windshield, either. It looked big and mean and ponderous, and it couldn't make the turn onto the down-ramp.

At least, not in one. That was the reason for all the manoeuvering. The van was shuffling back and forth, over-revving and crashing its gears, and with every move it gained at best only a few inches on the angle. As Frank watched, there was a screech of metal as some part of it kissed the barrier. He could almost sense the pressure-cooker frustration of those inside. It rocked on its wheels as the brakes went on and off, on and off, and the level was filled with the choking stink of its exhaust.

At last, the armoured van was aligned with the ramp. It bumped its way down to the level below.

And there, after less than a dozen yards of progress, it began the tortuous business of getting itself out of the end of the ramp and into the aisle.

No wonder they'd only managed to pull out three of the twelve, Frank was thinking. The other wire-jumpers probably died of old age while they were waiting.

He watched from hiding for a while longer. And then after they'd taken a few more shots at it and got themselves well and truly committed, he leaped up and ran.

Somebody saw him. It hardly seemed possible, but they did. He heard the brakes slam on, and then the horn started to sound with some urgency. The armoured van began to reverse, but without much danger of immediate success. Frank was running hard for the upper level now. Compared to the van, he was a bird.

The big Honda motorcycle lay almost where he'd seen it last; there were new scrape-marks on the concrete alongside it, indicating that the armoured van had nudged it out of the way in order to get past. Frank was hoping that this hadn't caused any damage because the way he had it planned in his mind, the bike was his ticket back to freedom.

Laying down the shotgun, he took hold of the handlebars and righted it. This took all of his strength, and then some. For a moment he almost thought that he wasn't going to manage it, but then the bike rocked upright and he kicked down the stand to hold it in place.

Two years. It hadn't been run in two years. But it was an

almost-new, top-of-the range model, and the storage conditions down here weren't exactly adverse, so Frank's hopes of getting it started were pretty high. He turned over the starter, and the sound of it reverberated under the concrete ceiling; it didn't catch, but it *did* sound healthy enough.

He'd go out the way that the armoured van had come in. All that stuff about infra-red beams and machine guns, they'd have to have them turned off for fear of killing their own. On a bike like this, he could be out and through their defenses before they knew what had hit them. Nobody would stop him. Nobody would get in his way, ever again. He'd been to hell and back; he could do anything. He tried the starter once more.

The bike started with a roar.

He was away.

The sound of its engine in the confined space was tremendous. He took off up the ramp like a demon, and had to use his foot like a speedway rider to get him around the narrow turn at the top. Only a few yards ahead was the entrance ramp; shuttered before, it now stood open to the big night sky and the air. God, he felt elated; he could taste it already. He opened the throttle wide, and went head-down for freedom.

The bike slammed on the brakes.

Frank didn't know what he'd done. He wasn't aware of doing anything at all. But the bike was slowing, and had almost come to a stop. He twisted the throttle hard over all the way, but nothing happened. He could feel his balance starting to go.

What the hell. He was almost there. He'd run for it.

But before he could start to dismount something weird started to happen, and it happened fast. The chrome safety bars on the sides of the bike wrenched themselves free and wrapped around his legs, effectively clamping them into place. Then the entire bike began to topple sideways, taking him with it. He fought to keep it upright, but there was nothing he could do. He was slammed down onto the ground, bike and everything, and a wrench of agony shot up from his leg as it was crunched between metal and concrete.

He wriggled, he squirmed. But now the bike was starting to rev again all on its own, and still it held him in a grip. The engine revved harder and harder as if gathering its power and then, in a sequence of rapid-action moves, the entire machine seemed to spring apart under him and then, spreading itself, to close around him again like a hand. It all happened so fast, he could hardly make out what was going on . . . and then he saw that the fork had dropped the front wheel and inverted itself over the handlebar and was pointing its twin prongs at his chest. Even as he looked, the painted metal seemed to skin back and a long, toothlike hook protruded from each.

The fork struck him like a snake, at the same moment that a number of other components and cables and widgets took a grab at the various available soft parts of his body. Frank tried to scream, but something flipped over his face from behind and got a sudden hold on his upper teeth and started to bend his head back hard, and then harder, and then far *too* hard.

With one tremendous surge of engine power, the bike re-inverted itself. Frank, at the centre of the process, burst like a depressurised egg as the hand became a bike again. The shell of him was crunched up into the structure of the machine, his face mashed into the manifold so that his last sensation in life was the smell of frying sweetbreads. The rest of him flew out in shreds or splashed down onto the ground beneath. The entire process had taken less than eight seconds, at the end of which the machine landed on its two wheels and flipped down its stand, put-putting away at the centre of a widening pool of blood and offal.

And then, just as the armoured truck came inching backwards up the ramp, it threw out a snout and sucked up all of the mess like a high-pressure vacuum, leaving little more than a fresh stain on the concrete.

The van went by. The only difference in the scene was that where previously the bike had been lying on its side, now it stood upright . . . but nobody seemed to notice it. As the truck was making its final withdrawal into the world again, the bike retched a little as a piece of bone stuck somewhere inside its digestive process. It flexed, and then it lengthened and narrowed slightly, and there was a crushing sound as the bone was powdered by the increased internal pressure.

The outside shutter-door rolled down, ending with a crash. The lights stayed on. There was silence through the plant, and silence in the parking garage.

Except for one discreet belch.

And later, when all the reports had been written and the fire blanket retrieved from the wire and the night shift had handed over to the day crew, there was a movement in the plant that went undetected by anyone as the big Honda flipped up its stand and motored along to a new position.

Then nothing much happened for a while.

And then, having given the matter some consideration, the beast opted for a change. It puffed out its cheeks, arched its back, and became a Volkswagen.

And then it continued the waiting game.

Joe R. Lansdale

Incident on and Off a Mountain Road

When Ellen camed to the moonlit mountain curve, her thoughts, which had been adrift with her problems, grounded, and she was suddenly aware that she was driving much too fast. The sign said CURVE: 30 MPH, and she was doing fifty.

She knew too that slamming on the brakes was the wrong move, so she optioned to keep her speed and fight the curve and make it, and she thought she could.

The moonlight was strong, so visibility was high, and she knew her Chevy was in good shape, easy to handle, and she was a good driver.

But as she negotiated the curve a blue Buick seemed to grow out of the ground in front of her. It was parked on the shoulder of the road, at the peak of the curve, its nose sticking out a foot too far, its rear end against the moon-wet, silver railing that separated the curve from a mountainous plunge.

Had she been going an appropriate speed, missing the Buick wouldn't have been a problem, but at her speed she was swinging too far right, directly in line with it, and was forced, after all, to use her brakes. When she did, the back wheels slid and the brakes groaned and the front of the Chevy hit the Buick and there was a sound like an explosion and then for a dizzy instant she felt as if she were in the tumblers of a dryer.

Through the windshield came: Moonlight. Blackness. Moonlight.

One high bounce and a tight roll and the Chevy came to rest upright with the engine dead, the right side flush against the railing. Another inch of jump or greater impact against the rail, and the Chevy would have gone over.

Ellen felt a sharp pain in her leg and reached down to discover that during the tumble she had banged it against something, probably the gear shift, and had ripped her stocking and her flesh. Blood was trickling into her shoe. Probing her leg cautiously with the tips of her fingers, she determined the wound wasn't bad and that all other body parts were operative.

She unfastened her seat belt, and as a matter of habit, located her purse and slipped its strap over her shoulder. She got out of the Chevy feeling wobbly, eased around front of it and saw the hood and bumper and roof were crumpled. A wisp of radiator steam hissed from beneath the wadded hood, rose into the moonlight and dissolved.

She turned her attentions to the Buick. Its tail end was now turned to her, and as she edged alongside it, she saw the front left side had been badly damaged. Fearful of what she might see, she glanced inside.

The moonlight shone through the rear windshield bright as a spotlight and revealed no one, but the back seat was slick with something dark and wet and there was plenty of it. A foul scent seeped out of a partially rolled down back window. It was a hot coppery smell that gnawed at her nostrils and ached her stomach.

God, someone had been hurt. Maybe thrown free of the car, or perhaps they had gotten out and crawled off. But when? She and the Chevy had been airborne for only a moment, and she had gotten out of the vehicle instants after it ceased to roll. Surely she would have seen someone get out of the Buick, and if they had been thrown free by the collision, wouldn't at least one of the Buick's doors be open? If it had whipped back and closed, it seemed unlikely that it would be locked, and all the doors of the Buick were locked, and all the glass was intact, and only on her side was it rolled down, and only a crack. Enough for the smell of the blood to escape, not enough for a person to slip through unless they were thin and flexible as a feather.

On the other side of the Buick, on the ground, between the back door and the railing, there were drag marks and a thick swathe of blood, and another swathe on the top of the railing; it glowed there in the moonlight as if it were molasses laced with radio-activity.

Ellen moved cautiously to the railing and peered over.

No one lay mangled and bleeding and oozing their guts. The ground was not as precarious there as she expected. It was pebbly and sloped out gradually and there was a trail going down it. The trail twisted slightly and as it deepened the foliage grew denser on either side of it. Finally it curlicued its way into the dark thicket of a forest below, and from the forest, host on the wind, came the strong turpentine tang of pines and something less fresh and not as easily identifiable.

Now she saw someone moving down there, floating up from the forest like an apparition; a white face split by silver—braces perhaps. She could tell from the way this someone moved that it was a man. She watched as he climbed the trail and came within examination range. He seemed to be surveying her as carefully as she was surveying him.

Could this be the driver of the Buick?

As he came nearer Ellen discovered she could not identify the expression he wore. It was neither joy or anger or fear or exhaustion or pain. It was somehow all and none of these.

When he was ten feet away, still looking up, that same odd expression on his face, she could hear him breathing. He was breathing with exertion, but not to the extent she thought him tired or injured. It was the sound of someone who had been about busy work.

She yelled down, "Are you injured?"

He turned his head quizzically, like a dog trying to make sense of a command, and it occurred to Ellen that he might be knocked about in the head enough to be disoriented.

"I'm the one who ran into your car," she said. "Are you all right?"

His expression changed then, and it was most certainly identifiable this time. He was surprised and angry. He came up the trail quickly, took held of the top railing, his fingers going into the blood there, and vaulted over and onto the gravel.

Ellen stepped back out of his way and watched him from a distance. The guy made her nervous. Even close up, he looked like some kind of spook.

He eyed her briefly, glanced at the Chevy, turned to look at the Buick.

"It was my fault," Ellen said.

He didn't reply, but returned his attention to her and continued to cock his head in that curious dog sort of way.

Ellen noticed that one of his shirt sleeves was stained with blood, and that there was blood on the knees of his pants, but he didn't act as if he were hurt in any way. He reached into his pants pocket and pulled out something and made a move with his wrist. Out flicked a lock-blade knife. The thin edge of it sucked up the moonlight and spat it out in a silver spray that fanned wide when he held it before him and jiggled it like a man working a stubborn key into a lock. He advanced toward her, and as he came, his lips split and pulled back at the corners, exposing, not braces, but metal capped teeth that matched the sparkle of his blade.

It occurred to her that she could bolt for the Chevy, but in the same mental flash of lightning, it occurred to her she wouldn't make it.

Ellen threw herself over the railing, and as she leapt, she saw out of the corner of her eye, the knife slashing the place she had occupied, catching moonbeams and throwing them away. Then the blade was out of her view and she hit on her stomach and skidded onto the narrow trail, slid downward, feet first. The gravel and roots tore at the front of her dress and ripped through her nylons and gouged her flesh. She cried out in pain and her sliding gained speed. Lifting her chin, she saw that the man was climbing over the railing and coming after her at a stumbling run, the knife held before him like a wand.

Her sliding stopped, and she pushed off with her hands to make it start again, not knowing if this was the thing to do or not, since the trail inclined sharply on her right side, and should she skid only slightly in that direction, she could hurtle off into blackness. But somehow she kept slithering along the trail and even spun around a corner and stopped with her head facing downward, her purse practically in her teeth.

She got up then, without looking back, and began to run into the woods, the purse beating at her side. She moved as far away from the trail as she could, fighting limbs that conspired to hit her across the face or hold her, vines and bushes that tried to tie her feet or trip her.

Behind her, she could hear the man coming after her, breathing heavily now, not really winded, but hurrying. For the first time in

INCIDENT ON AND OFF A MOUNTAIN ROAD

months, she was grateful for Bruce and his survivalist insanity. His passion to be in shape and for her to be in shape with him was paying off. All that jogging had given her the lungs of an ox and strengthened her legs and ankles. A line from one of Bruce's survivalist books came to her: *Do the unexpected.*

She found a trail amongst the pines, and followed it, then, abruptly broke from it and went back into the thicket. It was harder going, but she assumed her pursuer would expect her to follow a trail.

The pines became so thick she got down on her hands and knees and began to crawl. It was easier to get through that way. After a moment, she stopped scuttling and eased her back against one of the pines and sat and listened. She felt reasonably well hidden, as the boughs of the pines grew low and drooped to the ground. She took several deep breaths, holding each for a long moment. Gradually, she began breathing normally. Above her, from the direction of the trail, she could hear the man running, coming nearer. She held her breath.

The running paused a couple of times, and she could imagine the man, his strange, pale face turning from side to side, as he tried to determine what had happened to her. The sound of running started again and the man moved on down the trail.

Ellen considered easing out and starting back up the trail, making her way to her car and driving off. Damaged as it was, she felt it would still run, but she was reluctant to leave her hiding place and step into the moonlight. Still, it seemed a better plan than waiting. She didn't do something, the man could always go back topside himself and wait for her. The woods, covering acres and acres of land below and beyond, would take her days to get through, and without food and water and knowledge of the geography, she might never make it, could end up going in circles for days.

Bruce and his survivalist credos came back to her. She remembered something he had said to one of his self-defense classes, a bunch of red necks hoping and praying for a commie take-over so they could show their stuff. He had told them: "Utilize what's at hand. Size up what you have with you and how it can be put to use."

All right, she thought. All right, Brucey, you sonofabitch. I'll see what's at hand.

One thing she knew she had for sure was a little flashlight. It wasn't much, but it would serve for her to check out the contents of her purse. She located it easily, and without withdrawing it from her purse, turned it on and held the open purse close to her face to see what was inside. Before she actually found it, she thought of her nail file kit. Besides the little bottle of nail polish remover, there was an emery board and two metal files. The files were the ticket. They might serve as weapons; they weren't much, but they were something.

She also carried a very small pair of nail scissors, independent of the kit, the points of the scissors being less than a quarter inch. That wouldn't be worth much, but she took note of it and mentally catalogued it.

She found the nail kit, turned off the flash and removed one of the files and returned the rest of the kit to her purse. She held the file tightly, made a little jabbing motion with it. It seemed so light and thin and insignificant.

She had been absently carrying her purse on one shoulder, and now to make sure she didn't lose it, she placed the strap over her neck and slid her arm through.

Clenching the nail file, she moved on hands and knees beneath the pine boughs and poked her head out into the clearing of the trail. She glanced down it first, and there, not ten yards from her, looking up the trail, holding his knife by his side, was the man. The moonlight lay cold on his face and the shadows of the wind-blown boughs fell across him and wavered. It seemed as if she were leaning over a pool and staring down into the water and seeing him at the bottom of it, or perhaps his reflection on the face of the pool.

She realized instantly that he had gone down the trail a ways, became suspicious of her ability to disappear so quickly, and had turned to judge where she might have gone. And, as if in answer to the question, she had poked her head into view.

They remained frozen for a moment, then the man took a step up the trail, and just as he began to run, Ellen went backwards into the pines on her hands and knees.

She had gone less than ten feet when she ran up against a thick limb that lay close to the ground and was preventing her passage. She got down on her belly and squirmed beneath it, and as she was pulling her head under, she saw Moon Face crawling into the thicket, making good time; time made better, when he lunged suddenly and covered half the space between them, the knife missing her by fractions.

INCIDENT ON AND OFF A MOUNTAIN ROAD

Ellen jerked back and felt her feet falling away from her. She let go of the file and grabbed out for the limb and it bent way back and down with her weight. It lowered her enough for her feet to touch ground. Relieved, she realized she had fallen into a wash made by erosion, not off the edge of the mountain.

Above her, gathered in shadows and stray strands of moonlight that showed through the pine boughs, was the man. His metal-tipped teeth caught a moonbeam and twinkled. He placed a hand on the limb she held, as if to lower himself, and she let go of it.

The limb whispered away from her and hit him full in the face and knocked him back.

Ellen didn't bother to scrutinize the damage. Turning, she saw that the wash ended in a slope and that the slope was thick with trees growing out like great, feathered spears thrown into the side of the mountain.

She started down, letting the slant carry her, grasping limbs and tree trunks to slow her descent and keep her balance. She could hear the man climbing down and pursuing her, but she didn't bother to turn and look. Below she could see the incline was becoming steeper, and if she continued, it would be almost straight up and down with nothing but the trees for support, and to move from one to the other, she would have to drop, chimpanzee-like, from limb to limb. Not a pleasant thought.

Her only consolation was that the trees to her right, veering back up the mountain, were thick as cancer cells. She took off in that direction, going wide, and began plodding upwards again, trying to regain the concealment of the forest.

She chanced a look behind her before entering the pines, and saw that the man, who she had come to think of as Moon Face, was some distance away.

Weaving through a mass of trees, she integrated herself into the forest, and as she went the limbs began to grow closer to the ground and the trees became so thick they twisted together like pipe cleaners. She got down on her hands and knees and crawled between limbs and around tree trunks and tried to lose herself among them.

To follow her, Moon Face had to do the same thing, and at first she heard him behind her, but after a while, there were only the sounds she was making.

She paused and listened.

Nothing.

Glancing the way she had come, she saw the intertwining limbs she had crawled under mixed with penetrating moonbeams, heard the short bursts of her breath and the beating of her heart, but detected no evidence of Moon Face. She decided the head start she had, all the weaving she had done, the cover of the pines, had confused him, at least temporarily.

It occurred to her that if she had stopped to listen, he might have done the same, and she wondered if he could hear the pounding of her heart. She took a deep breath and held it and let it out slowly through her nose, did it again. She was breathing more normally now, and her heart, though still hammering furiously, felt as if it were back inside her chest where it belonged.

Easing her back against a tree trunk, she sat and listened, watching for that strange face, fearing it might abruptly burst through the limbs and brush, grinning its horrible teeth, or worse, that he might come up behind her, reach around the tree trunk with his knife and finish her in a bloody instant.

She checked and saw that she still had her purse. She opened it and got hold of the file kit by feel and removed the last file, determined to make better use of it than the first. She had no qualms about using it, knew she would, but what good would it do? The man was obviously stronger than she, and crazy as the pattern in a scratch quilt.

Once again, she thought of Bruce. What would he have done in this situation? He would certainly have been the man for the job. He would have relished it. Would probably have challenged old Moon Face to a one on one at the edge of the mountain, and even with a nail file, would have been confident that he could take him.

Ellen thought about how much she hated Bruce, and even now, shed of him, that hatred burned bright. How had she gotten mixed up with that dumb, macho bastard in the first place? He had seemed enticing at first. So powerful. Confident. Capable. The survivalist stuff had always seemed a little nutty, but at first no more nutty than an obsession with golf or a strong belief in astrology. Perhaps had she known how serious he was about it, she wouldn't have been attracted to him in the first place.

No. It wouldn't have mattered. She had been captivated by him, by his looks and build and power. She had nothing but her own libido and stupidity to blame. And worse yet, when things turned sour, she had stayed and let them sour even more. There had been good moments, but they were quickly eclipsed by Bruce's determination to be ready for the Big Day, as he referred to it. He knew it was coming, if he was somewhat vague on who was bringing it. But someone would start a war of some sort, a nuclear war, a war in the streets, and only the rugged individualist, well-armed and well-trained and strong of body and will would survive beyond the initial attack. Those survivors would then carry out guerrilla warfare, hit and run operations, and eventually win back the country from . . . whoever. And if not win it back, at least have some kind of life free of dictatorship.

It was silly. It was every little boy's fantasy. Living by your wits with gun and knife. And owning a woman. She had been the woman. At first Bruce had been kind enough, treated her with respect. He was obviously on the male chauvinist side, but originally it had seemed harmless enough, kind of Old World charming. But when he moved them to the mountains, that charm had turned to domination, and the small crack in his mental state widened until it was a deep, dark gulf.

She was there to keep house and to warm his bed, and any opinions she had contrary to his own were stupid. He read survivalist books constantly and quoted passages to her and suggested she look the books over, be ready to stand tall against the oncoming aggressors.

By the time he had gone completely over the edge, living like a mountain man, ordering her about, his eyes roving from side to side, suspicious of her every move, expecting to hear on his shortwave at any moment World War Three had started, or that race riots were overrunning the U.S., or that a shiny probe packed with extraterrestrial invaders brandishing ray guns had landed on the White House lawn, she was trapped in his cabin in the mountains with him holding the keys to her Chevy and his jeep.

For a time she feared he would become paranoid enough to imagine she was one of the "bad guys" and put a .357 round through her chest. But now she was free of him, escaped from all that . . . only to be threatened by another man; a moon-faced, silver-toothed monster with a knife.

She returned once again to the question, what would Bruce do, outside of challenging Moon Face in hand to hand combat? Sneaking past him would be the best bet, making it back to the

Chevy. To do that Bruce would have used guerrilla techniques. "Take advantage of what's at hand," he always said.

Well, she had looked to see what was at hand, and that turned out to be a couple of finger nail files, one of them lost up the mountain.

Then maybe she wasn't thinking about this in the right way. She might not be able to out fight Moon Face, but perhaps she could out think him. She had out thought Bruce, and he had considered himself a master of strategy and preparation.

She tried to put herself in Moon Face's head. What was he thinking? For the moment he saw her as his prey, a frightened animal on the run. He might be more cautious because of that trick with the limb, but he'd most likely chalk that one up to accident—which it was for the most part . . . But what if the prey turned on him?

There was a sudden cracking sound, and Ellen crawled a few feet in the direction of the noise, gently moved aside a limb. Some distance away, discerned faintly through a tangle of limbs, she saw light and detected movement, and knew it was Moon Face. The cracking sound must have been him stepping on a limb.

He was standing with his head bent, looking at the ground, flashing a little pocket flashlight, obviously examining the drag path she had made with her hands and knees when she entered into the pine thicket.

She watched as his shape and the light bobbed and twisted through the limbs and tree trunks, coming nearer. She wanted to run, but didn't know where to.

"All right," she thought. "All right. Take it easy. Think."

She made a quick decision. Removed the scissors from her purse, took off her shoes and slipped off her panty hose and put her shoes on again.

She quickly snipped three long strips of nylon from her damaged panty hose and knotted them together, using the sailor knots Bruce had taught her. She cut more thin strips from the hose—all the while listening for Moon Face's approach—and used all but one of them to fasten her fingernail file, point out, securely to the tapered end of one of the small, flexible pine limbs, then she tied one end of the long nylon strip she had made around the limb, just below the file, and crawled backwards, pulling the limb with her, bending it deep. When she had it back as far as she could manage, she took a death grip on the nylon strip, and using it to keep the limb's position taut, crawled around the trunk of a small pine and curved the nylon strip about it and made a loop knot at the base of a sapling that crossed her knee-drag trail. She used her last strip of nylon to fasten to the loop of the knot, and carefully stretched the remaining length across the trail and tied it to another sapling. If it worked correctly, when he came crawling through the thicket, following her, his hands or knees would hit the strip, pull the loop free, and the limb would fly forward, the file stabbing him, in an eye if she were lucky.

Pausing to look through the boughs again, she saw that Moon Face was on his hands and knees, moving through the thick foliage toward her. Only moments were left.

She shoved pine needles over the strip and moved away on her belly, sliding under the cocked sapling, no longer concerned that she might make noise, in fact hoping noise would bring Moon Face quickly.

Following the upward slope of the hill, she crawled until the trees became thin again and she could stand. She cut two long strips of nylon from her hose with the scissors, and stretched them between two trees about ankle high.

That one would make him mad if it caught him, but the next one would be the corker.

She went up the path, used the rest of the nylon to tie between two saplings, then grabbed hold of a thin, short limb and yanked at it until it cracked, worked it free so there was a point made from the break. She snapped that over her knee to form a point at the opposite end. She made a quick mental measurement, jammed one end of the stick into the soft ground, leaving a point facing up.

At that moment came evidence her first snare had worked—a loud swishing sound as the limb popped forward and a cry of pain. This was followed by a howl as Moon Face crawled out of the thicket and onto the trail. He stood slowly, one hand to his face. He glared up at her, removed his hand. The file had struck him in the cheek; it was covered with blood. Moon Face pointed his blood-covered hand at her and let out an accusing shriek so horrible she retreated rapidly up the trail. Behind her, she could hear Moon Face running.

The trail curved upward and turned abruptly. She followed the curve a ways, looked back as Moon Face tripped over her first strip and hit the ground, came up madder, charged even more violently up the path. But the second strip got him and he fell forward, throwing his hands out. The spike in the trail hit him low in the throat.

She stood transfixed at the top of the trail as he did a pushup and came to one knee and put a hand to his throat. Even from a distance, and with only the moonlight to show it to her, she could see that the wound was dreadful.

Good.

Moon Face looked up, stabbed her with a look, started to rise. Ellen turned and ran. As she made the turns in the trail the going improved and she theorized that she was rushing up the trail she had originally come down.

This hopeful notion was dispelled when the pines thinned and the trail dropped, then leveled off, then tapered into nothing. Before she could slow up, she discovered she was on a sort of peninsula that jutted out from the mountain and resembled an irregular shaped diving board from which you could leap off into night-black eternity.

In place of the pines on the sides of the trail were numerous scarecrows on poles, and out on the very tip of the peninsula, somewhat dispelling the diving board image, was a shack made of sticks and mud and brambles.

After pausing to suck in some deep breaths, Ellen discovered on closer examination that it wasn't scarecrows bordering her path after all. It was people.

Dead people. She could smell them.

There were at least a dozen on either side, placed upright on poles, their feet touching the ground, their knees slightly bent. They were all fully clothed, and in various states of deterioration. Holes had been poked through the backs of their heads to correspond with the hollow sockets of their eyes, and the moonlight came through the holes and shined through the sockets, and Ellen noted with a warm sort of horror that one wore a white sun dress and pink, plastic shoes, and through its head she could see stars. On the corpse's finger was a wedding ring, and the finger had grown thin and withered and the ring was trapped there by knuckle bone alone.

The man next to her was fresher. He too was eyeless and holes had been drilled through the back of his skull, but he still wore glasses and was fleshy. There was a pen and pencil set in his coat pocket. He wore only one shoe.

There was a skeleton in overalls, a wilting cigar stuck between his teeth. A fresh UPS man with his cap at a jaunty angle, the moon through his head, and a clipboard tied to his hand with string. His legs had been positioned in such a way it seemed as if he were walking. A housewife with a crumpled, nearly disintegrated grocery bag under her arm, the contents having long fallen through the worn, wet bottom to heap at her feet in a mass of colorless boxes and broken glass. A withered corpse in a ballerina's tutu and slippers, rotting grapefruits tied to her chest with cord to simulate breasts, her legs arranged in such a way she seemed in mid-dance, up on her toes, about to leap or whirl.

The real horror was the children. One pathetic little boy's corpse, still full of flesh and with only his drilled eyes to show death, had been arranged in such a way that a teddy bear drooped from the crook of his elbow. A toy metal tractor and a plastic truck were at his feet.

There was a little girl wearing a red, rubber clown nose and a propeller beenie. A green plastic purse hung from her shoulder by a strap and a doll's legs had been taped to her palm with black electrician's tape. The doll hung upside down, holes drilled through its plastic head so that it matched its owner.

Things began to click. Ellen understood what Moon Face had been doing down here in the first place. He hadn't been in the Buick when she struck it. He was disposing of a body. He was a murderer who brought his victims here and set them up on either side of the pathway, parodying the way they were in life, cutting out their eyes and punching through the backs of their heads to let the world in.

Ellen realized numbly that time was slipping away, and Moon Face was coming, and she had to find the trail up to her car. But when she turned to run, she froze.

Thirty feet away, where the trail met the last of the pines, squatting dead center in it, arms on his knees, one hand loosely holding the knife, was Moon Face. He looked calm, almost happy, in spite of the fact a large swathe of dried blood was on his cheek and the wound in his throat was making a faint whistling sound as air escaped it.

He appeared to be gloating, savoring the moment when he would set his knife to work on her eyes, the gray matter behind them, the bone of her skull.

A vision of her corpse propped up next to the child with the teddy bear, or perhaps the skeletal ballerina, came to mind; she could see herself hanging there, the light of the moon falling through her empty head, melting into the path.

Then she felt anger. It boiled inside her. She determined she was not going to allow Moon Face his prize easily. He'd earn it.

Another line from Bruce's books came to her.

Consider your alternatives.

She did, in a flash. And they were grim. She could try charging past Moon Face, or pretend to, then dart into the pines. But it seemed unlikely she could make the trees before he overtook her. She could try going over the side of the trail and climbing down, but it was much too steep there, and she'd fall immediately. She could make for the shack and try and find something she could fight with. The last idea struck her as the correct one, the one Bruce would have pursued. What was his quote? "If you can't effect an escape, fall back and fight with what's available to you."

She hurried to the hut, glancing behind her from time to time to check on Moon Face. He hadn't moved. He was observing her calmly, as if he had all the time in the world.

When she was about to go through the doorless entry way, she looked back at him one last time. He was in the same spot, watching, the knife held limply against his leg. She knew he thought he had her right where he wanted her, and that's exactly what she wanted him to think. A surprise attack was the only chance she had. She just hoped she could find something to surprise him with.

She hastened inside and let out an involuntary rasp of breath.

The place stank, and for good reason. In the center of the little hut was a folding card table and some chairs, and seated in one of the chairs was a woman, the flesh rotting and dripping off her skull like candle wax, her eyes empty and holes in the back of her head. Her arm was resting on the table and her hand was clamped around an open bottle of whiskey. Beside her, also without eyes, suspended in a standing position by wires connected to the roof, was a man. He was a fresh kill. Big, dressed in khaki pants and shirt and work shoes. In one hand a doubled belt was taped, and wires were attached in such a way that his arm was drawn back as if ready to strike. Wires were secured to his lips and pulled tight behind his head so that he was smiling in a ghoulish way. Foil gum wrappers were fixed to his

teeth, and the moonlight gleaming through the opening at the top of the hut fell on them and made them resemble Moon Face's metal-tipped choppers.

Ellen felt queasy, but fought the sensation down. She had more to worry about than corpses. She had to prevent herself from becoming one.

She gave the place a quick pan. To her left was a rust-framed roll-away bed with a thin, dirty mattress, and against the far wall was a baby crib, and next to that a camper stove with a small frying pan on it.

She glanced quickly out the door of the hut and saw that Moon Face had moved onto the stretch of trail bordered by the bodies. He was walking very slowly, looking up now and then as if to appreciate the stars.

Her heart pumped another beat.

She moved about the hut, looking for a weapon.

The frying pan.

She grabbed it, and as she did, she saw what was in the crib. What belonged there. A baby. But dead. A few months old. It's skin thin as plastic and stretched tight over pathetic, little rib bones. Eyes gone, holes through its head. Burnt match stubs between blackened toes. It wore a diaper and the stink of feces wafted from it and into her nostrils. A rattle lay at the foot of the crib.

A horrible realization rushed through her. The baby had been alive when taken by this mad man, and it had died here, starved and tortured. She gripped the frying pan with such intensity her hand cramped.

Her foot touched something.

She looked down. Large bones were heaped there—discarded Mommies and Daddies, for it now occurred to her that was who the corpses represented.

Something gleamed amongst the bones. A gold cigarette lighter.

Through the doorway of the hut she saw Moon Face was halfway down the trail. He had paused to nonchalantly adjust the UPS man's clipboard. The geek had made his own community here, his own family, people he could deal with—dead people—and it was obvious he intended for her to be part of his creation.

Ellen considered attacking straight-on with the frying pan when Moon Face came through the doorway, but so far he had proven strong enough to take a file in the cheek and a stick in the throat, and despite the severity of the latter wound, he had kept on coming. Chances were he was strong enough to handle her and her frying pan.

A back-up plan was necessary. Another one of Bruce's pronouncements. She recalled a college friend, Carol, who used to use her bikini panties to launch projectiles at a teddy bear propped on a chair. This graduated to an apple on the bear's head. Eventually, Ellen and her dorm sisters got into the act. Fresh panties with tight elastic and marbles for ammunition were ever ready in a box by the door, the bear and an apple were in constant position. In time, Ellen became the best shot of all. But that was ten years ago. Expertise was long gone, even the occasional shot now and then was no longer taken . . . Still . . .

Ellen replaced the frying pan on the stove, hiked up her dress and pulled her bikini panties down and stepped out of them and picked up the lighter.

She put the lighter in the crotch of the panties and stuck her fingers into the leg loops to form a fork and took hold of the lighter through the panties and pulled it back, assured herself the elastic was strong enough to launch the projectile.

All right. That was a start.

She removed her purse, so Moon Face couldn't grab it and snare her, and tossed it aside. She grabbed the whiskey bottle from the corpse's hand and turned and smashed the bottom of it against the cook stove. Whiskey and glass flew. The result was a jagged weapon she could lunge with. She placed the broken bottle on the stove next to the frying pan.

Outside, Moon Face was strolling toward the hut, like a shy teenager about to call on his date.

There were only moments left. She glanced around the room, hoping insanely at the last second she would find some escape route, but there was none.

Sweat dripped from her forehead and ran into her eye and she blinked it out and half-drew back the panty sling with its golden projectile. She knew her makeshift weapon wasn't powerful enough to do much damage, but it might give her a moment of distraction, a chance to attack him with the bottle. If she went at him straight on with it, she felt certain he would disarm her and make short work of her, but if she could get him off guard . . .

She lowered her arms, kept her makeshift slingshot in front of

INCIDENT ON AND OFF A MOUNTAIN ROAD

her, ready to be cocked and shot.

Moon Face came through the door, ducking as he did, a sour sweat smell entering with him. His neck wound whistled at her like a teapot about to boil. She saw then that he was bigger than she first thought. Tall and broad shouldered and strong.

He looked at her and there was that peculiar expression again. The moonlight from the hole in the roof hit his eyes and teeth, and it was as if that light was his source of energy. He filled his chest with air and seemed to stand a full two inches taller. He looked at the woman's corpse in the chair, the man's corpse supported on wires, glanced at the playpen.

He smiled at Ellen, squeaked more than spoke, "Bubba's home, Sissie."

I'm not Sissie yet, thought Ellen. Not yet.

Moon Face started to move around the card table and Ellen let out a blood-curdling scream that caused him to bob his head high like a rabbit surprised by headlights. Ellen jerked up the panties and pulled them back and let loose the lighter. It shot out of the panties and fell to the center of the card table with a clunk.

Moon Face looked down at it.

Ellen was temporarily gripped with paralysis, then she stepped forward and kicked the card table as hard as she could. It went into Moon Face, hitting him waist high, startling, but not hurting him.

Now! thought Ellen, grabbing her weapons. Now!

She rushed him, the broken bottle in one hand, the frying pan in the other. She slashed out with the bottle and it struck him in the center of the face and he let out a scream and the glass fractured and a splash of blood burst from him and in that same instant Ellen saw that his nose was cut half in two and she felt a tremendous throb in her hand. The bottle had broken in her palm and cut her.

She ignored the pain and as Moon Face bellowed and lashed out with the knife cutting the front of her dress but not her flesh, she brought the frying pan around and caught him on the elbow and the knife went soaring across the room and behind the rollaway bed.

Moon Face froze, glanced in the direction the knife had taken. He seemed empty and confused without it.

Ellen swung the pan again. Moon Face caught her wrist and jerked her around and she lost the pan and was sent hurtling toward the bed, where she collapsed on the mattress. The bed slid down and smashed through the thin wall of sticks and a foot of the bed stuck out into blackness and the great drop below. The bed tottered slightly, and Ellen rolled off of it, directly into the legs of Moon Face. As his knees bent, and he reached for her, she rolled backwards and went under the bed and her hand came to rest on the knife. She grabbed it, rolled back toward Moon Face's feet, reached out quickly and brought the knife down on one of his shoes and drove it in as hard as she could.

A bellow from Moon Face. His foot leaped back and it took the knife with it. Moon Face screamed, "Sissie! You're hurting me!"

Moon Face reached down and pulled the knife out, and Ellen saw his foot come forward, and then he was grabbing the bed and effortlessly jerking it off of her and back, smashing it into the crib, causing the child to topple out of it and roll across the floor, the rattle clattering behind it. He grabbed Ellen by the back of her dress and jerked her up and spun her around to face him, clutched her throat in one hand and held the knife close to her face with the other, as if for inspection; the blade caught the moonlight and winked.

Beyond the knife, she saw his face, pathetic and pained and white. His breath, sharp as the knife, practically wilted her. His neck wound whistled softly. The remnants of his nose dangled wet and red against his upper lip and cheek and his teeth grinned a moon-lit, metal good-bye.

It was all over, and she knew it, but then Bruce's words came back to her in a rush. "When it looks as if you're defeated, and there's nothing left, try anything."

She twisted and jabbed out at his eyes with her fingers and caught him solid enough that he thrust her away and stumbled backwards. But only for an instant. He bolted forward, and Ellen stooped and grabbed the dead child by the ankle and struck Moon Face with it as if it were a club. Once in the face, once in the midsection. The rotting child burst into a spray of desiccated flesh and innards and she hurled the leg at Moon Face and then she was circling around the roll-away bed, trying to make the door. Moon Face, at the other end of the bed, saw this, and when she moved for the door, he lunged in that direction, causing her to jump back to the end of the bed. Smiling, he returned to his end, waited for her next attempt.

She lurched for the door again, and Moon Face deep-stepped

INCIDENT ON AND OFF A MOUNTAIN ROAD

that way, and when she jerked back, Moon Face jerked back too, but this time Ellen bent and grabbed the end of the bed and hurled herself against it. The bed hit Moon Face in the knees, and as he fell, the bed rolled over him and he let go of the knife and tried to put out his hands to stop the bed's momentum. The impetus of the roll-away carried him across the short length of the dirt floor and his head hit the far wall and the sticks cracked and hurtled out into blackness, and Moon Face followed and the bed followed him, then caught on the edge of the drop and the wheels buried up in the dirt and hung there.

Ellen had shoved so hard she fell face down, and when she looked up, she saw the bed was dangling, shaking, the mattress slipping loose, about to glide off into nothingness.

Moon Face's hands flicked into sight, clawing at the sides of the bed's frame. Ellen gasped. He was going to make it up. The bed's wheels were going to hold.

She pulled a knee under her, cocking herself, then sprang forward, thrusting both palms savagely against the bed. The wheels popped free and the roll-away shot out into the dark emptiness.

Ellen scooted forward on her knees and looked over the edge. There was blackness, a glimpse of the mattress falling free, and a pale object, like a white-washed planet with a great vein of silver in it, jetting through the cold expanse of space. Then the mattress and the face were gone and there was just the darkness and a distant sound like a water balloon exploding.

Ellen sat back and took a breather. When she felt strong again and felt certain her heart wouldn't tear through her chest, she stood up and looked around the room. She thought a long time about what she saw.

She found her purse and panties, went out of the hut and up the trail, and after a few wrong turns, she found the proper trail that wound its way up the mountain side to where her car was parked. When she climbed over the railing, she was exhausted.

Everything was as it was. She wondered if anyone had seen the cars, if anyone had stopped, then decided it didn't matter. There was no one here now, and that's what was important.

She took the keys from her purse and tried the engine. It turned over. That was a relief.

She killed the engine, got out and went around and opened the trunk of the Chevy and looked down at Bruce's body. His face looked like one big bruise, his lips were as large as sausages. It made her happy to look at him.

A new energy came to her. She got him under the arms and pulled him out and managed him over to the rail and grabbed his legs and flipped him over the railing and onto the trail. She got one of his hands and started pulling him down the path, letting the momentum help her. She felt good. She felt strong. First Bruce had tried to dominate her, had threatened her, had thought she was weak because she was a woman, and one night, after slapping her, after raping her, while he slept a drunken sleep, she had pulled the blankets up tight around him and looped rope over and under the bed and used the knots he had taught her, and secured him.

Then she took a stick of stove wood and had beat him until she was so weak she fell to her knees. She hadn't meant to kill him, just punish him for slapping her around, but when she got started she couldn't stop until she was too worn out to go on, and when she was finished, she discovered he was dead.

That didn't disturb her much. The thing then was to get rid of the body somewhere, drive on back to the city and say he had abandoned her and not come back. It was weak, but all she had. Until now.

After several stops for breath, a chance to lie on her back and look up at the stars, Ellen managed Bruce to the hut and got her arms under his and got him seated in one of the empty chairs. She straightened things up as best she could. She put the larger pieces of the baby back in the crib. She picked Moon Face's knife up off the floor and looked at it and looked at Bruce, his eyes wide open, the moonlight from the roof striking them, showing them to be dull as scratched glass.

Bending over his face, she went to work on his eyes. When she finished with them, she pushed his head forward and used the blade like a drill. She worked until the holes satisfied her. Now if the police found the Buick up there and came down the trail to investigate, and found the trail leading here, saw what was in the shack, Bruce would fit in with the rest of Moon Face's victims. The police would probably conclude Moon Face, sleeping here with his "family", had put his bed too close to the cliff and it had broken through the thin wall and he had tumbled to his death.

She liked it.

She held Bruce's chin, lifted it, examined her work.

"You can be Uncle Brucey," she said, and gave Bruce a pat on the shoulder. "Thanks for all your advice and help, Uncle Brucey. It's what got me through." She gave him another pat.

She found a shirt—possibly Moon Face's, possibly a victims—on the opposite side of the shack, next to a little box of Harlequin Romances, and she used it to wipe the knife, pan, all she had touched, clean of her prints, then she went out of there, back up to her car.

(For Jo Foshee)

Steppin Out, Summer, '68

Buddy drank another swig of beer and when he brought the bottle down he said to Jake and Wilson, "I could sure use some pussy."

"We could all use some," Wilson said, "problem is we don't never get any."

"That's the way I see it too," Jake said.

"You don't get any," Buddy said. "I get plenty, you can count on that."

"Uh huh," Wilson said. "You talk pussy plenty good, but I don't ever see you with a date. I ain't never even seen you walking a dog, let alone a girl. You don't even have a car, so how you gonna get with a girl?"

"That's the way I see it too," Jake said.

"You see what you want," Buddy said. "I'm gonna be getting me a Chevy soon. I got my eye on one."

"Yeah?" Wilson said. "What one?"

"Drew Carrington's old crate."

"Shit," Wilson said, "that motherfucker caught on fire at a streetlight and he run it off in the creek."

"They got it out," Buddy said.

"They say them flames jumped twenty feet out from under the hood before he run it off in there," Jake said.

"Water put the fire out," Buddy said.

"Uh huh," Wilson said, "after the motor blowed up through the hood. They found that motherfucker in a tree out back of Old

Maud Page's place. One of the pistons fell out of it and hit her on the head while she was picking up apples. She was in the hospital three days."

"Yeah," Jake said. "And I hear Carrington's in Dallas now, never got better from the accident. Near drowned and some of the engine blew back into the car and hit him in the nuts, castrated him, fucked up his legs. He can't walk. He's on a wheeled board or something, got some retard that pulls him around."

"Them's just stories," Buddy said. "Motor's still in the car. Carrington got him a job in Dallas as a mechanic. He didn't get hurt at all. Old Woman Page didn't get hit by no piston either. It missed her by a foot. Scared her so bad she had a little stroke. That's why she was in the hospital."

"You seen the motor?" Wilson asked. "Tell me you've seen it."

"No," Buddy said, "but I've heard about it from good sources, and they say it can be fixed."

"Jack it up and drive another car under it," Wilson said, "it'll be all right."

"That's the way I see it too," Jake said.

"Listen to you two," Wilson said. "You know it all. You're real operators. I'll tell you morons one thing, I line up a little of the hole that winks and stinks, like I'm doing tonight, you won't get none of it."

Wilson and Jake shuffled and eyed each other. An unspoken, but clear message passed between them. They had never known Buddy to actually get any, or anyone else to know of him getting any, but he had a couple of years on them, and he might have gotten some, way he talked about it, and they damn sure knew they weren't getting any, and if there was a chance of it, things had to be patched up.

"Car like that," Wilson said, "if you worked hard enough, you might get it to run. Some new pistons or something . . . What you got lined up for tonight?"

Buddy's face put on some importance. "I know a gal likes to do the circle, you know what I mean?"

Wilson hated to admit it, but he didn't. "The circle?"

"Pull the train," Buddy said. "Do the team. You know, fuck a bunch a guys, one after the other."

"Oh," Wilson said.

"I knew that," Jake said.

"Yeah," Wilson said. "Yeah sure you did." Then to Buddy: "When you gonna see this gal?"

Buddy, still important, took a swig of beer and pursed his lips and studied the afternoon sky. "Figured I'd walk on over there little after dark. It's a mile or so."

"Say she likes to do more than one guy?" Wilson asked.

"Way I hear it," Buddy said, "she'll do 'em till they ain't able to do. My cousin, Butch, he told me about her."

Butch. The magic word. Wilson and Jake eyed each other again. There could be something in this after all. Butch was twenty, had a fast car, could play a little bit on the harmonica, bought his own beer, cussed in front of adults, and most importantly, he had been seen with women.

Buddy continued. "Her name's Sally. Butch said she cost five dollars. He's done her a few times. Got her name off a bathroom wall."

"She cost?" Wilson asked.

"Think some gal's going to do us all without some money for it?" Buddy said.

Again, an unspoken signal passed between Wilson and Jake. There could be truth in that.

"Butch gave me her address, said her pimp sits on the front porch and you go right up and negotiate with him. Says you talk right, he might take four."

"I don't know," Wilson siad. "I ain't never paid for it."

"Me neither," said Jake.

"Ain't neither one of you ever had any at all, let alone paid for it," Buddy said.

Once more, Wilson and Jake were struck with the hard and painful facts.

Buddy looked at their faces and smiled. He took another sip of beer. "Well, you bring your five dollars, and I reckon you can tag along with me. Come by the house about dark and we'll walk over together."

"Yeah, well, all right," Wilson said. "I wish we had a car."

"Keep wishing," Buddy said. "You boys hang with me, we'll all be riding in Carrington's old Chevy before long. I've got some prospects."

* * *

It was just about dark when Wilson and Jake got over to Buddy's neighborhood, which was a long street with four houses on it widely spaced. Buddy's house was the ugliest of the four. It looked ready to nod off its concrete blocks at any moment and go crashing into the unkempt yard and die in a heap of rotting lumber and squeaking nails. Great strips of graying Sherwin Williams flat-white paint hung from it in patches, giving it the appearance of having a skin disease. The roof was tin and loved the sun and pulled it in and held it so that the interior basked in a sort of slow simmer until well after sundown. Even now, late in the day, a rush of heat came off the roof and rippled down the street like the last results of a nuclear wind.

Wilson and Jake came up on the house from the side, not wanting to go to the door. Buddy's mother was a grumpy old bitch in a brown bathrobe and bunny rabbit slippers with an ear missing on the left foot. No one had ever seen her wearing anything else, except now and then she added a shower cap to her uniform, and no one had ever seen her, with or without the showercap, except through the screenwire door. She wasn't thought to leave the house. She played radio contests and had to be near the radio at strategic times throughout the day so she could phone if she knew the answer to something. She claimed to be listening for household tips, but no one had ever seen her apply any. She also watched her daughter's soap operas, though she never owned up to it. She always pretended to be reading, kept a Reader's Digest cracked so she could look over it and see the tv.

She wasn't friendly either. Times Wilson and Jake had come over before, she'd met them at the screen door and wouldn't let them in. She wouldn't even talk to them. She'd call back to Buddy inside, "Hey, those hoodlum friends of yours are here."

Neither Wilson or Jake could see any sort of relationship developing between them and Buddy's mother, and they had stopped trying. They hung around outside the house under the open windows until Buddy came out. There were always interesting things to hear while they waited. Wilson told Jake it was educational.

This time, as before, they sidled up close to the house where they could hear. The television was on. A laugh track drifted out to them. That meant Buddy's sister LuWanda was in there watching. If it wasn't on, it meant she was asleep. Like her mother, she was drawing a check. Back problems plagued the family. Except for

Buddy's pa. His back was good. He was in prison for sticking up a liquor store. What little check he was getting for making license plates probably didn't amount to much.

Now they could hear Buddy's mother. Her voice had a quality that made you think of someone trying to talk while fatally injured; like she was lying under an overturned refrigerator, or had been thrown free of a car and had hit a tree.

"LuWanda, turn that thing down. You know I got bad feet."

"You don't listen none with your feet, Mama," LuWanda said. Her voice was kind of slow and lazy, faintly squeaky, as if hoisted from her throat by a hand-over pulley.

"No," Buddy's mother said. "But I got to get up on my old tired feet and come in here and tell you to turn it down."

"I can hear you yelling from the bedroom good enough when your radio ain't too high."

"But you still don't turn it down."

"I turn it down anymore, I won't be able to hear it."

"Your old tired mother, she ought to get some respect."

"You get about half my check," LuWanda said, "ain't that enough. I'm gonna get out of here when I have the baby."

"Yeah, and I bet that's some baby, way you lay up with anything's got pants."

"I hardly never leave the house to get the chance," LuWanda said. "It was pa done it before he tried to knock-over that liquor store."

"Watch your mouth, young lady. I know you let them in through the windows. I'll be glad to see you go, way you lie around here an watch that old tv. You ought to do something educational. Read the Reader's Digest like I do. There's tips for living in those, and you could sure profit some."

"Could be something to that all right," LuWanda said. "Pa read the Reader's Digest and he's over in Huntsville. I bet he likes there better than here. I bet he has a better time come night."

"Don't you start that again, young lady."

"Way he told me," LuWanda said, "I was always better with him than you was."

"I'm putting my hands right over my ears at those lies. I won't hear them."

"He sure had him a thrust, didn't he Mama?"

"Ooooh, you . . . you little shit, if I should say such a thing.

You'll get yours in hell, sister."

"I been getting plenty of hell here."

Wilson leaned against the house under the window and whispered to Jake. "Where the hell's Buddy?"

This was answered by Buddy's mother's shrill voice. "Buddy, you are *not* going out of this house wearing them nigger shoes."

"Oh, Mama," Buddy said, "these ain't nigger shoes. I bought these over at K-Woolens."

"That's right where the niggers buy their things," she said.

"Ah Mama," Buddy said.

"Don't you Mama me. You march right back in there and take off them shoes and put on something else. And get you a pair of pants that don't fit so tight people can tell which side it's on."

A moment later a window down from Wilson and Jake went up slowly. A hand holding a pair of shoes stuck out. The hand dropped the shoes and disappeared.

Then the screen door slammed and Wilson and Jake edged around to the corner of the house for a peek. It was Buddy coming out, and his mother's voice came after him, "Don't you come back to this house with a disease, you hear?"

"Ah, Mama," Buddy said.

Buddy was dressed in a long-sleeved paisley shirt with the sleeves rolled up so tight over his biceps they bulged as if actually full of muscle. He had on a pair of striped bell-bottoms and tennis shoes. His hair was combed high and hard and it lifted up on one side; it looked as if an oily squirrel were clinging precariously to the side of his head.

When Buddy saw Wilson and Jake peeking around the corner of the house, his chest got full and he walked off the porch with a cool step. His mother yelled from inside the house, "And don't walk like you got a corncob up you."

That cramped Buddy's style a little, but he sneered and went around the corner of the house trying to look like a man who knew things.

"Guess you boys are ready to stretch a little meat," Buddy said. He paused to locate an almost flat half-pack of Camels in his back pocket. He pulled a cigarette out and got a match from his shirt pocket and grinned and held his hand by his cheek and popped the match with his thumb. It sparked and he lit the cigarette and puffed. "Those things with filters, they're for sissies."

"Give us one of those," Wilson said.

"Yeah, well, all right, but this is it," Buddy said. "Only pack I got till I collect some money owed me."

Wilson and Jake stuck smokes in their faces and Buddy snapped another match and lit them up. Wilson and Jake coughed some smoke clouds.

"Sshhhh," Buddy said. "The old lady'll hear you."

They went around to the back window where Buddy had dropped the shoes and Buddy picked them up and took off the ones he had on and slipped on the others. They were smooth and dark and made of alligator hide. Their toes were pointed. Buddy wet his thumb and removed a speck of dirt from one of them. He put his tennis shoes under the house, brought a flat little bottle of clear liquid out from there.

"Hooch," Buddy said, and winked. "Bought it off Old Man Hoyt."

"Hoyt?" Wilson said. "He sells hooch?"

"Makes it himself," Buddy said. "Get you a quart for five dollars. Got five dollars and he'll sell to bottle babies."

Buddy saw Wilson eyeing his shoes appreciatively.

"Mama don't like me wearing these," he said. "I have to sneak them out."

"They're cool," Jake said. "I wish I had me a pair like 'em."

"You got to know where to shop," Buddy said.

As they walked the night became rich and cool and the moon went up and it was bright with a fuzzy ring around it. Crickets chirped. The streets they came to were little more than clay, but there were more houses than in Buddy's neighborhood, and they were in better shape. Some of the yards were mowed. The lights were on in the houses along the street, and the three of them could hear televisions talking from inside houses as they walked.

They finished off the street and turned onto another that was bordered by deep woods. They crossed a narrow wooden bridge that went over Mud Creek. They stopped and leaned on the bridge railing and watched the dark water in the moonlight. Wilson remembered when he was ten and out shooting birds with a BB gun, he had seen a dead squirrel in the water, floating out from under the bridge, face down, as if it were snorkling. He had watched it sail on down the creek and out of sight. He had popped at it and all around it with his BB gun for as long as the gun had the distance. The memory made him nostalgic for his youth and he tried to remember what he had done with his old Daisy air rifle. Then it came to him that his dad had probably pawned it. He did that sort of thing now and then, when he fell off the wagon. Suddenly a lot of missing items over the years began to come together. He'd have to get him some kind of trunk with a lock on it and nail it to the floor or something. It wasn't nailed down, it and everything in it might end up at the pawn shop for strangers to paw over.

They walked on and finally came to a long street with houses at the end of it and the lights there seemed less bright and the windows the lights came out of much smaller.

"That last house before the street crosses," Buddy said, "that's the one we want."

Wilson and Jake looked where Buddy was pointing. The house was dark except for a smudgy porch light and a sick yellow glow that shone from behind a thick curtain. Someone was sitting on the front porch doing something with their hands. They couldn't tell anything about the person or about what the person was doing. From that distance the figure could have been whittling or masturbating.

"Ain't that nigger town on the other side of the street?" Jake said. "This gal we're after, she a nigger? I don't know I'm ready to fuck a nigger. I heard my old man say to a friend of his that Mammy Clewson will give a hand job for a dollar and a half. I might go that from a nigger, but I don't know about putting it in one."

"House we want is on this side of the street, before nigger town," Buddy said. "That's a full four foot difference. She ain't a nigger. She's white trash."

"Well . . . all right," Jake said. "That's different."

"Everybody take a drink," Buddy said, and he unscrewed the lid on the fruit jar and took a jolt. "Wheee. Straight from the horse."

Buddy passed the jar to Wilson and Wilson drank and nearly threw it up. "Goddamn," he said. "Goddamn. He must run that stuff through a radiator hose or something."

Jake took a turn, shivered as if in the early throes of an epileptic fit. He gave the jar back to Buddy. Buddy screwed the lid on and they walked on down the street, stopped opposite the house they wanted and looked at the man on the front porch, for they could clearly see now it was a man. He was old and toothless and he was shelling peas from a big paper sack into a little white wash pan.

"That's the pimp," Buddy whispered. He opened up the jar and took a sip and closed it and gave it to Wilson to hold. "Give me your money."

They gave him their five dollars.

"I'll go across and make the arrangements," Buddy said. "When I signal, come on over. The pimp might prefer we go in the house one at a time. Maybe you can sit on the porch. I don't know yet."

The three smiled at each other. The passion was building.

Buddy straightened his shoulders, pulled his pants up, and went across the street. He called a howdy to the man on the porch.

"Who the hell are you?" the old man said. It sounded as if his tongue got in the way of his words.

Buddy went boldly up to the house and stood at the porch steps. Wilson and Jake could hear him from where they stood, shuffling their feet and sipping from the jar. He said, "We come to buy a little pussy. I hear you're the man to supply it."

"What's that?" the old man said, and he stood up. When he did, it was obvious he had a problem with his balls. The right side of his pants looked to have a baby's head in it.

"I was him," Jake whispered to Wilson, "I'd save up my share of that pussy money and get me a truss."

"What is that now?" the old man was going on. "What is that you're saying, you little shit?"

"Well now," Buddy said cocking a foot on the bottom step of the porch like someone who meant business, "I'm not asking for free. I've got fifteen dollars here. It's five a piece ain't it? We're not asking for anything fancy. We just want to lay a little pipe."

A pale light went on inside the house and a plump, blond girl appeared at the screen door. She didn't open it. She stood there looking out.

"Boy, what in hell are you talking about?" the old man said. "You got the wrong house."

"No one here named Sally?" Buddy asked.

The old man turned his head toward the screen and looked at the plump girl.

"I don't know him, Papa," she said. "Honest."

"You sonofabitch," the old man said to Buddy, and he waddled down the step and swung an upward blow that hit Buddy under the chin and flicked his squirrel-looking hair-do out of shape, sent him hurtling into the front yard. The old man got a palm under his oversized balls and went after Buddy, walking like he had something heavy tied to one leg. Buddy twisted around to run and the old man kicked out and caught him one in the seat of the pants, knocked him stumbling into the street.

"You little bastard," the old man yelled, "don't you come sniffing around here after my daughter again, or I'll cut your nuts off."

Then the old man saw Wilson and Jake across the street. Jake, unable to stop himself, nervously lifted a hand and waved.

"Git on out of here, or I'll let Blackie out," the old man said. "He'll tear your asses up."

Buddy came on across the street, trying to step casually, but moving briskly just the same. "I'm gonna get that fucking Butch," he said.

The old man found a rock in the yard and threw it at them. It whizzed by Buddy's ear and he and Jake and Wilson stepped away lively.

Behind them they heard a screen door slam and the plump girl whined something and there was a whapping sound, like a fan belt come loose on a big truck, then they heard the plump girl yelling for mercy and the old man cried "Slut" once, and they were out of there, across the street, into the black side of town.

They walked along a while, then Jake said, "I guess we could find Mammy Clewson."

"Oh, shut up," Buddy said. "Here's your five dollars back. Here's both your five dollars back. The both of you can get her to do it for you till your money runs out."

"I was just kidding," Jake said.

"Well don't," Buddy said. "That Butch, I catch him, right in the kisser, man. I don't care how big and mean he is. Right in the kisser."

They walked along the street and turned left up another. "Let's get out of boogie town," Buddy said. "All these niggers around here, it makes me nervous."

When they were well up the street and there were no houses, they turned down a short dirt street with a bridge in the middle of it that went over the Sabine river. It wasn't a big bridge because the river was narrow there. Off to the right was a wide pasture. To the left a church. They crossed into the back church yard. There were a couple of wooden pews sitting out there under an oak. Buddy went over there and sat down.

"I thought you wanted to get away from the boogies?" Wilson said.

"Naw," Buddy said. "This is all right. This is fine. I'd like for a nigger to start something. I would. That old man back there hadn't been so old and had his balls fucked up like that, I'd have kicked his ass."

"We wondered what was holding you back," Wilson said.

Buddy looked at Wilson, didn't see any signs of sarcasm.

"Yeah, well, that was it. Give me the jar. There's some other women I know about. We might try something later on, we feel like it."

But a cloud of unspoken resignation, as far as pussy was concerned, had passed over them, and they labored beneath its darkness with their fruit jar of hooch. They sat and passed the jar around and the night got better and brighter. Behind them, off in the woods, they could hear the Sabine river running along. Now and then a car would go down or up the street, cross over the bridge with a rumble, and pass out of sight beyond the church, or if heading in the other direction, out of sight behind trees.

Buddy began to see the night's fiasco as funny. He mellowed. "That Butch, he's something, ain't he? Some joke, huh?"

"It was pretty funny," Jake said, "seeing that old man and his balls coming down the porch after you. That thing was any more ruptured, he'd need a wheel barrow to get from room to room. Shit, I bet he couldn't have turned no dog on us. He'd had one in there, it'd have barked."

"Maybe he calls Sally Blackie," Wilson said. "Man, we're better off she didn't take money. You see that face. She could scare crows."

"Shit," Buddy said, sniffing at the jar of hooch. "I think Hoyt puts hair oil in this. Don't that smell like Vitalis to you?"

He held it under Wilson's nose, then Jake's.

"It does," Wilson said. "Right now, I wouldn't care if it smelled like sewer. Give me another swig."

"No," Buddy said standing up, wobbling, holding the partially filled jar in front of him. "Could be we've discovered a hair tonic we could sell. Buy it from Hoyt for five, sell it to guys to put on their heads for ten. We could go into business with Old Man Hoyt. Make a fortune."

Buddy poured some hooch into his palm and rubbed it into his hair, fanning his struggling squirrel-do into greater disarray. He gave the jar to Jake, got out his comb and sculptured his hair with it. Hooch ran down from his hairline and along his nose and cheeks. "See that," he said, holding out his arms as if he were styling. "Shit holds like glue."

Buddy seemed an incredible wit suddenly. They all laughed. Buddy got his cigarettes and shook one out for each of them. They lipped them. They smiled at one another. They were great friends. This was a magnificent and important moment in their lives. This night would live in memory forever.

Buddy produced a match, held it close to his cheek like always, smiled and flicked it with his thumb. The flaming head of the match jumped into his hair and lit the alcohol Buddy had combed into it. His hair flared up, and a circle of fire, like a halo for the devil, wound its way around his scalp and licked at his face and caught the hooch there on fire. Buddy screamed and bolted beserkly into a pew, tumbled over it and came up running. He looked like the Human Torch on a mission.

Wilson and Jake were stunned. They watched him run a goodly distance, circle, run back, hit the turned over pew again and go down.

Wilson yelled, "Put his head out."

Jake reflexively tossed the contents of the fruit jar at Buddy's head, realizing his mistake a moment too late. But it was like when he waved at Sally's pa. He couldn't help himself.

Buddy did a short tumble, came up still burning; in fact, he appeared to be more on fire than before. He ran straight at Wilson and Jake, his tongue out and flapping flames.

Wilson and Jake stepped aside and Buddy went between them, sprinted across the church yard toward the street.

"Throw dirt on his head!" Wilson said. Jake threw down the jar and they went after him, watching for dirt they could toss.

Buddy was fast for someone on fire. He reached the street well ahead of Wilson and Jake and any discovery of available dirt. But he didn't cross the street fast enough to beat the dump truck. Its headlights hit him first, then the left side of the bumper clipped him on the leg and he did a high complete flip, his blazing head resembling some sort of wheeled fireworks display. He landed on the bridge railing on the far side of the street with a crack of bone and a barking noise. With a burst of flames around his head, he fell off the bridge and into the water below.

The dump truck locked up its brakes and skidded.

Wilson and Jake stopped running. They stood looking at the spot where Buddy had gone over, paralyzed with disbelief.

The dump truck driver, a slim white man in overalls and a cap, got out of the truck and stopped at the rear of it, looked at where Buddy had gone over, looked up and down the street. He didn't seem to notice Wilson and Jake. He walked briskly back to the truck, got in, gunned the motor. The truck went away fast, took a right on the next street hard enough the tires protested like a cat with its tail in a crack. It backfired once, then there was only the distant sound of the motor and gears being rapidly shifted.

"Sonofabitch!" Wilson yelled.

He and Jake ran to the street, paused, looked both ways in case of more dump trucks, and crossed. They glanced over the railing.

Buddy lay with his lower body on the bank. His left leg was twisted so that his shoe pointed in the wrong direction. His dark, crisp head was in the water. He was straining his neck to lift his blackened, eyeless face out of the water; white wisps of smoke swirled up from it and carried with it the smell of barbecued meat. His body shifted. He let out a groan.

"Goddamn," Wilson said. "He's alive. Let's get him."

But at that moment there was splashing in the water. A log came sailing down the river, directly at Buddy's head. The log opened its mouth and grabbed Buddy by the head and jerked him off the shore. A noise like walnuts being cracked and a muffled scream drifted up to Wilson and Jake.

"An alligator," Jake said, and noted vaguely how closely its skin and Buddy's shoes matched.

Wilson darted around the railing, slid down the incline to the water's edge. Jake followed. They ran alongside the bank.

The water turned extremely shallow, and they could see the shadowy shape of the gator as it waddled forward, following the path of the river, still holding Buddy by the head. Buddy stuck out of the side of its mouth like a curmudgeon's cigar. His arms were flapping and so was his good leg.

Wilson and Jake paused running and tried to get their breath. After some deep inhalations, Wilson said, "Gets in the deep water, it's all over." He grabbed up an old fence post that had washed onto the bank and began running again, yelling at the gator as he went. Jake looked about, but didn't see anything to hit with. He ran after Wilson.

The gator, panicked by the noisy pursuit, crawled out of the shallows and went into the high grass of a connecting pasture, ducking under the bottom strand of a barbed wire fence. The wire caught one of Buddy's flailing arms and ripped a flap of flesh from it six inches long. Once on the other side of the wire his good leg kicked up and the fine shine on his alligator shoes flashed once in the moonlight and fell down.

Wilson went through the barb wire and after the gator with his fence post. The gator was making good time, pushing Buddy before it, leaving a trail of mashed grass behind it. Wilson could see it's tail weaving in the moonlight. It's stink trailed behind it like fumes from a busted muffler.

Wilson put the fence post on his shoulder and ran as hard as he could, managed to close in. Behind him came Jake, huffing and puffing.

Wilson got alongside the gator and hit him in the tail with the fence post. The gator's tail whipped out and caught Wilson's ankles and knocked his feet from under him. He came down hard on his butt and lost the fence post.

Jake grabbed up the post and broke right as the gator turned in that direction. He caught the beast sideways and brought the post down on its head, and when it hit, Buddy's blood jumped out of the gator's mouth and landed in the grass and on Jake's shoes. In the moonlight it was the color of cough syrup.

Jake went wild. He began to hit the gator brutally, running alongside it, following its every twist and turn. He swung the fence post mechanically, slamming the gator in the head. Behind him Wilson was saying, "You're hurting Buddy, you're hurting Buddy," but Jake couldn't stop, the frenzy was on him. Gator blood was flying, bursting out of the top of the reptile's head. Still, it held to Buddy, not giving up an inch of head. Buddy wasn't thrashing or kicking anymore. His legs slithered along in the grass as the gator ran; he looked like one of those dummies they throw off cliffs in old cowboy movies.

Wilson caught up, started kicking the gator in the side. The gator started rolling and thrashing and Jake and Wilson hopped like

rabbits and yelled. Finally the gator quit rolling. It quit crawling. Its sides heaved.

Jake continued to pound it with the post and Wilson continued to kick it. Eventually its sides quit swelling. Jake kept hitting it with the post until he staggered back and fell down in the grass exhausted. He sat there looking at the gator and Buddy. The gator trembled suddenly and spewed gator shit into the grass. It didn't move again.

After a few minutes, Wilson said, "I don't think Buddy's alive."

Just then, Buddy's body twitched.

"Hey, hey, you see that?" Jake said.

Wilson was touched with wisdom. "He's alive, the gator might be too."

Wilson got on his knees about six feet from the gator's mouth and bent over to see if he could see Buddy in there. All he could see were the gator's rubbery lips and the sides of its teeth and a little of Buddy's head shredded between them, like gray cheese on a grater. He could smell both the sour smell of the gator and the stink of burnt meat.

"I don't know if he's alive or not," Wilson said. "Maybe if we could get him out of its mouth, we could tell more."

Jake tried to wedge the fence post into the gator's mouth, but that didn't work. It was as if the great jaw was locked with a key.

They watched carefully, but Buddy didn't show any more signs of life.

"I know," Wilson said. "We'll carry him and the gator up to the road, find a house and get some help."

The gator was long and heavy. The best they could do was get hold of its tail and pull it and Buddy along. Jake managed this with the fence post under his arm. He didn't trust the gator and wouldn't give it up.

They went across an acre of grass and came to a barbed wire fence that bordered the street where Buddy had been hit by the dump truck. The bridge was in sight.

They let go of the gator and climbed through the wire. Jake used the fence post to lift up the bottom strand, and Wilson got hold of the gator's tail and tugged the beast under, along with Buddy.

Pulling the gator and Buddy alongside the road, they watched for house lights. They went past the church on the opposite side of the road and turned left where the dump truck had turned right and backfired. They went alongside the street there, occasionally allowing the gator and Buddy to weave over into the street itself. It was hard work steering a gator and its lunch.

They finally came to a row of houses. The first one had an old Ford pickup parked out beside it and lot of junk piled in the yard. Lawn mowers, oily rope, overturned freezers, wheels, fishing reels and line, bicycle parts, and a busted commode. A tarp had been pulled half-heartedly over a tall stack of old shop creepers. There was a light on behind one window. The rest of the houses were dark.

Jake and Wilson let go of the gator in the front yard, and Wilson went up on the porch, knocked on the door, stepped off the porch and waited.

Briefly thereafter, the door opened a crack and a man called out, "Who's out there? Don't you know it's bed time?"

"We seen your light on," Wilson said.

"I was in the shitter. You trying to sell me a brush or a book or something this time of night, I won't be in no good temper about it. I'm not through shitting either."

"We got a man hurt here," Wilson said. "A gator bit him."

There was a long moment of quiet. "What you want me to do? I don't know nothin' about no gator bites. I don't even know who you are. You might be with the Ku Kluxers."

"He's . . . He's kind of hung up with the gator," Wilson said.

"Just a minute," said the voice.

Moments later a short, fat black man came out. He was shirtless and barefooted, wearing overalls with the straps off his shoulders, dangling at his waist. He had a ball bat in his hand. He came down the steps and looked at Wilson and Jake carefully, as if expecting them to spring. "You stand away from me with that fence post, hear," he said. Jake took a step back and this seemed to satisfy the man. He took a look at the gator and Buddy.

He went back up the porch and reached inside the door and turned on the porch light. A child's face stuck through the crack in the door, said, "What's out there, papa?"

"You get your ass in that house, or I'll kick it," the black man said. The face disappeared.

The black man came off the porch again, looked at the gator and Buddy again, walked around them a couple of times, poked the gator with the ball bat, poked Buddy too.

He looked at Jake and Wilson. "Shit," he said. "You peckerwoods is crazy. That motherfucker's dead. He's dead enough for two men. He's deader than I ever seen anybody."

"He caught on fire," Jake offered suddenly, "and we tried to put his head out, and he got hit by a truck, knocked in the river, and the gator got him . . . We seen him twitch a little a while back . . . The fella, Buddy, not the gator, I mean."

"Them's nerves," the black man said. "You better dig a hole for this man-jack, skin that ole gator out and sell his hide. They bring a right smart price sometimes. You could probably get something for them shoes too, if'n they clean up good."

"We need you to help us load him up into your pickup and take him home," Jake said.

"You ain't putting that motherfucker in my pickup," the black man said. "I don't want no doings with you honkey motherfuckers. They'll be claiming I sicked that gator on him."

"That's silly," Wilson said. "You're acting like a fool."

"Uh-huh," said the black man, "and I'm gonna go on acting like one here in my house."

He went briskly up the porch steps, closed the door and turned out the light. A latch was thrown.

Wilson began to yell. He used the word nigger indiscriminately. He ran up on the porch and pounded on the door. He cussed a lot.

Doors of houses down the way opened up and people moved onto their front porches like shadows, looked at where the noise was coming from.

Jake, standing there in the yard with his fence post, looked like a man with a gun. The gator and Buddy could have been the body of their neighbor. The shadows watched Jake and listened to Wilson yell a moment, then went back inside.

"Goddamn you," Wilson yelled. "Come on out of there so I can whip your ass, you hear me? I'll whip your black ass."

"You come on in here, cocksucker," came the black man's voice from the other side of the door. "Come on in, you think you can. You do, you'll be trying to shit you some twelve gauge shot, that's what you'll be trying to do."

At mention of the twelve gauge, Wilson felt a certain calm descend on him. He began to acquire perspective. "We're leaving," he said to the door. "Right now." He backed off the porch. He spoke softly so only Jake could hear: "Boogie motherfucker."

"What we gonna do now?" Jake said. He sounded tired. All the juice had gone out of him.

"I reckon," Wilson said, "we got to get Buddy and the gator on over to his house."

"I don't think we can carry him that far," Jake said. "My back is hurting already."

Wilson looked at the junk beside the house. "Wait a minute." He went over to the junk pile and got three shop creepers out from under the tarp and found some hanks of rope. He used the rope to tie the creepers together, end to end. When he looked up, Jake was standing beside him, still holding the fence post. "You go on and stay by Buddy," Wilson said. "Turn your back too long, them niggers will be all over them shoes."

Jake went back to his former position.

Wilson collected several short pieces of rope and a twist of wire and tied them together and hooked the results to one of the creepers and used it as a handle. He pulled his contraption around front by Buddy and the gator. "Help me put 'em on there," he said.

They lifted the gator onto the creepers. He fit with only his tail overlapping. Buddy hung to the side, off the creepers, causing them to tilt.

"That won't work," Jake said.

"Well, here now," Wilson said, and he got Buddy by the legs and turned him. The head and neck were real flexible, like they were made of chewing gum. He was able to lay Buddy straight out in front of the gator. "Now we can pull the gator down a bit, drag all of its tail. That way we got 'em both on there."

When they got the gator and Buddy arranged, Wilson doubled the rope and began pulling. At first it was slow going, but after a moment they got out in the road and the creepers gained momentum and squeaked right along. Jake used his fence post to punch at the edges of the creepers when they swung out of line.

An ancient, one-eyed Cocker Spaniel with a foot missing, came out and sat at the edge of the road and watched them pass. He barked once when the alligator's tail dragged by in the dirt behind the creepers, then he went and got under a porch.

They squeaked on until they passed the house where Sally lived. They stopped across from it for a breather and to listen. They didn't hear anyone screaming and they didn't hear any beatings going on.

They started up again, kept at it until they came to Buddy's street. It was deadly quiet, and the moon had been lost behind a cloud and everything was dark.

At Buddy's house, the silver light of the tv strobed behind the living room curtains. Wilson and Jake stopped on the far side of the street and squatted beside the creepers and considered their situation.

Wilson got in Buddy's back pocket and pulled the smokes out and found that though the package was damp from the water, a couple of cigarettes were dry enough to smoke. He gave one to Jake and took the other for himself. He got a match from Buddy's shirt pocket and struck it on a creeper, but it was too damp to light.

"Here," Jake said, and produced a lighter. "I stole this from my old man in case I ever got any cigarettes. It works most of the time." Jake clicked it repeatedly and finally it sparked well enough to light. They lit up.

"We knock on the door, his mom is gonna be mad," Jake said. "Us bringing home Buddy and an alligator, and Buddy wearing them shoes."

"Yeah," Wilson said. "You know, she don't know he went off with us. We could put him in the yard. Maybe she'll think the gator attacked him there."

"What for," Jake said, "them shoes? He recognized his aunt or something?" He began laughing at his own joke, but if Wilson got it he didn't give a sign. He seemed to be thinking. Jake quit laughing, scratched his head and looked off down the street. He tried to smoke his cigarette in a manful manner.

"Gators come up in yards and eat dogs now and then," Wilson said after a long silence. "We could leave him, and if his Mama don't believe a gator jumped him, that'll be all right. The figuring of it will be a town mystery. Nobody would ever know what happened. Those niggers won't be talking. And if they do, they don't know us from anybody else anyway. We all look alike to them."

"I was Buddy," Jake said, "that's the way I'd want it if I had a couple friends involved."

"Yeah, well," Wilson said, "I don't know I really liked him so much."

Jake thought about that. "He was all right. I bet he wasn't going to get that Chevy though."

"If he did," Wilson said, "there wouldn't have been no motor in it, I can promise you that. And I bet he never got any pussy neither."

They pulled the creepers across the road and tipped gator and Buddy onto the ground in front of the porch steps.

"That'll have to do," Wilson whispered.

Wilson crept up on the porch and over to the window, looked through a crack in the curtain and into the living room. Buddy's sister lay on the couch asleep, her mouth open, her huge belly bobbing up and down as she breathed. A half-destroyed bag of Cheetos lay beside the couch. The tv light flickered over her like saintly fire.

Jake came up on the porch and took a look.

"Maybe if she lost some pounds and fixed her hair different," he said.

"Maybe if she was somebody else," Wilson said.

They sat on the porch steps in the dark and finished smoking their cigarettes, watching the faint glow of the television through the curtain, listening to the tinny sound of a late night talk show.

When Jake finished his smoke, he pulled the alligator shoes off Buddy and checked them against the soles of his own shoes. "I think these dudes will fit me. We can't leave 'em on him. His Mama sees them, she might not consent to bury him."

He and Wilson left out of there then, pulling the creepers after them.

Not far down the road, they pushed the creepers off in a ditch and continued, Jake carrying the shoes under his arm. "These are all right," he said. "I might can get some pussy wearing these kind of shoes. My Mama don't care if I wear things like this."

"Hell, she don't care if you cut your head off," Wilson said.

"That's the way I see it," Jake said.

(For Gary Raisor)

JOURNAL ENTRIES

A week to remember . . .

After this, my little white page friend, you shall have greater security, kept under not only lock and key, but you will have a hiding place. If I were truly as smart as I sometimes think I am, I wouldn't write this down. I know better. But, I am compelled.

Compulsion. It comes out of nowhere and owns us all. We put a suit and tie and hat on the primitive part of our brain and call it manners and civilization, but ultimately, it's just a suit and tie and a hat. The primitive brain is still primitive, and it compels, pulses to the same dark beat that made our less civilized ancestors and the primordial ooze before them throb to simple, savage rhythms of sex, death and destruction.

Our nerves call out to us to touch and taste life, and without our suits of civilization, we can do that immediately. Take what we need if we've muscle enough. Will enough. But all dressed up in the trappings of civilization, we're forced to find our thrills vicariously. And eventually, that is not enough. Controlling our impulses that way is like having someone eat our food for us. No taste. No texture. No nourishment. Pitiful business.

Without catering to the needs of our primitive brains, without feeding impulses, trying instead to get what we need through books and films and the lives of the more adventurous, we cease to live. We wither. We bore ourselves and others. We die. And are glad of it.

Whatcha gonna do, huh?

JOE R. LANSDALE

Saturday Morning, June 10th, Through Saturday 17th:

I haven't written in a while, so I'll cover a few days, beginning with a week ago today.

It was one of those mornings when I woke up on the wrong side of the bed, feeling a little out of sorts, mad at the wife over something I've forgotten and she probably hasn't forgotten, and we grumbled down the hall, into the kitchen, and there's our dog, a Siberian Husky—my wife always refers to him as a Suburban Husky because of his pampered life style, though any resemblance to where we live and suburbia requires a great deal of faith—and he's smiling at us, and then we see why he's smiling. Two reasons: (1) He's happy to see us. (2) He feels a little guilty.

He has reason to feel guilty. Not far behind him, next to the kitchen table, was a pile of shit. I'm not talking your casual little whoopsie-doo, and I'm not talking your inconvenient pile, and I'm not talking six to eight turds the size of large bananas. I'm talking a certified, pure-dee, goddamn prize winning SHIT. There were enough dog turds there to shovel out in a pickup truck and dump on the lawn and let dry so you could use them to build a adobe hut big enough to park your car in.

And right beside this sterling deposit, was a lake of piss wide enough and deep enough to go rowing on.

I had visions of a Siberian Husky hat and slippers, or possibly a nice throw rug for the bedroom, a necklace of dog claws and teeth; maybe cut that smile right out of his face and frame it.

But the dog-lover in me took over, and I put him outside in his pen where he cooled his dew-claws for a while. Then I spent about a half-hour cleaning up dog shit while my wife spent the same amount of time keeping our two year old son, Kevin, known to me as Fruit of My Loins, out of the shit.

Yep, Oh Great White Page of a Diary, he was up now. It always works that way. In times of greatest stress, in times of greatest need for contemplation or privacy, like when you're trying to get that morning piece off the Old Lady, the kid shows up, and suddenly it's as if you've been deposited inside an ant farm and the ants are crawling and stinging. By the time I finished cleaning up the mess, it was time for breakfast, and I got to tell you, I didn't want anything that looked like link sausage that morning.

THE PHONE WOMAN

So Janet and I ate, hoping that what we smelled while eating was the aroma of disinfectant and not the stench of shit wearing a coat of disinfectant, and we watched the kid spill his milk eighty-lebben times and throw food and drop stuff on the floor, and me and the wife we're fussing at each other more and more, about whatever it was we were mad about that morning—a little item intensified by our dog's deposits—and by the time we're through eating our meal, and Janet leaves me with Fruit of My Loins and his View Master and goes out to the laundry room to do what the room is named for—probably went out there to beat the laundry clean with rocks or bricks, pretending shirts and pants were my head—I'm beginning to think things couldn't get worse. About that time the earth passes through the tail of a comet or something, some kind of dimensional gate is opened, and the world goes weird.

There's a knock at the door.

At first I thought it was a bird pecking on the glass, it was that soft. Then it came again and I went to the front door and opened it, and there stood a woman about five-feet tall wearing a long, wool coat, and untied, flared-at-the-ankles shoes, and a ski cap decorated with a silver pin. The wool ski cap was pulled down so tight over her ears her face was pale. Keep in mind that it was probably eighty degrees that morning, and the temperature was rising steadily, and she was dressed like she was on her way to plant the flag at the summit of Everest. Her age was hard to guess. Had that kind of face. She could have been twenty-two or forty-two.

She said, "Can I use your phone, mister? I got an important call to make."

Well, I didn't see any ready-to-leap companions hiding in the shrubbery, and I figured if she got out of line I could handle her, so I said, "Yeah, sure. Be my guest," and let her in.

The phone was in the kitchen, on the wall, and I pointed it out to her, and me and Fruit of My Loins went back to doing what we were doing, which was looking at the View Master. We switched from Goofy to Winnie the Pooh, the one about Tigger in the tree, and it was my turn to look at it, and I couldn't help but hear that my guest's conversation with her mother was becoming stressful—I knew it was her mother because she addressed her by that title—and suddenly Fruit of My Loins yelled, "Wook, Daddy Wook."

I turned and "wooked", and what do I see but what appears to be some rare tribal dance, possibly something having originated in higher altitudes where the lack of oxygen to the brain causes wilder abandon with the dance steps. This gal was all over the place. Fred Astair with a hot coat hanger up his ass couldn't have been any brisker. I've never seen anything like it. Then, in mid-dossey-do, she did a leap like cheerleaders do, one of those things where they kick their legs out to the side, open up like a nut-cracker and kick the palms of their hands, then she hit the floor on her ass, spun, and wheeled as if on a swivel into the hallway and went out of sight. Then there came a sound from in there like someone on speed beating the bongos. She hadn't dropped the phone either. The wire was stretched tight around the corner and was vibrating like a big fish was on the line.

I dashed over there and saw she was lying crosswise in the hallway, bamming her head against the wall, clutching at the phone with one hand and pulling her dress up over her waist with the other, and she was making horrible sounds and rolling her eyes, and I immediately thought: this is it, she's gonna die. Then I saw she wasn't dying, just thrashing, and I decided it was an epileptic fit.

I got down and took the phone away from her, took hold of her jaw, got her tongue straight without getting bit, stretched her out on the floor away from the wall, picked up the phone and told her mama, who was still fussing about something or another, that things weren't so good, hung up on her in mid-sentence and called the ambulance.

I ran out to the laundry room, told Janet a strange woman was in our hallway pulling her dress over her head and that an ambulance was coming. Janet, bless her heart, has become quite accustomed to weird events following me around, and she went outside to direct the ambulance, like one of those people at the airport with light sticks.

I went back to the woman and watched her thrash awhile, trying to make sure she didn't choke to death, or injure herself, and Fruit of My Loins kept clutching my leg and asking me what was wrong. I didn't know what to tell him.

After what seemed a couple of months and a long holiday, the ambulance showed up with a whoop of siren, and I finally decided the lady was doing as good as she was going to do, so I went outside. On either side of my walk were all these people. It's like Bradbury's story "The Crowd". The one where when there's an accident all these strange people show up out of nowhere and stand around and watch.

THE PHONE WOMAN

I'd never seen but two of these people before in my life, and I've been living in this neighborhood for years.

One lady immediately wanted to go inside and pray for the woman, who she somehow knew, but Janet whispered to me there wasn't enough room for our guest in there, let alone this other woman and her buddy, God, so I didn't let her in.

All the other folks are just a jabbering, and about all sorts of things. One woman said to another: "Mildred, how you been?"

"I been good. They took my kids away from me this morning, though. I hate that. How you been?"

"Them hogs breeding yet?" one man says to another, and the other goes into not only are they breeding, but he tells how much fun they're having at it.

Then here comes the ambulance boys with a stretcher. One of the guys knew me somehow, and he stopped and said, "You're that writer, aren't you?"

I admitted it.

"I always wanted to write. I got some ideas that's make a good book and a movie. I'll tell you about 'em. I got good ideas, I just can't write them down. I could tell them to you and you could write them up and we could split the money."

"Could we talk about this later?" I said. "There's a lady in there thrashing in my hallway."

So they went in with the stretcher, and after a few minutes the guy I talked to came out and said, "We can't get her out of there and turned through the door. We may have to take your back door out."

That made no sense to me at all. They brought the stretcher through and now they were telling me they couldn't carry it out. But I was too addled to argue and told them to do what they had to do.

Well, they managed her out the back door without having to remodel our home after all, and when they came around the edge of the house I heard the guy I'd talked to go, "Ahhh, damn, I'd known it was her I wouldn't have come."

I thought they were going to set her and the stretcher down right there, but they went on out to the ambulance and jerked open the door and tossed her and the stretcher inside like they were tossing a dead body over a cliff. You could hear that stretcher strike the back of the ambulance and bounce forward and slide back again.

I had to ask: "You know her?"

"Dark enough in the house there, I couldn't tell at first. But when we got outside, I seen who it was. She does this all the time, but not over on this side of town in a while. She don't take her medicine on purpose so she'll have fits when she gets stressed, or she fakes them, like this time. Way she gets attention. Sometimes she hangs herself, cuts off her air. Likes the way it feels. Sexual or something. She's damn near died half-dozen times. Between you and me, wish she'd go on and do it and save me some trips."

And the ambulance driver and his assistant were out of there. No lights. No siren.

Well, the two people standing in the yard that we knew were still there when I turned around, but the others, like mythical creatures, were gone, turned to smoke, dissolved, become one with the universe, whatever. The two people we knew, elderly neighbors, said they knew the woman, who by this time, I had come to think of as the Phone Woman.

"She goes around doing that," the old man said. "She stays with her mamma who lives on the other side of town, but they get in fights on account of the girl likes to hang herself sometimes for entertainment. Never quite makes it over the ridge, you know, but gets her mother worked up. They say her mother used to do that too, hang herself, when she was a girl. She outgrew it. I guess the girl there ... you know I don't even know her name ... must have seen her mamma do that when she was little, and it kind of caught on. She has that 'lepsy stuff too, you know thrashing around and all, biting on her tongue?"

I said I knew and had seen a demonstration of it this morning.

"Anyway," he continued, "they get in fights and she comes over here and tries to stay with some relatives that live up the street there, but they don't cotton much to her hanging herself to things. She broke down their clothes line post last year. Good thing it was old, or she'd been dead. Wasn't nobody home that time. I hear tell they sometimes go off and leave her there and leave rope and wire and stuff laying around, sort of hoping, you know. But except for that time with the clothesline, she usually does her hanging when someone's around. Or she goes in to use the phone at houses and does what she did here."

"She's nutty as a fruitcake," said the old woman. "She goes back on behind here to where that little trailer park is, knocks on doors where the wet backs live, about twenty to a can, and they ain't got no phone, and she knows it. She's gotten raped couple times doing that, and it ain't just them Mex's that have got to her. White folks, niggers. She tries to pick who she thinks will do what she wants. She wants to be raped. It's like the hanging. She gets some kind of attention out of it, some kind of loving. Course, I ain't saying she chose you cause you're that kind of person."

I assured her I understood.

The old couple went home then, and another lady came up, and sure enough, I hadn't seen her before either, and she said, "Did that crazy ole girl come over here and ask to use the phone, then fall down on you and flop?"

"Yes, m'am."

"Does that all the time."

Then this woman went around the corner of the house and was gone, and I never saw her again. In fact, with the exception of the elderly neighbors and the Phone Woman, I never saw any of those people again and never knew where they came from. Next day there was a soft knock on the door. It was the Phone Woman again. She asked to use the phone.

I told her we'd had it taken out.

She went away and I saw her several times that day. She'd come up our street about once every half hour, wearing that same coat and hat and those sad shoes, and I guess it must have been a hundred and ten out there. I watched her from the window. In fact I couldn't get any writing done because I was watching for her. Thinking about her lying there on the floor, pulling her dress up, flopping. I thought too of her hanging herself now and then, like she was some kind of suit on a hanger.

Anyway, the day passed and I tried to forget about her, then the other night, Monday probably, I went out on the porch to smoke one of my rare cigars (about four to six a year), and I saw someone coming down the dark street, and from the way that someone walked, I knew it was her, the Phone Woman.

She went on by the house and stopped down the road a piece and looked up and I looked where she was looking, and through the trees I could see what she saw. The moon.

We both looked at it a while, and she finally walked on, slow, with her head down, and I put my cigar out well before it was finished and went inside and brushed my teeth and took off my clothes, and tried to go to sleep. Instead I lay there for a long time and thought about her, walking those dark streets, maybe thinking about her mom, or a lost love, or a phone, or sex in the form of rape because it was some kind of human connection, about hanging herself because it was attention and it gave her a sexual high . . . and then again, maybe I'm full of shit and she wasn't thinking about any of these things.

Then it struck me suddenly, as I lay there in bed beside my wife, in my quiet house, my son sleeping with his teddy bear in the room across the way, that maybe she was the one in touch with the world, with life, and that I was the one gone stale from civilization. Perhaps life had been civilized right out of me.

The times I had truly felt alive, in touch with my nerve centers, were in times of violence or extreme stress.

Where I had grown up, in Mud Creek, violence simmered underneath everyday life like lava cooking beneath a thin crust of earth, ready at any time to explode and spew. I had been in fights, been cut by knives. I once had a job bouncing drunks. I had been a bodyguard in my earlier years, had illegally carried a .38. On one occasion, due to a dispute the day before while protecting my employer, who sometimes dealt with a bad crowd, a man I had insulted and hit with my fists, pulled a gun on me, and I had been forced to pull mine. The both of us ended up with guns in our faces, looking into each other's eyes, knowing full well our lives hung by a thread and the snap of a trigger.

I had killed no one, and had avoided being shot. The Mexican stand-off ended with us both backing away and running off, but there had been that moment when I knew it could all be over in a flash. Out of the picture in a blaze of glory. No old folks home for me. No drool running down my chin and some young nurse wiping my ass, thinking how repulsive and old I was, wishing for quitting time so she could roll up with some young stud some place sweet and cozy, open her legs to him with a smile and a sigh, and later a passionate scream, while in the meantime, back at the old folks ranch, I lay in the bed with a dead dick and an oxygen mask strapped to my face.

Something about the Phone Woman had clicked with me. I understood her suddenly. I understood then that the lava that had boiled beneath the civilized facade of my brain was no longer boiling. It might be bubbling way down low, but it wasn't boiling, and

THE PHONE WOMAN

the realization of that went all over me and I felt sad, very, very sad. I had dug a grave and crawled into it and was slowly pulling the dirt in after me. I had a home. I had a wife. I had a son. Dirt clods all. Dirt clods filling in my grave while life simmered somewhere down deep and useless within me.

I lay there for a long time with tears on my cheeks before exhaustion took over and I slept in a dark world of dormant passion.

Couple days went by, and one night after Fruit of My Loins and Janet were in bed, I went out on the front porch to sit and look at the stars and think about what I'm working on—a novella that isn't going well—and what do I see but the Phone Woman, coming down the road again, walking past the house, stopping once more to look at the moon.

I didn't go in this time, but sat there waiting, and she went on up the street and turned right and went out of sight. I walked across the yard and went out to the center of the street and watched her back going away from me, mixing into the shadows of the trees and houses along the street, and I followed.

I don't know what I wanted to see, but I wanted to see something, and I found for some reason that I was thinking of her lying there on the floor in my hallway, her dress up, the mound of her sex, as they say in porno novels, pushing up at me. The thought gave me an erection, and I was conscious of how silly this was, how unattractive this woman was to me, how odd she looked, and then another thought came to me: I was a snob. I didn't want to feel sexual towards anyone ugly or smelly in a winter coat in the dead of summer.

But the night was cool and the shadows were thick, and they made me feel all right, romantic maybe, or so I told myself.

I moved through a neighbor's backyard where a dog barked at me a couple of times and shut up. I reached the street across the way and looked for the Phone Woman, but didn't see her.

I took a flyer, and walked on down the street toward the trailer park where those poor illegal aliens were stuffed in like sardines by their unscrupulous employers, and I saw a shadow move among shadows, and then there was a split in the trees that provided the shadows, and I saw her, the Phone Woman. She was standing in a yard under a great oak, and not far from her was a trailer. A pathetic air conditioner hummed in one of its windows.

She stopped and looked up through that split in the trees above, and I knew she was trying to find the moon again, that she had staked out spots that she traveled to at night; spots where she stood and looked at the moon or the stars or the pure and sweet black eternity between them.

Like the time before, I looked up too, took in the moon, and it was beautiful, as gold as if it were a great glob of honey. The wind moved my hair, and it seemed solid and purposeful, like a lovers soft touch, like the beginning of foreplay. I breathed deep and tasted the fragrance of the night, and my lungs felt full and strong and young.

I looked back at the woman and saw she was reaching out her hand to the moon. No, a low limb. She touched it with her finger tips. She raised her other hand, and in it was a short, thick rope. She tossed the rope over the limb and made a loop and pulled it taught to the limb. Then she tied a loop to the other end, quickly expertly, and put that around her neck.

Of course, I knew what she was going to do. But I didn't move. I could have stopped her, I knew, but what was the point? Death was the siren she had called on many a time, and finally, she had heard it sing.

She jumped and pulled her legs under her and the limb took her jump and held her. Her head twisted to the left and she spun about on the rope and the moonlight caught the silver pin on her ski cap and it threw out a cool beacon of silver light, and as she spun, it hit me once, twice, three times.

On the third spin her mouth went wide and her tongue went out and her legs dropped down and hit the ground and she dangled there, unconscious.

I unrooted my feet and walked over there, looking about as I went.

I didn't see anyone. No lights went on in the trailer.

I moved up close to her. Her eyes were open. Her tongue was out. She was swinging a little, her knees were bent and the toes and tops of her silly shoes dragged the ground. I walked around and around her, an erection pushing at my pants. I observed her closely, tried to see what death looked like.

She coughed. A little choking cough. Her eyes shifted toward

THE PHONE WOMAN

me. Her chest heaved. She was beginning to breathe. She made a feeble effort to get her feet under her, to raise her hands to the rope around her neck.

She was back from the dead.

I went to her. I took her hands, gently pulled them from her throat, let them go. I looked into her eyes. I saw the moon there. She shifted so that her legs held her weight better. Her hands went to her dress. She pulled it up to her waist. She wore no panties. Her bush was like a nest built between the boughs of a snow-white elm.

I remembered the day she came into the house. Everything since then, leading up to this moment, seemed like a kind of perverse mating ritual. I put my hand to her throat. I took hold of the rope with my other hand and jerked it so that her knees straightened, then I eased behind her, put my forearm against the rope around her throat, and I began to tighten my hold until she made a soft noise, like a virgin taking a man for the first time. She didn't lift her hands. She continued to tug her dress up. She was trembling from lack of oxygen. I pressed myself against her buttocks, moved my hips rhythmically, my hard-on bound by my underwear and pants. I tightened the pressure on her throat.

And choked her.

And choked her.

She gave up what was left of her life with a shiver and a thrusting of her pelvis, and finally she jammed her buttocks back into me and I felt myself ejaculate, thick and hot and rich as shaving foam.

Her hands fell to her side. I loosened the pressure on her throat but clung to her for a while, getting my breath and my strength back. When I felt strong enough, I let her go. She swung out and around on the rope and her knees bent and her head cocked up to stare blindly at the gap in the trees above, at the honey-golden moon.

I left her there and went back to the house and slipped into the bedroom and took off my clothes. I removed my wet underwear carefully and wiped them out with toilet paper and flushed the paper down the toilet. I put the underwear in the clothes hamper. I put on fresh and climbed into bed and rubbed my hands over my wife's buttocks until she moaned and woke up. I rolled her on her stomach and mounted her and made love to her. Hard, violent love, my forearm around her throat, not squeezing, but thinking about the Phone Woman, the sound she had made when I choked her from behind, the way her buttocks had thrust back into me at the end. I closed my eyes until in my ears the sound that Janet made was the sound the Phone Woman made and I could visualize her there in the moonlight, swinging by the rope.

When it was over, I held Janet and she kissed me and joked about my arm around her throat, about how it seemed I had wanted to choke her. We laughed a little. She went to sleep. I let go of her and moved to my side of the bed and looked at the ceiling and thought about the Phone Woman. I tried to feel guilt. I could not. She had wanted it. She had tried for it many times. I had helped her do what she had never been able to manage. And I had felt alive again. Doing something on the edge. Taking a risk.

Well, journal, here's the question: Am I a sociopath?

No. I love my wife. I love my child. I even love my Suburban husky. I have never hunted and fished, because I thought I didn't like to kill. But there are those who want to die. It is their one moment of life; to totter on the brink between light and darkness, to take the final, dark rush down a corridor of black, hot pain.

So, Oh Great White Pages, should I feel guilt, some inner torment, a fear that I am at heart a cold-blooded murderer?

I think not.

I gave the sweet gift of truly being alive to a woman who wanted someone to participate in her moment of joy. Death ended that, but without the threat of it, her moment would have been nothing. A stage rehearsal for a highschool play in street clothes.

Nor do I feel fear. The law will never suspect me. There's no reason to. The Phone Woman had a record of near suicides. It would never occur to anyone to think she had died by anyone's hand other than her own.

I feel content, in touch again with the lava beneath the primal crust. I have allowed it to boil up and burst through and flow, and now it has gone down once more. But it's no longer a distant memory. It throbs and rolls and laps just below, ready to jump and give me life. Are there others out there like me? Or better yet, others for me, like the Phone Woman?

Most certainly.

And now I will recognize them. The Phone Woman has taught me that. She came into my life on a silly morning and brought me adventure, took me away from the grind, and then she brought me more, much, much more. She helped me recognize the fine but perfect line between desire and murder; let me know that there are happy victims and loving executioners.

I will know the happy victims now when I see them, know who needs to be satisfied. I will give them their desire, while they give me mine.

This last part with the Phone Woman happened last night and I am recording it now, while it is fresh, as Janet sleeps. I think of Janet in there and I have a hard time imagining her face. I want her, but I want her to be the Phone Woman, or someone like her.

I can feel the urge rising up in me again. The urge to give someone that tremendous double-edged surge of life and death.

Its like they say about sex. Once you get it, you got to have it on a regular basis. But it isn't sex I want. It's something like it, only sweeter.

I'll wrap this up. I'm wired. Thinking that I'll have to wake Janet and take the edge off my need, imagine that she and I are going to do more than fornicate; that she wants to take that special plunge and that she wants me to shove her.

But she doesn't want that. I'd know. I have to find that in my dreams, when I nestle down into the happy depths of the primitive brain.

At least until I find someone like the Phone Woman, again, that is. Someone with whom I can commit the finest of adultry.

And until that search proves fruitful and I have something special to report, dear diary, I say, goodnight.

(For Ed Gorman)

Drive-In Date

The line into the Starlite Drive-In that night was short. Monday nights were like that. Dave and Merle paid their money at the ticket house and Dave drove the Ford to a spot up near the front where there were only a few cars. He parked in a space with no one directly on either side. On the left the first car was four speakers away, on the right, six speakers.

Dave said, "I like to be up close so it all looks bigger than life. You don't mind do you?"

"You ask me that every time," Merle said. "You don't never ask me that when we're driving in, you ask when we're parked."

"You don't like it, we can move."

"No. I like it. I'm just saying, you don't really care if I like it. You just ask."

"Politeness isn't a crime."

"No, but you ought to mean it."

"I said we can move."

"Hell no, stay where you are. I'm just saying when you ask me what I like, you could mean it."

"You're a testy motherfucker tonight. I thought coming to see a monster picture would cheer you up."

"You're the one likes 'em, and that's why you come. It wasn't for me, so don't talk like it was. I don't believe in monsters, so I can't enjoy what I'm seeing. I like something that's real. Cop movie. Things like that."

"I tell you, Merle, there's just no satisfying you, man. You'll feel better when they cut the lot lights and the movie starts. We can get our date then."

"I don't know that makes me feel better."

"You done quit liking pussy?"

"Watch your mouth. I didn't say that. You know I like pussy. I like pussy fine."

"Whoa. Aren't we fussy? Way you talk, you're trying to convince me. Maybe it's butt holes you like."

"Goddamnit, don't start on the butt holes."

Dave laughed and got out a cigarette and lipped it. "I know you did that one ole gal in the butt that night." Dave reached up and tapped the rearview mirror. "I seen you in the mirror here."

"You didn't see nothing," Merle said.

"I seen you get in her butt hole. I seen that much."

"What the hell you doing watching? It ain't good enough for you by yourself, so you got to watch someone else get theirs?"

"I don't mind watching."

"Yeah, well, I bet you don't. You're like one of those fucking perverts."

Dave snickered, popped his lighter and lit his cigarette. The lot lights went out. The big lights at the top of the drive-in screen went black. Dave rolled down the window and pulled the speaker in and fastened it to the door. He slapped at a mosquito on his neck.

"Won't be long now," Dave said.

"I don't know I feel up to it tonight."

"You don't like this first feature, the second's some kind of mystery. It might be like a cop show."

"I don't mean the movies."

"The girl?"

"Yeah. I'm in a funny mood."

Dave smoked for a moment. "Merle, this is kind of a touchy subject, but you been having trouble, you know, getting a bone to keep, I'll tell you, that happens. It's happened to me. Once."

"I'm not having trouble with my dick, okay?"

"If you are, it's no disgrace. It'll happen to a man from time to time."

"My tool is all right. It works. No problem."

"Then what's the beef?"

"I don't know. It's a mood. I feel like I'm going through a kind of, I don't know, mid-life crisis or something."

DRIVE-IN DATE

"Mood, huh? Let me tell you, when she's stretched out on that back seat, you'll be all right, crisis or no crisis. Hell, get her butt hole if you want it, I don't care."

"Don't start on me."

"Who's starting? I'm telling you, you want her butt hole, her ear, her goddamn nostril, that's your business. Me, I'll stick to the right hole, though."

"Think I don't know a snide remark when you make it?"

"I hope you do, or I wouldn't make it. You don't know I'm making one, what's the fun in making it?" Dave reached over and slapped Merle playfully on the arm. "Lighten up, boy. Let's see a movie, get some pussy. Hey, you feel better if I went and got us some corn and stuff . . . That'd do you better, wouldn't it?"

Merle hesitated. "I guess."

"Back in a jiffy."

Dave got out of the car.

Fifteen minutes and Dave was back. He had a cardboard box that held two bags of popcorn and some tall drinks. He set the box on top of the car, opened the door then got the box and slid inside. He put the box on the seat between them.

"How much I owe you?" Merle said.

"Not a thing. You get it next time . . . Think how much more expensive this would be we had to pay for her to eat too."

"A couple or three dollars. So what? That gonna break us?"

"No, but it's beer money. You think about it."

Merle sat and thought about it.

The big white drive-in screen was turned whiter by the projector light, then there was a flicker and images moved on the screen: Ads for the concession. Coming attractions.

Dave got his popcorn, started eating. He said, "I'm getting kind of horny thinking about her. You see the legs on that bitch?"

"Course I seen the legs. You don't know from legs. A woman's got legs is all you care, and you might not care about that. Couple of stumps would be all the same to you."

"No, I don't care for any stumps. Got to be feet on one end, pussy on the other. That's legs enough. But this one, she's got some

235

good ones. Hell, you're bound to've noticed how good they were."

"I noticed. You saying I'm queer or something? I noticed. I noticed she's got an ankle bracelet on the right leg and she wears about a size ten shoe. Biggest goddamn feet I've ever seen on a woman."

"Now, it comes out. You wanted to pick the date, not me?"

"I never did care for a woman with big feet. You got a good looking woman all over and you get down to them feet and they look like something goes on either side of a water plane . . . Well, it ruins things."

"She ain't ruined. Way she looks, big feet or not, she ain't ruined. Besides, you don't fuck the feet . . . Well, maybe *you* do. Right after the butt hole."

"You gonna push one time too much, Dave. One time too much."

"I'm just kidding, man. Lighten up. You don't ever lighten up. Don't we deserve some fun after working like niggers all day?"

Merle sighed. "You got to use that nigger stuff? I don't like it. It makes you sound ignorant. Will, he's colored and I like him. He's done me all right. Man like that, he don't deserve to be called nigger."

"He's all right at the plant, but you go by his house and ask for a loan."

"I don't want to borrow nothing from him. I'm just saying people ought to get their due, no matter what color they are. Nigger is an ugly word."

"You like boogie better, Martin Luther? How about coon or shine? I was always kind of fond of burrhead or wooly myself."

"There's just no talking to you, is there?"

"Hell, you like niggers so much, next date we set up, we'll make it a nigger. Shit, I'd fuck a nigger. It's all pink on the inside, ain't that what you've heard?"

"You're a bigot is what you are."

"If that means I'm not wanting to buddy up to coons, then, yeah, that's what I am." Dave thumped his cigarette butt out the window. "You got to learn to lighten up, Merle. You don't, you'll die. My uncle, he couldn't never lighten up. Gave him a spastic colon, all that tension. He swelled up until he couldn't wear his pants. Had to get some stretch pants, one of those running suits, just so he could have on clothes. He eventually got so bad they had to go in and operate. You can bet he wishes he didn't do all that worrying now. It didn't get him a thing but sick. He didn't get a better life on account of that worry, now did he? Still lives over in that apartment where he's been living, on account of he got so sick from worry he couldn't work. They're about to throw him out of there, and him a grown man and sixty years old. Lost his good job, his wife—which he ought to know is a good thing—and now he's doing little odd shit here and there to make ends meet. Going down to catch the day work truck with the winos and niggers—Excuse me. Afro-Americans, Colored Folks, whatever you prefer.

"Before he got to worrying over nothing, he had him some serious savings and was about ready to put some money down on a couple of acres and a good double wide."

"I was planning on buying me a double wide, that'd make me worry. Them old trailers ain't worth a shit. Comes a tornado, or just a good wind, and you can find those fuckers at the bottom of the Gulf of Mexico next to the regular trailers. Tornado will take a double wide easy as any of the others."

Dave shook his head. "You go from one thing to the other, don't you? I know what a tornado can do. It can take a house, too. Your house. That don't matter. I'm not talking about mobile homes here, Merle. I'm talking about living. It's a thing you better attend to. You're forty goddamn years old. Your life's half over . . . I know that's a cold thing to say, but there you have it. It's out of my mouth. I'm forty this next birthday, so I'm not just putting the doom on you. It's a thing ever man's got to face. Getting over the hill. Before I die, I'd like to think I did something fun with my life. It's the little things that count. I want to enjoy things, not worry them away. Hear what I'm saying, Merle?"

"Hard not to, being in the goddamn car with you."

"Look here, way we work, we deserve to lighten up a little. You haul your ashes first. That'll take some edge off."

"Well . . ."

"Naw, go on."

"All right . . . But, one thing . . ."

"What?"

"Don't do me no more butt hole jokes, okay? One friend to another, Dave, no more butt hole jokes."

"It bothers you that bad, okay. Deal."

Merle climbed over the seat and got on his knees in the floorboard. He took hold of the back seat and pulled. It was rigged with a hinge. It folded down. He got on top of the folded down seat and bent and looked into the exposed trunk. The young woman's face was turned toward him, half of her cheek was hidden by the spare tire. There was a smudge of grease on her nose.

"We should have put a blanket back here," Merle said. "Wrapped her in that. I don't like 'em dirty."

"She's got pants on," Dave said. "You take them off, the part that counts won't be dirty."

"That part's always dirty. They pee and bleed out of it don't they? Hell, hot as it is back here, she's already starting to smell."

"Oh, bullshit." Dave turned and looked over the seat at Merle. "You can't get pleased, can you? She ain't stinking. She didn't even shit her pants when she checked out. And she ain't been dead long enough to smell, and you know it. Quit being so goddamn contrary." Dave turned back around and shook out a cigarette and lit it.

"Blow that out the window, damnit," Merle said. "You know that smoke works my allergies."

Dave shook his head and blew smoke out the window. He turned up the speaker. The ads and commercials were over. The movie was starting.

"And don't be looking back here at me neither," Merle said.

Merle rolled the woman out of the trunk, across the seat, onto the floorboard and up against him. He pushed the seat back into place and got hold of the woman and hoisted her onto the back seat. He pushed her tee-shirt up over her breasts. He fondled her breasts. They were big and firm and rubbery cold. He unfastened her shorts and pulled them over her shoes and ripped her panties apart at one side. He pushed one of her legs onto the floorboard and gripped her hips and pulled her ass down a little, got it cocked to a position he liked. He unfastened and pulled down his jeans and boxer shorts and got on her.

Dave roamed an eye to the rearview mirror, caught sight of Merle's butt bobbing. He grinned and puffed at his cigarette. After a while, he turned his attention to the movie.

* * *

DRIVE-IN DATE

When Merle was finished he looked at the woman's dead eyes. He couldn't see their color in the dark, but he guessed blue. Her hair he could tell was blond.

"How was it?" Dave asked.

"It was pussy. Hand me the flashlight."

Dave reached over and got the light out of the glove box and handed it over the seat. Merle took it. He put it close to the woman's face and turned it on.

"She's got blue eyes," Merle said.

"I noticed that right off when we grabbed her," Dave said. "I thought then you'd like that, being how you are about blue eyes."

Merle turned off the flashlight, handed it to Dave, pulled up his pants and climbed over the seat. On the screen a worm-like monster was coming out of the sand on a beach.

"This flick isn't half bad," Dave said. "It's kind of funny, really. You don't get too good a look at the monster though . . . That all the pussy you gonna get?"

"Maybe some later," Merle said.

"You feeling any better?"

"Some."

"Yeah, well, why don't you eat some popcorn while I get me a little. Want a cigarette? You like a cigarette after sex, don't you?"

"All right."

Dave gave Merle a cigarette, lit it. Merle sucked the smoke in deeply.

"Better?" Dave asked.

"Yeah, I guess."

"Good." Dave thumped his cigarette out the window. "I'm gonna take my turn now. Don't let nothing happen on the movie. Make it wait."

"Sure."

Dave climbed over the seat. Merle tried to watch the movie. After a moment, he quit. He turned and looked out his window. Six speakers down he could see a Chevy rocking.

"Got to be something more to life than this?" Merle said without turning to look at Dave.

"I been telling you," Dave said, "this is life, and you better start enjoying. Get you some orientation before it's too late and it's all over but the dirt in the face . . . Talk to me later. Right now this is what I want out of life. Little later, I might want a drink."

Merle shook his head.

Dave lifted the woman's leg and hooked her ankle over the front seat. Merle looked at her foot, the ankle bracelet dangling from it. "I bet that damn foot's more a size eleven than a ten," Merle said. "Probably buys her shoes at the ski shop."

Dave hooked her other ankle over the back seat, on the package shelf. "Like I said, it's not the feet I'm interested in."

Merle shook his head again. He rolled down his window and thumped out some ash and turned his attention to the Chevy again. It was still rocking.

Dave shifted into position in the back seat. The Ford began to rock. The foot next to Merle vibrated, made little dead hops.

From the back seat Dave began to chant: "Give it to me, baby. Give it to me. Am I your Prince, baby? Am I your goddamn King? Take that anaconda, bitch. Take it!"

"For heaven's sake," Merle said.

Five minutes later Dave climbed into the front seat, said, "Damn. Damn good piece."

"You act like she had something to do with it," Merle said.

"Her pussy, ain't it?"

"We're doing all the work. We could cut a hole in the seat back there and get it that good."

"That ain't true. It ain't the hole does it, and it damn sure ain't the personality, it's how they look. That flesh under you. Young. Firm. Try coming in an ugly or fat woman and you'll see what I mean. You'll have some troubles. Or maybe you won't."

"I don't like 'em old or fat."

"Yeah, well, I don't see the live ones like either one of us all that much. The old ones or the fat ones. Face it, we've got no way with live women. And I don't like the courting. I like to know I see one I like, I can have her if I can catch her."

Merle reached over and shoved the woman's foot off the seat. It fell heavily into the floorboard. "I'm tired of looking at that slat. Feet like that, they ought to have paper bags over them."

* * *

When the second feature was over, they drove to Dave's house and parked out back next to the tall board fence. They killed the lights and sat there for awhile, watching, listening.

No movement at the neighbors.

"You get the gate," Dave said, "I'll get the meat."

"We could just go on and dump her," Merle said. We could call it a night."

"It's best to be careful. The law can look at sput now and know who it comes from. We got to clean her up some."

Merle got out and opened the gate and Dave got out and opened the trunk and pulled the woman out by the foot and let her fall on her face to the ground. He reached in and got her shorts and put them in the crook of his arm, then bent and ripped her torn panties the rest of the way off and stuffed them in a pocket of her shorts and stuffed the shorts into the front of his pants. He got hold of her ankle and dragged her through the gate.

Merle closed the gate as Dave and the corpse came through. "You got to drag her on her face?" he said.

"She don't care," Dave said.

"I know, but I don't like her messed up."

"We're through with her."

"When we let her off, I want her to be, you know, okay."

"She ain't okay now, Merle. She's dead."

"I'm don't want her messed up."

Dave shrugged. He crossed her ankles and flipped her on her back and dragged her over next to the house and let go of her by the water hose. He uncoiled the hose and took the nozzle and inserted it up the woman with a sound like a boot being withdrawn from mud, and turned the water on low.

When he looked up from his work, Merle was coming out of the house with a six-pack of beer. He carried it over to the redwood picnic table and sat down. Dave joined him.

"Have a Lone Star," Merle said.

Dave twisted the top off one. "You're thinking on something, I can tell."

"I was thinking we ought to take them alive," Merle said.

Dave lit a cigarette and looked at him. "We been over this. We take one alive she might scream or get away. We could get caught easy enough."

"We could kill her when we're finished. Way we're doing, we

could buy one of those blow up dolls, put it in the glove box and bring it to the drive-in."

"I've never cottoned to something like that. Even jacking off bothers me. A man ought to have a woman."

"A dead woman?"

"That's the best kind. She's quiet. You haven't got to put up with clothes and makeup jabber, keeping up with the Jones' jabber, getting that promotion jabber. She's not gonna tell you no in the middle of the night. Ain't gonna complain about how you put it to her. One stroke's as good as the next to a dead bitch."

"I kind of like hearing 'em grunt, though. I like being kissed."

"Rape some girl, think she'll want to kiss you?"

"I can make her."

"Dead's better. You don't have to worry yourself about how happy she is. You don't pay for nothing. If you got a live woman, one you're married to even, you're still paying for pussy. If you don't pay in money, you'll pay in pain. They'll smile and coo for a time, but stay out late with the boys, have a little financial stress, they all revert to just what my mama was. A bitch. She drove my daddy into an early grave, way she nagged, and the old sow lived to be ninety. No wonder women live longer than men. They worry men to death.

"Like my uncle I was talking about. All that worry . . . Hell, that was his wife put it on him. Wanting this and wanting that. When he got sick, had that operation and had to dip into his savings, she was out of there. They'd been married thirty years, but things got tough, you could see what those thirty years meant. He didn't even come out of that deal with a place to put his dick at night."

"Ain't all women that way."

"Yeah they are. They can't help it. I'm not blaming them. It's in them, like germs. In time, they all turn out just the same."

"I'm talking about raping them, though, not marrying them. Getting kissed."

"You're with the kissing again. You been reading Cosmo or something? What's this kiss stuff? You get hungry, you eat. You get thirsty, you drink. You get tired, you sleep. You get horny, you kill and fuck. You use them like a product, Merle, then when you get through with the product, you throw out the package. Get a new one when you need it. This way you always got the young ones, the tan ones, no matter how old or fat or ugly you get. You don't have to see a pretty woman get old, see that tan turn her face to leather.

DRIVE-IN DATE

You can keep the world bright and fresh all the time. You listen to me, Merle. It's the best way."

Merle looked at the woman's body. Her head was turned toward him. Her eyes looked to have filled with milk. Water was running out of her and pooling on the grass and starting to spurt from between her legs. Merle looked away from her, said, "Guess I'm just looking for a little romance. I had me a taste of it, you know. It was all right. She could really kiss."

"Yeah, it was all right for a while, then she ran off with a sand nigger."

"Arab, Dave. She ran off with an Arab."

"He was here right now, you'd call him an Arab?"

"I'd kill him."

"There you are. Call him an Arab or a sand nigger, you'd kill him, right?"

Merle nodded.

"Listen," Dave said. "Don't think I don't understand what you're saying. Thing I like about you, Merle, is you aren't like those guys down at the plant, come in do your job, go home, watch a little TV, fall asleep in the chair dreaming about some magazine model cause the old lady won't give out, or you don't want to think about her giving out on account of the way she's got ugly. Thing is, Merle, you know you're dissatisfied. That's the first step to knowing there's more to life than the old grind. I appreciate that in you. It's a kind of sensitivity some men don't like to face. Think it makes them weak. It's a strength, is what it is, Merle. Something I wish I had more of."

"That's damn nice of you to say, Dave."

"It's true. Anybody knows you, knows you feel things deeply. And I don't want you to think that I don't appreciate romance, but you get our age, you got to look at things a little straighter. I can't see any romance with an old woman anyway, and a young one, she ain't gonna have me . . . Unless it's the way we're doing it now."

Merle glanced at the corpse. Water was spewing up from between her legs like a whale blowing. Her stomach was a fat, white mound.

"We don't get that hose out of her," Merle said, "she's gonna blow the hell up."

"I'll get it," Dave said. He went over and turned off the water and pulled the hose out of her and put his foot on her stomach and began to pump his leg. Water gushed from her and her stomach began to flatten. "She was all right, wasn't she, Merle?"

"'Cept for them feet, she was fine."

They drove out into the pines and pulled off to the side of a little dirt road and parked. They got out and went around to the trunk and Dave unlocked it. They looked at the young woman's body for a moment, then they each took a leg and jerked her from the trunk, and with her legs spread like a wishbone, they dragged her into the brush and dropped her on the edge of an incline coated in blackberry briars.

"Man," Dave said. "Taste that air. This is the prettiest night I can remember."

"It's nice," Merle said.

Dave put a boot to the woman and pushed, she went rolling down the incline in a white moon-licked haze and crashed into the brush at the bottom. Dave pulled her shorts from the front of his pants and tossed them after her.

"Time they find her, the worms will have had some pussy too," Dave said.

They got in the car and Dave started it up and eased down the road.

"Dave?"

"Yeah?"

"You're a good friend," Merle said. "The talk and all, it done me good. Really."

Dave smiled, clapped Merle's shoulder. "Hey, it's all right. I been seeing this coming in you for a time, since the girl before last . . . You're all right now, though. Right?"

"Well, I'm better."

"That's how you start."

They drove a piece. Merle said, "But I got to admit to you, I still miss being kissed."

Dave laughed. "You and the kiss. You're some piece of work buddy . . . I got your kiss. Kiss my ass."

Merle grinned. "Way I feel, your ass could kiss back, I just might."

DRIVE-IN DATE

   Dave laughed again. They drove out of the woods and onto the highway. The moon was high and bright.

(For Gary Goldstein)

Robert R. McCammon

Afterword
the Judge

Listen up.

When you walk into my courtroom, don't you sneer. Don't you scowl or make a face or think you're somebody, because when you step through my door I own you. I'll tell you how to walk and talk, I'll tell you how to stand there and listen, I'll tell you everything you need to know, I'll tell you when to think and when to shut up thinking.

I'm telling you right now. Clear the slop out of your head. Knock the long-haired, homo jungle-bunny artsy-fartsy hippie yuppie shitzie rap heavy metal Satanic filth out from between your ears, my friend.

Because I'm the Judge, and what I say is the only way.

So. You're a reader, are you?

Heard of those.

Maybe you'd like to know what you're doing in my courtroom. Well, the book found in your possession is obscene and unlawful. Anything titled "Night Visions" has got to be pretty sick, if you want my honest opinion. You can call it a book if you want to, but trash like this isn't going to be tolerated. Not in my courtroom. Because I'm in charge here.

I've seen you before, haven't I? Yes, I think I have. You see, I have a long memory. I believe you've been brought to my attention before. I believe you were among those who said children—God-fearing children, with all their energy and willingness to do a good day's work for an honest wage—should not be allowed in the coal mines, or to learn a craft at the spindles, or operate the gears of the stone-crushing machines. Now exactly what did you hope to gain by that? Don't you understand that America's heart is its workplace? And when you take children—full of energy and willing to work their hands to the bone for an honest wage—out of that workplace, you hurt the heart of America? Don't you understand that by taking children out of the workplace, you make the prices go up for everyone else? And what would children be doing if they weren't earning an honest day's wage? Lazy children become lazy adults, my friend. You've got to train them well and early, the earlier the better. Free enterprise, low prices, well-trained adults: that's what you get when children are in the workplace. Don't you understand that?

No, I don't care to hear what you have to say.

Oh yes, I do remember you. You were the one with the big mouth. You were the one saying you smelled something burning. Well, no one else seemed to notice, did they? Over the whole world, who noticed such a thing as that? Even the kikes didn't notice it. They walked on in, just walked on in, and they were greedy because they thought they were getting showers when they knew there was a war on and water was rationed. They knew it. But oh no, they just walked on into the showers to use up some of that rationed water, and they didn't care about little children or sick old people, they just cared about themselves. And you were the one who said you smelled something burning, when all over the world nobody else even sniffed the wind. But God has a way of taking care of things, my friend. God balances the scales, and you'd better believe He knows what he's doing. If all those greedy kikes hadn't walked in to take showers, what would the world's population be today? We wouldn't have room to draw a breath, would we? And just think how many more criminals there would be, and how many more prisons we'd have to build. My friend, you're very liberal with other people's money, aren't you? Well, think of this: do you know what they did with those tons and tons of kike ashes? You don't know a thing about history, do you? They used those ashes as fertilizer! With those ashes, they grew bounty harvests of wheat that went out to feed their nation! They put those ashes in the earth, and up sprang wonders! With the food that grew from those ashes, little starving children were fed, and sick men and women made healthy. Besides,

THE JUDGE

if it hadn't happened like it did, there wouldn't be any Israel today, and a lot of those Jews born in Israel have come to Hollywood to make movies that have thrilled millions and broken all kinds of box-office records.

But you had to say something about burning, didn't you?

Oh, now I've got you placed! You were one of those beatniks carrying a sign that said "Ban The Bomb". Well, thank the Lord Almighty we didn't ban the bomb! If we'd listened to you and your kind, we'd be in our graves right this minute! The Statue of Liberty would be holding a hammer and sickle! But because we didn't listen to you, the Berlin Wall is down and we're the winners. Yes sir, we've won it all! They're going to lick our boots and we're going to have the power to tell them when to jump and how high and they'll do it because they don't know running a country is just like running a business. Well, we're the winners now. We're the big dog on the block, because we didn't ban the bomb. And if we had, where would our energy program be right now? Do you know how many people rely on nuclear power? Do you have any idea how important nuclear power is to the lives and well-being of the generations of future Americans? And all that crap about the nuclear reactors being unsafe and radiation in the air, the food and the water, and some idiot saying that back in 19whenever a little bit of concrete cracked and some radiation floated out! Where are the records, I ask? Where is the proof? Besides, nobody cares about that. They care about the important things, like the sanctity of our flag. They care about shouting down a two-cent tax on gasoline and cigarettes for money to educate somebody else's kid in some other state. They care about the God-given right to bear firearms and hunt a deer with the semi-automatic weapon of their choice. Those are the important things. Give me a comedy on Saturday night, a roof over my head, bread on my table and a Nintendo for the kids and I am satisfied.

But not you. Oh, no. Your record speaks for itself.

Tell me something. What did standing in that park, getting hosed down with a mob of coloreds get you?

I have a dream. Now those are pretty words, aren't they? Well, the man who said them was a so-called preacher, a professional speaker, so why shouldn't they be pretty words? Oh, that man knew how to incite a crowd, didn't he? But he was laughing at them all the time, he was laughing at them, because he was having affairs with women just like his buddy President Camelot was. So you stood out there in that park and got hosed down and you smelled the breath of dogs and felt their teeth and you rode on a schoolbus and would not drink water from the proper fountain and you wanted to go to college and vote and where is that dream now?

I'll tell you where it is, my friend, if you're man enough to hear it.

That dream was speeding like a runaway car, and it hit the wall of reality and shattered and nobody knows how to put that dream back together again. It's like you can't find the parts anymore, and the blueprints died in Memphis. Are you man enough to hear this?

You gave up.

Oh, you still holler. You still whine, but it's the whimper of a whipped dog. But that dream got in a needle and in a vial and you can buy one for five dollars on a corner and you can slink on into a house where other whipped dogs burn dreams and suck the blue flames into their lungs and then you can dream, dream, dream, you can dream until Len Bias slamdunks and Marion Berry praises God and all the coloreds who went to their graves dreaming get up and tapdance in bony chorus lines.

You really ought to smile more, my friend.

Since you're a reader, tell me: where are the colored writers? I don't see any. You know, reading itself is kind of a dying bird, isn't it? And it seems to me that what most publishers put out is just the same thing over and over again, except with different covers. Reading can't compare with watching television. Who wants to read, when you can *watch*? Not me. I want to be entertained, I don't want to have to work at entertaining myself. Well, most writers are starting to write books like tv shows, anyway, aren't they? Just action, action, more action, car crashes, stick that knife in, give me a shooting, speed it up faster, faster, ahhhhhh now we come to the end. At last. You have to give the people what they want, it seems to me. And what they want is blood and action, hearts and flowers. Something with a happy ending. If they want reality, they can watch the news. Which is, of course, why no one in his right mind watches the news.

Your face is very clear to me now.

It was you singing "Give Peace A Chance". It was you who stuck a flower into the loaded rifle of a National Guardsman. It was you who burned a candle to protest the Vietnam War. It was you

THE JUDGE

who caused all those fine brave boys to come home stained with defeat.

I hope you're satisfied with yourself, you coward.

It was you who started this environmental crap, wasn't it? What good is a world with dolphins in it if you can't order a nice piece of tuna in a seafood restaurant? Tell me what whales ever did for me, that my heart should bleed. See this gavel? That's about how smart a whale is. It was you who smelled burning again, down in the Amazon. There you go again, taking jobs away from foreigners. You know what happens when you take away jobs from foreigners? They come to America begging for handouts. So let them alone, before our taxes get any higher! Yeah, I'll bet you even think meat stinks, don't you?

It was you, it's always you. Saying a woman should have a choice, saying AIDS isn't God's way of exterminating the queers, saying the homeless aren't in those cardboard boxes by their own free will, saying American industry is sick. Well, if it is sick it's because we took children out of the workplace and each generation grew up lazier than the last. It's always you, saying pornography should masquerade as art and corrupt our little children, saying that Satan worshippers and jungle-bunnies should be free to spew whatever bile they like on our airwaves.

This is still America, by God.

And I'm in charge now.

You know, a lot of people say they don't know what pornography is. I do know what it is.

It's anything I don't like.

Take this so-called book you've been arrested for reading. I think that's a fine title, don't you? *Night Visions Eight*. You mean to tell me there've been seven more books like this one? And what does "night visions" mean, anyway? Is it like a fever? A sickness? Yes, it's a sickness, isn't it? Looking through some of these so-called stories gives me "night visions", that's for sure.

Are these the so-called writers? John Farris? Stephen Gallagher? Joe Lansdale? I think I may have met those men in my courtroom at one time or another. You see, I have a long memory.

Yeah, let's just take a look at some of these titles. Oh, here's a fine one: "Hairshirt". I'll bet that's one my grandmother would just love to curl up with. "Good Morning, Daddy". I can already smell the reek of obscenity. "Dead Man's Handle". Uh huh, pornography and worship of death. "Hunter, Killer". That's a long way from being pleasant. isn't it? I don't want to even look at "Drive-In Date", because I know it's filth. I see the Lord's name taken in vain in "Steppin' Out, Summer, '68". Yes, that would be a summer a person like you might remember, wouldn't it?

When are you going to learn, my friend?

Reading this obscenity is not going to be allowed anymore.

Oh, yes, I know what these stories are called. Cautionary tales, isn't that right? And some people might try to say these stories have some worth and meaning? Well, those people are very, very sick. I don't have to stick my nose in a sewer to know what's flowing down there. And I don't have to read this book to know these so-called writers need to be put away and re-educated as to what makes good, entertaining writing. Look at what they were able to do with Elvis Presley. He was sick in the head and couldn't sing a note until they put him in those movies, and then he sang some wonderful, wholesome songs.

This *Night Visions Eight* needs a great big dose of wholesome, if you ask me.

No, I'm not going to read it. Not a single story. I don't care to waste my time. If I was to read a book, it would either be the Holy Bible or Donald Trump's autobiography. Now there's a man who ought to be President.

Let me set you straight on something, my friend.

If so-called books like *Night Visions Eight* were thrown on a bonfire and burned until the ashes flew in the wind, the world would be a lot kinder and gentler. People don't need to look into mirrors, and think, and get all stirred up about things. People just need to salute the flag, know the national anthem, pray to God on their knees and watch television.

I pronounce you subversive and dangerous to our society. You will be taken from this courtroom and confined in a place where your opinions and ideas will wither and die. When that happens, I may let you join the rest of us again.

But don't count on it.

I know you. Oh yes, I know who you are. Your name's been on my list for a long, long time.

Well, this is my courtroom. I'm the Judge, and what I say is the only way.

THE JUDGE

And before too much longer, we're going to pour the gasoline and strike the matches and then we'll see what Mr. Mark Homo Twain and Mr. Edgar Dopehead Poe and Mr. Stephen Blasphemy King and Mr. J.D. Satanist Salinger have to say when their mouths are eaten up by the fire.

And oh, what a lovely fire that shall be.

This Farris and Gallagher and Lansdale, they're going to be silenced too. I'll see to it, personally.

Understand this, my friend.

I'm all in favor of freedom of speech.

Just as long as I agree with what's being said.

Next case.